SAVING SHADOWS

SHADOWS LANDING #1

KATHLEEN BROOKS

An original work of Kathleen Brooks. *Saving Shadows* copyright @ 2018 by Kathleen Brooks.

❀ Created with Vellum

To my mother, Marcia, my father, Milo, and their 49 years of marriage. A true inspiration of a lifetime of love.
Plus they made me, so in a way they're responsible for all these books.

To my family, Pat, Mike, Craig, Cris, Kathy, Erik, Tracie, Marc and Joey.
To my friends, Kathy, Aoife, Chris, Candy, Heather, Melissa, Katie, Maggie, Kate, Ava, Jana, Renee, Ruth, Cali, Jan, and so many others that I hold so dear to me.

And to the readers in Kathleen's Blossom Café.
You all have been inspiring in your kindness, support, and love.

To my husband, Chris. Thank you for not having a man bun, for making me laugh every day, and for being my rock. I love you!

Bluegrass Series

Bluegrass State of Mind

Risky Shot

Dead Heat

Bluegrass Brothers

Bluegrass Undercover

Rising Storm

Secret Santa: A Bluegrass Series Novella

Acquiring Trouble

Relentless Pursuit

Secrets Collide

Final Vow

Bluegrass Singles

All Hung Up

Bluegrass Dawn

The Perfect Gift

The Keeneston Roses

Forever Bluegrass Series

Forever Entangled

Forever Hidden

Forever Betrayed

Forever Driven

Forever Secret

Forever Surprised

Forever Concealed

Forever Devoted

Forever Hunted

Forever Guarded

Forever Notorious (coming in 2019)

Shadows Landing Series

Saving Shadows

Sunken Shadows (coming later in 2019)

Women of Power Series

Chosen for Power

Built for Power

Fashioned for Power

Destined for Power

Web of Lies Series

Whispered Lies

Rogue Lies

Shattered Lies

PROLOGUE

Ellery St. John felt her heart beating so hard it might burst out of her chest. Fear. Panic. Death. They were all after her. She screamed, but it was only inside her head. For in her head, the incident was on a loop playing over and over again.

Night. Darkness. Rain. Terror. Ellery knew someone was going to kill her. She heard the sound of her high heels on the wet cobblestone as she ran for her car. She saw her reflection in the driver's window when she reached for the handle. Time slowed.

Her hair was damp, there was rain dripping down her forehead and into her eyes. In one split second she knew she wasn't going to make it. Her mouth opened as she screamed. She saw a hand rise behind her in the reflection of the window, tightly clenched around a hard object. Ellery tried to jump back as she pulled the handle, but it was too late. The scream fighting to get free was silenced as her world went black.

ELLERY DIDN'T KNOW how long it had been or how many times the loop of her attack played over and over in her head. Her body shivered. That had to mean she was alive. So she fought. She fought the darkness. She fought the fear. She fought the death trying to take her.

With monumental effort, she cracked an eyelid. The wind howled. The rain pummeled. All she saw was darkness. She felt as if she were being tossed back and forth. Her body listed to one side and slammed into something hard. Her head exploded at every jostle.

"Help." That one word croaked from her lips. It took all her mental focus and all her body's energy, but she finally managed the one word.

"It's too late for help."

A figure stood over her, cloaked in a long, hooded raincoat. No matter how hard she tried she couldn't make out if it was a man or a woman. The voice was covered by the thunder and hard pounding rain so she barely heard it. She couldn't decipher if the voice was a man or woman. The figure approached as Ellery tried to fight back. She swung an arm, but it was limp as it slapped harmlessly against the arms reaching down for her.

"No," she tried to yell as the hands gripped her. They pulled her up and pushed her against the hard wall, and then she was falling. Her breath was taken when she hit the water. Pain exploded in her head as her legs dropped like anchors into the ocean water. Her eyes closed as the pain called her into the darkness once again.

"Just let the water take you," the voice called to her.

Ellery tried to open her eyes but couldn't. She didn't know where she was or how she'd gotten there. She struggled against the darkness trying to drag her under. For a split second, she only saw dark and dangerous clouds in the night sky as rain fell upon her. The choppy ocean waters covered her arms, her chest, and then finally her head. Her body didn't, or couldn't, react as the water dragged her into the darkness.

Charleston a little ways out in the Atlantic Ocean. The surge would be big, which meant he really did need to secure his boat.

Flipping on the light to the kitchen, Gavin dug around the closet by the back door for his boots, raincoat, and flashlight. He stuffed his bare feet into the boots that reached his knees and zipped up his jacket. He could try the hood, but it would be a bigger pain to keep on than to just admit his head was going to get wet. He picked up the flashlight and unlocked his door. It flung open with the wind and Gavin trudged outside. The gusts ripped at his jacket as he used force to shut the door. The sustained winds were around seventy-five miles per hour, so it was barely at hurricane strength, but walking still presented a challenge.

Palmetto branches, some of his neighbors unsecured lawn chairs, and other debris rolled around the backyard as he battled his way down the grassy slope toward the dock. The water levels were already high, but his floating dock would be fine. His house was up a hill, so flooding wasn't a major concern either. This was more of a pain in the ass than anything but the way his boat was slamming into his dock worried him. He needed to secure the boat better and then he'd go back to bed.

The wooded dock was slippery, and Gavin held out his arms to balance himself. It was as if he were walking on an old tilt-a-whirl ride as waves crashed around him. Using his flashlight, Gavin located the ropes that had given way. He opened the storage box built onto the dock that he used for seating and pulled out new ropes and two extra bumpers. He tied the bumpers to the dock and when the boat rocked away from him, he tossed the bumpers into the raging waters.

He was wet, tired, and aggravated he hadn't tied the boat securely in the first place as he went to work. He'd taken the boat out fishing after a long day in the office, and when he'd gotten back he'd been too tired to do a proper job. Well, this sure as hell taught him to do it right the first time.

Lightning crashed in the distance toward Charleston, and Gavin turned to the oncoming storm. Wind and rain lashed against his face as the storm raged in the Atlantic Ocean. They wouldn't take a direct hit, but it would be enough to send the ocean waters racing inland. Gavin was turning back to the house when something caught his eye. Something white stood out in the dark waters racing toward the end of his dock. It was probably someone's overturned kayak, partially submerged. Gavin thought about leaving it as he looked at his warm, and more importantly, dry house. He was about to walk toward his house when he thought better of it. He'd want someone to rescue his boat if it broke free.

Gavin flashed his light on it again as he tried to gauge where the kayak would hit his dock so he could grab it. It was going to skirt by the edge, so he set his flashlight on the dock so the wind blew it against his storage container and not into the water. He lay on his stomach so he wouldn't fall in and waited for the overturned kayak to come to him. Rain pelted him as streams of water caused his eyes to stay half closed. He blinked through the water and saw the small boat bob in the waves. It went under for a second and then popped back up. As it was pushed closer to him, Gavin narrowed his eyes and lifted a hand to shield them from the onslaught of rain. The boat wasn't partially submerged like he thought.

Gavin's heart sped up when he realized what he thought was the side of the kayak were really arms wrapped around a log. What he thought was the submerged end of a kayak was really a person's legs underwater. And the white underbelly of the kayak was actually a raincoat on a body. A disturbingly still body.

"Hey!" Gavin yelled, but the body didn't respond. All he could see was wet hair plastered to a head. From this distance he couldn't tell if the body was a man or woman. He tried yelling again, but the howling wind ripped the words from his mouth as the waves carried the person up and down and sometimes under.

Medical school and his tour in the Charleston hospital only further instilled his desire to help people. His cousin Wade had joined the Coast Guard for the same reason. They'd talked about it when Wade had joined and while Gavin was in med school. They'd all grown up in Shadows Landing, and Gavin had swum these waters more times than he could count—even when they were rough. As the wind blew harder, the waves carried the person toward him, however, the direction indicated the body would stay out of reach.

Gavin pushed himself up and pulled off his boots. The wind yanked them from the dock and sent them flying against the storage box. He unlocked the lid, tossed in the boots and his raincoat and closed it before stepping to the end of the dock. It was still warm enough that he was comfortable in nothing but a pair of athletic shorts. The rain stung his body as if the drops were thousands of little needles pricking his skin.

The person went up a wave and then down again. When they were about to pass the dock, Gavin jumped. In the air, the wind pushed him to the left, but he'd calculated that when he'd made his move. He kicked with the waves and strong current, letting nature slam him against the unconscious person.

Gavin didn't have time to do an assessment as the water crashed upon them, carrying them quickly past his property. He only had time to notice the figure was a woman as he wrapped an arm around her and the log and began kicking with all his might in a slow diagonal toward the shore. His lungs burned as he coughed up water. His legs shook, his abdominal muscles were tense, and his shoulders burned from the exertion, but then he was finally able to reach out with his right hand and grasp the ladder to his neighbor's dock. The waters and winds did their best to rip the woman from his grasp as he hooked his leg and arm through the ladder. Leaning to the right he used his body weight to pull the woman against the current.

"Come on!" he yelled as nature worked against him. His left arm was under her arm and around her chest as he held on tightly to her side and pulled her free from the log. The log disappeared as he used all his strength to pull the woman up the three feet to the dock.

With his muscles fatigued and his body ready to give up, Gavin pulled as hard as he could. The woman rose with the wave and when the wave fell, he yanked her hard. Her limp, waterlogged body was pulled against his cold, shaking core. Gavin struggled to prop her onto the ladder as he climbed over and up the ladder before falling onto the deck in a seated position. He leaned over the edge and grabbed her hands that he'd tucked around one of the rungs of the ladder. He pulled her up toward him. His body fell backward, landing hard on the wooden dock as the woman's body surged upward and partially onto the dock, ending with her head in his lap.

Gavin took deep breaths to refuel his body then reached for her neck. He pushed her hair aside and searched for a pulse. It was barely there, but her breathing was so shallow her lips had begun to turn blue. Gavin scooted back, dragging the woman with him until she lay flat on her back, and he began CPR. After some chest compressions and a deep breath blown into her cold lips, the woman's eyes fluttered open a second before a whole gallon of ocean water was thrown up. She looked disappointed for a second before she groaned, her eyelids fluttered shut, and she passed back out. Gavin felt her pulse and tracked her breathing. Both were steadier now. "Thank goodness," he whispered before he bent to pick her up.

He stretched her arms and legs out and then hefted her into a fireman's carry position around his back. He held tight to her arm and leg as he began to battle the wind through his neighbor's yard and then across the debris landmines in his own. By the time he kicked open his door, he was close to collapsing from nature's best attempt at defeating him. But he refused to give up as he closed and locked the door. He rushed through the living room, turning left into the hallway, and pushing open the door that led to his office, the exam room, and then the surgical room.

When Gavin had bought the house, he'd turned the old formal greeting room into an exam room and a small surgical room. Then he'd turned the formal dining room into an office. His cousin Ridge was a builder and had done the conversion and had also built an entrance and waiting area to the side of the house.

Gavin sat the woman on the surgical table and began a quick exam. Her body temperature was low, her face was pale, and he found a gash on the back of her head. He needed to get her dry, warm, and hooked up to an IV quickly. He unzipped her white raincoat and gently removed it to expose a simple, yet elegant black dress. What was this woman doing in the ocean during a hurricane? As he undressed her, he felt along her body for any injuries. He was in full professional mode, not even noting her full breasts, flat stomach, and curved hips as he grabbed a towel and roughly dried her. Her skin began to pink with the increased circulation as he reached for an exam gown and slipped her arms through it to cover her before running into the living room for a blanket.

When he made it back into the room, the woman's body was shivering, but color was returning to her lips. He tucked her in tight and moved efficiently, starting an IV and taking her vitals again. Her temperature was slowly rising. He hooked her up to a monitor and was relieved when both her blood pressure and pulse began to stabilize. Gavin didn't want to leave her, but he needed to have her transported to Charleston Memorial Hospital for a head scan. To do that, he needed to get dressed and call into town.

Gavin rushed from the exam room, out into the hallway, and up the stairs to the master bedroom. He shoved off his soaking wet shorts and slid into sweatpants and a long sleeve T-shirt before grabbing his cell phone and racing back downstairs with a warm pair of socks in his hand. He entered the exam room, and even though he knew the likelihood was low, he hoped to be greeted by the woman's open eyes. Instead, he found her completely unmoved and unchanged.

Gavin dialed the hospital's ER desk number as he bent to put the thick socks on the woman's tiny feet. A harried nurse answered briskly, "BethAnn here."

"BethAnn, it's Doctor Gavin Faulkner. I need a helicopter or an ambulance in Shadows Landing."

"Hiya Doc. Status?" BethAnn asked, cutting to the chase.

He knew most of the doctors and nurses at Charleston's main hospital, and they'd be all hands on deck tonight.

"Unconscious woman with a head wound."

"Bless your heart, Doc. You're not going to get emergency services with a little ol' thing like that. Not tonight. Besides, the road out of town is flooded, and we're grounded until the wind calms down. As long as she's not critical, as in about to die any second, she's best to stay put with you."

"It was worth a shot. I'll monitor overnight and bring her in as soon as possible. Thanks BethAnn."

"You can thank me by saying a prayer for us. A hurricane and a full moon. Someone done gone and pissed off a higher power. You stay dry, Doc," BethAnn ordered before hanging up.

Gavin had one more shot at getting the woman into the hospital, and he'd give it a try. He pulled up his contacts and called his cousin Wade in the Coast Guard. Wade answered, but over his voice, Gavin heard the roar of waves and wind.

"I found a woman in the river. She's unconscious with a head wound. Can you pick her up for a hospital transport?"

"Sorry Gav," he barely heard Wade yell over the growing sound of helicopter blades. "I'm about to fly out to help a sinking fishing boat. We don't have a single free bird tonight. If it's not critical, stay put. The worst is over and the waters will start receding some when the tide moves out."

"Stay safe," Gavin yelled back and got a quick "Yup" before Wade hung up and went off with his crew for a rescue. Gavin turned and looked at the woman. Her shivering was lessening, so he pulled up a chair and slid his hand into hers. "You're safe now," he told her as he watched the steady beat of her heart on the monitor. When he deemed her stable, he stood up and gathered his supplies to suture her head wound. He rolled the woman onto her side and was rewarded with a low groan. "It's okay. You're safe, but you have a nasty cut on your head. I'm going to administer something to numb it. You'll feel a prick and then a little bit of a burn, but you won't feel a thing as I sew it up," he said, talking to her as he did exactly what he told her he was going to do. He believed even unconscious people could hear what was going on. Now, they may not be able to process it, but his soothing voice might keep her calm.

Gavin pushed her hair from the wound as he cleaned it and grimaced. There were several gashes as if something hard and pointy had hit her head. It was amazing it hadn't killed her. The wounds were deep, and he could see her skull in places. "Here we go. You'll be good as new in no time."

GAVIN LET out a breath as he pulled the medical gloves from his hands and threw them away. He placed the woman on her back but angled her head so she wouldn't be lying on her wounds. Then he cleaned the small surgical room, dimmed the lights so they wouldn't hurt her eyes when she woke, and took his seat next to her again.

"Come back to me," Gavin said softly as he took her hand in his and leaned forward. "You're safe now."

He watched for any sign she heard him, but the woman did not wake while time went on and the winds and rain died down.

2

The waters covered her head, dragging her down. Ellery opened her eyes, but in the dark night she couldn't see under the water. She struggled to swim to the surface, but she couldn't tell which way was up. There was nothing but darkness surrounding her. Something hit her leg and she screamed, water filling her mouth as the last breath escaped her lungs.

She didn't finish the thought that it could be a shark as she swam in the opposite direction. Her high heels fell from her feet as she frantically fought toward the surface. Her lungs burned, her vision seemed to be blurring, and the water was constantly pulling at her.

Her fingers broke free first then her head. With a gasp, she dragged water and air into her lungs before a coughing spasm hit. Waves pushed her under as lightning flashed above the ocean. Frantically, Ellery fought to reach the surface and once she did, she looked around, but there was nothing. Just open water and the city in the distance. The city lights from Charleston flickered as heavy sheets of rain fell. Just the thought of swimming that far had her head spinning. She didn't know what had happened or why she was there. As she tried to think, the pain in her head intensified.

Ellery lifted a hand to the pain on the back of her head, and when she pulled it away her fingers were dark with blood. Blood, ocean, sharks . . . Ellery struggled to keep her head above water. Black dots danced in her eyes and before she knew it, she threw up champagne and ocean water. She struggled to kick toward the city but too soon she grew weak and dizzy. A dark shadow lay ahead in the water and Ellery froze. Too bad the ocean didn't. The waves, wind, and tide pushed her forward. As Ellery prepared to fight off a shark, the water dropped her right on it—a log.

She felt tears fall as she pulled her bleeding head and the upper part of her body out of the water and wrapped her arms around the ocean-weathered log. It smelled of the ocean, and barnacles clung to it as tightly as she did. The black dots danced until there was nothing but darkness. But then she remembered her body being pushed, air forcing itself in, and warm lips touching hers. When her eyes fluttered open, the handsomest face she'd ever seen was bent over hers. It must be heaven and she must be getting a kiss from an angel. But then she threw up and the darkness took her once again. Until now.

Ellery's eyes shot open. It took a moment for them to focus. Even though she felt as if she were still drifting in the ocean, she realized she wasn't. Slowly, she turned her head to the right. It looked as if she was in some kind of hospital. But it was so quiet. And something was holding down her hand. Panic flared again until she slowly turned her aching and throbbing head to find a hand clasping hers.

It wasn't just a hand. A man was asleep against the exam table she was lying on. He held her hand with his and was leaning forward, resting his head on his other arm, which was resting on the table close to her thigh. She couldn't see his face. All she could see was his dark brown hair. It was short, yet messy. As if he'd gone to bed with wet hair and now it was sticking out in every direction. But who was he? He wore sweats and a T-shirt. Not your standard doctor or nurse attire.

Ellery made a tiny move to sit up and groaned out loud. Her vision blurred as she was hit with a wave of nausea. The man's head shot up.

"You're awake," he said calmly, even though she could tell he was relieved. "How do you feel?"

"Like I might throw up on you," Ellery said with a very scratchy voice. Her throat was so dry. It was then she really took a look at the man and gasped. It was the man from her dreams—the man whose lips had pulled her from death.

He quickly stood and walked across the room. He returned with a curved pan in case she had to throw up and a disposable cup filled with water. "Try small sips," he said, setting the pan in her lap before putting one strong arm behind her and slowly helping her sit up. Waves of nausea crashed into her as her head spun wildly out of control.

The man pulled out a penlight and began to examine her as she tentatively took her first sip of water. "Who are you? Where am I?" Ellery asked.

The man lowered the light. "I'm sorry. You must be very confused. My name is Dr. Gavin Faulkner. This is my house and clinic. I was securing my boat in the middle of the night when I found you floating in the water during the hurricane. I jumped in and got you out, but you were unconscious. I tried to get you transported to Charleston Memorial Hospital, but the helicopters weren't flying with the high winds, and the roads are flooded, so we can't get you into town."

"Am I on Mount Pleasant?" she asked of the island across from Charleston. He really was the man of her dreams. And he'd saved her.

"No, Shadows Landing. We're a little inland from Charleston."

She knew of the small town with the interesting past. "Barbeque Festival," she muttered before taking another small sip of water.

Doctor Faulkner grinned, and his eyes reminded her of the Spanish moss that hung from the oak trees in and around Charleston. They were green with a hint of gray, and when he smiled, they brightened.

"That's right. And what's your name?"

"Ellery."

Doctor Faulkner smiled again. "Nice to meet you, Ellery. You have a concussion. You've been hit by something very hard. I'll call the sheriff and see if he can get someone to help get you back to Charleston. You'll need to be admitted to the hospital for observation and get a head scan to make sure there isn't a brain bleed, although you're not currently showing symptoms of one."

"No!" Ellery's stomach churned. Something tugged at her mind, almost crippling her with pain as the memories tried to fight their way free.

"It's okay. Relax," Doctor Faulkner said gently as he rubbed her back with one hand and held her hair back with the other as she vomited up even more ocean water. Her head felt as if it were going to blow off. The black spots were back, and they weren't just dancing. They were going full mosh pit crazy.

The darkness began to drag her under. With one last

effort, she tried to make her mouth move as the doctor lowered her back onto the exam table. "Don't tell anyone I'm here. Please." And then she was lost again in the darkness.

GAVIN LOOKED down at the woman who had passed out again. He felt her pulse, took her vitals, and sat back to watch her. She was stable and knew who she was. As night turned to morning, he wondered about her. Why didn't she want anyone to know where she was? What had happened to her? The head wound, the water rescue, the fear. Gavin had seen enough boating accidents to know the injuries and the demeanor didn't fit. He didn't think Ellery was a victim of an accident. Instead, she matched up with victims of violence. Something very bad had happened to this woman.

Her face was lined with worry as she was trapped in a replay of her nightmare. Gavin took her hand in his and saw the tension in her face ease. "You're safe, Ellery. I'll take care of you."

Gavin pushed a strand of her now dry hair from her face. It was a golden blonde color and her eyes were the color of the sky on a clear summer day. Her nose was pert, her cheekbones high, and her lips full. Was she married? Did her husband or boyfriend hurt her? Gavin was interrupted from further speculation by a knock on the door.

Reluctantly, he took his hand from hers, pulled the blanket to her shoulders, and headed to his front door. When he didn't hurry to answer it, there was an increase in the banging before he heard the sound of a key being inserted in the front door. Before Gavin could open it, the door swung open and his sister Harper strode in. She was wearing jean shorts, monogramed knee-high rain boots, and a strappy shirt. Her shoulder-length brown hair was freshly highlighted with some dark blonde as she blew in like the hurricane had the night before.

"What took you so long?" Harper asked as she walked right into his house. She cringed when she looked in the mirror and muttered something about humidity and hair before putting her long hair into some kind of sloppy bun with a grimace on her face.

"I have a patient," Gavin answered. "Did you get any damage from the storm?"

Harper snorted. "Not because of the weather. Gator and Junior got into it after having a couple of my hurricane specials."

Gavin shook his head. His sister owned Shadows Bar where all the locals gathered at night for some drinks or to play pool or darts. Whenever there was a hurricane, she offered two-for-one hurricane drinks. "I told you that was going to get you in trouble. Do I need to patch them up?"

"Nah," Harper said, sitting on the couch and crossing her legs. "Gator won pretty easily. I tried to tell Junior not to get into a wrestling match with a man who hunts alligators for a living, but you know Junior."

Yes, yes he did. Gator looked about what you would expect from a man nicknamed Gator. Six feet tall and two hundred fifteen pounds of country muscle with a beard and a University of South Carolina fighting gamecocks baseball cap that Gavin had never seen removed in twenty years. His skin was tan and leathery from all his time in the water with the gators. Junior, on the other hand, was barely five foot eight in his work boots and maybe weighed one forty if he was soaking wet. He was the town handyman.

"Did Junior have his hammer on him?" Gavin asked.

"You know he doesn't go anywhere without it," Harper

said with a sigh. "Which is why I had to leap over the bar top, knock Junior off his stool, and tussle that hammer from him before Gator pulled his hunting knife."

Gavin narrowed his eyes and scanned his sister again. "Is that why you're favoring your left arm?"

"Yeah. Can you look at it? I'm worried I dislocated the darn thing again." For as beautiful as Harper was, she was equally powerful in mind and body. She also didn't hesitate to use that power to break up fights.

"You need to stop getting involved in bar fights. You should have let the sheriff handle it."

"Couldn't. The sheriff was down at Stephen's," Harper said, emphasizing the "f" sound as Stephen did. And you never called him just Stephen. It didn't matter that he was only a couple years older than Gavin, the second he'd gotten his Ph.D. in American history focused on southern studies, he'd insisted everyone call him Professor Stephen Adkins or if he was really feeling pretentious, Dr. Adkins. It once led to a very embarrassing incident when Gator's younger cousin, Turtle, came into the bar bleeding and asking if the doctor was there. Stephen had answered before Gavin could but passed out when he'd turned around and saw blood from a slice across Turtle's arm.

"What did Stephen need?" Gavin asked when he knew he shouldn't. It would only make him mad.

"He demanded the sheriff fortify the historical center while he preserved the historical documents," Harper said with a roll of her eyes much like his, but only deeper green.

Gavin felt his blood pressure rise. "Shadows Landing Historical Center is the most fortified building in town."

"Don't I know it," Harper muttered and then hissed as Gavin pushed her shoulder back into place. "Thanks, Gav."

His sister popped off the couch and placed a kiss on his

cheek. "I'm off to have breakfast with the girls. See you soon."

"Bye, Harper. Tell them I say hi."

The girls consisted of their cousin, Tinsley, and an old family friend who had recently been widowed and had moved back to Shadows Landing. Edie Greene Wecker's husband had been killed in action. Edie's brother, Walker, was Gavin's best friend and was the only survivor of the Navy SEAL mission that had taken her husband's life. Now Edie was back in Shadows Landing, and Walker was happily married in Keeneston, Kentucky. The whole Faulkner family was spoiling Edie, probably to the point she'd go running back to Virginia or to Keeneston if they didn't back off, but she was practically family and family helped family.

Speaking of helping . . . Gavin turned toward the kitchen. He'd make Ellery some broth to see if that would calm her stomach and help strengthen her. As he cooked, Ellery's blue eyes never seemed far from his mind. He was a doctor. He healed people. But he'd never felt so protective of a patient before. He didn't want to only heal her, he wanted to care for her.

3

Ellery was drawn from her deep sleep by a delicious smell. Her stomach rumbled and cramped almost painfully as she opened her eyes. Dr. Faulkner smiled softly at her as he held a bowl of soup.

"I thought you might be hungry."

"I'm starving," she said, finding the black dots had receded. While she felt weak and wrung out like a wet dishtowel, it was still better than the first time she had awoken. "What time is it?"

"It's almost noon," he told her as he held the bowl for her. Her hand shook as she lifted the spoon to her mouth. Dr. Faulkner held the bowl close to her mouth to make it easier for her to eat but let her move at her own pace. The first sip was like a burst of flavor. Her stomach growled as the soothing broth calmed her sore throat.

"Who knew broth could taste like a five star meal?" she joked as she took another sip. By the fifth, her hand shook less and her body felt more grounded. When she finished, the doctor set the bowl down and turned to her.

"I think we need to talk now."

Dread filled her, but she nodded. Every time she thought about her missing memories, her head rewarded her with stabbing pain.

"Do you want to sit up?" the doctor asked.

"Yes, please," she said as the doctor moved the back of the table to a sitting position. She leaned against it and realized she no longer wore her clothes. "Dr. Faulkner, what happened to my clothes?"

"They're over there," he said, pointing to the countertop. "I had to get you dry and warm. And please, call me Gavin."

Gavin. Ellery sighed. The man was tall and strong, and she'd heard his voice in her dreams telling her she was safe. His voice kept her from going too deeply into the darkness.

"I didn't get a chance before, but thank you for saving me. I'm so relieved you weren't hurt." Ellery watched as he pulled his seat close to her and sat down. At some point he'd changed out of his sweats and into scrubs. She also noticed it was no longer completely quiet. She heard the muted sounds of conversation coming from somewhere behind one of the doors.

"You're welcome. I'm relieved you're doing as well as you are. But now, the not so fun part. Paperwork."

He held up a clipboard, and Ellery smiled when she really wanted to groan.

"Full name?" Gavin asked.

"Ellery," Ellery said before stopping suddenly. Pain shot through her head, and she raised a hand to rub her temple.

"Ellery what?" Gavin asked.

"It's floating right there, but I can't think of it."

She closed her eyes as her head hurt more. Then she felt his hand on her leg, right above her knee. "Ellery, it's okay. Some memory loss is expected after the trauma you've been through. Let's just answer what you can, okay?" The heat from his hand and the way he gently squeezed her leg calmed her.

"Okay. What's next?" she asked, taking a deep breath.

"Do you know where you live?"

"Charleston," Ellery said quickly. But then she frowned. She could see the inside of her home, except it was blurred so much she couldn't pick out details.

"Do you know what you do for a living?" Gavin asked as he continued to gently hold her leg.

"It's like everything is blurry. I see colors. Lots of colors." Ellery was growing irritated, and her heart felt as if it was going to burst.

"Parents?"

"Dead. I know that much."

"You're doing very well, Ellery. Things will come back to you as the swelling goes down. You were hit on the back of the head."

The image of a car window reflection of something menacing arcing through the air raced through her mind. Her body shivered, and she didn't realize she'd reached for Gavin until he was by her side holding her. "What do you remember?"

"I was reaching for a car door, and I saw something in the window swing at me. I feel fear when I think of it."

"Was it nighttime or daytime?" Gavin asked as his arm wrapped around her shoulder, holding her other shoulder against his chest. She felt warm and safe when she was close to him. She didn't know if it was because he'd rescued her or because she knew he wasn't involved with whatever it was in Charleston that sent panic racing through her at the thought of going back.

"Night. It was raining."

"You're doing well, Ellery. Let's continue. Are you married?"

Ellery looked down at her hands. No ring or indention on her left hand. Her right hand bore a blue topaz ring encircled with a halo of small diamonds. "I can't remember, but I don't think so. This ring. It was my great-grandmother's. Her name was Ellery too. I'm named after her." She looked up and smiled at Gavin. She could remember some things, and that made her feel hopeful.

"Do you remember anything about your medical history? What's your birthdate?"

"November 7th." Ellery's heart sped up as she remembered. "I'm twenty-eight years old. I broke my arm four-wheeling when I was fifteen. I'm allergic to sunflower seeds."

She watched as Gavin wrote everything down. "I have no doubt you'll get your full memory back. Don't push it, though. Just let it happen." He set the clipboard down and ran his hand over her arm to grasp her hands. "Can you think of anyone you'd like me to call?"

"Tibbie," Ellery said on a rush as the name burst from her mind.

"Who's Tibbie?" Gavin asked.

The pain shot into her head as she became frustrated again. "Ugh. I can't remember."

"I can call the sheriff—"

"No!" Ellery said, the pain stabbing her head now as her heart raced. "I don't know why, but no one can know where I am. I think my life depends on it."

Gavin nodded as he began the calming rub of his hand on her back. "Sheriff Granger Fox is one of my good friends. But I won't say anything to him if you don't want me to. I do have another option if you'd allow it."

"What's that?" Ellery asked suspiciously.

"I have family in Kentucky who could find out your identity, address, and such."

"Do they know anyone in Charleston?" Ellery asked. Kentucky was pretty far away. Maybe far enough that whatever darkness had tried to hurt her couldn't reach.

"I don't know, but they have no ties to the city. The only ties I know about are to my family."

She looked at Gavin. He hadn't given her any reason not to trust him. "Okay. If they promise to not tell anyone anything about me."

"Would you feel better if you talked to them too?" Gavin asked.

"Yes," she said instantly. She desperately wanted the missing puzzle pieces of her memory back.

Gavin pulled out his phone, and a minute later a handsome man holding an infant in his arms showed up on his screen. "Hey cuz, what's up?"

"I need your help," Gavin told the attractive man with hazel eyes.

"You got it. Sweetheart, can you take Ash? Gavin needs my help."

A woman with auburn hair appeared and bent down to slide the baby into her arms. "Does he need help finding a girlfriend? Nora at the Fluff and Buff has been asking about . . ." The woman then turned to the screen and smiled after a quick flash of surprise. Ellery had leaned over to see the baby and the woman caught sight of her. "I guess Gavin doesn't need my help after all. Hi, I'm Sienna Parker."

"Um, Ellery," she said, smiling back at the woman.

"How long have you known Gavin?" Sienna asked, taking a seat next to her husband and taking over the conversation.

"A couple hours," Ellery said, looking to Gavin for help. She wasn't his girlfriend, and she expected Gavin to inform them of that. But when he didn't, she continued, "Gavin rescued me from flood waters during the hurricane."

"That's so romantic." Sienna sighed.

"And it's why I need to talk to Ryan. Love to you and the family, but it's official business."

Sienna rolled her eyes and went to get up, but Ellery stopped her. She didn't know why, but the woman exuded caring and understanding, even over the phone. "It's okay if she stays."

"I knew I liked you," Sienna said with a wink as she sat back down. "But what do you need the FBI for?"

"FBI!" Ellery practically shrieked. "I told you no one could know about me."

"It's okay, Ellery. Ryan won't say a word, will you?"

"I can't say anything unless you tell me what's going on," Ryan said patiently. But Ellery was already moving to stand up.

"Ellery," Sienna said calmly. "Please sit down. What can we do to help you?"

Ellery took a seat. They wanted to help. They weren't going to turn her over to whoever hurt her. They were offering help to a complete stranger, and soon Ellery found herself telling Sienna all that she could remember.

"You poor thing!" Sienna cried. "I want to give you a hug so badly right now."

"Sweetheart," Ryan said, shaking his head, "can I offer Ellery my help or do you two want to go ahead and plan your girls' trip now and call me when you're done?" Ellery laughed at the loving teases the two tossed at each other. It was clear they were deeply in love and blissfully happy in their marriage.

"Have Gavin give you my number. I expect to hear from you soon. Now, I'll let y'all get down to business while I change Ash."

When Sienna disappeared from view, Ryan leaned forward. "So, you think the person who hurt you has enough power to find you if you go to the local police?"

"I don't know. I don't even know where I was when I got hit and can't guess at who would want to kill me. I don't know anything right now except I'm scared," Ellery admitted. Gavin put his arm around her again. She leaned into him, unconsciously seeking his protection.

"I'm going to snap your picture and run it and your information through an untraceable search. It won't be on the FBI network so there's no way anyone will be able to trace it," Ryan reassured her.

"Nash?" Gavin asked, and Ryan nodded.

"He's a friend who can operate in the shadows of the law because he's security for a foreign prince and has the lovely ability to claim diplomatic immunity. Does that meet with your approval?" Ryan asked her.

"If Gavin trusts you both, I do too."

"Smile," Ryan said. "I'll call you as soon as I have something. Feel better, Ellery, and Gavin, let us know if you need any help."

"Thanks, cuz."

Gavin ended the video call right as there was a knock on the door. He stood and called for the person to enter. A young woman around twenty-five with sun-kissed blonde hair and scrubs with a low V-neck poked her head in. "Doctor, room one is waiting."

"Thank you, Sadie."

Sadie looked at Ellery with curiosity before closing the

door. "You have other patients, and here I am taking up all your time. If you could tell me where the nearest hotel—"

"You're not staying at a hotel. If I can't get you to a hospital, you're staying here so I can watch you." Gavin turned off the IV and unhooked it from her hand. "Do you think you can walk a bit?" Gavin held out his hand to help her from the table.

Ellery grimaced when she put pressure on her legs. It was as if her whole body was bruised and beaten. Gavin put his arm around her waist and led her through a second door into his office then out into a hallway. "This is my house. I'm going to set you here on the couch. Bathroom is there. Kitchen is through there. Make yourself at home. If you need anything, just shout. I'll be able to hear you. I shouldn't be too long. Are you sure you're okay to be left alone? Sadie can come sit with you if you'd like."

"No," Ellery said quickly. She didn't want the perky nurse to stare at her or ask too many questions. "I'll be fine. Thank you, Gavin."

Ellery sat on the couch and watched the doctor stride from the room. She looked around and felt herself relax. It was a comfortable room with pictures on the bookcase, large windows, and a fluffy blanket. It may be hot outside, but the air conditioner was keeping it nice and cool. Ellery managed to get up and walk around, taking in the beautiful artwork hanging on the walls. They were splendid. She looked closely and saw them signed by "Tinsley."

After a turn around the living room and a trip to the bathroom where she stood under the hot water of the shower for what felt like forever, Ellery was exhausted. She curled up on the couch, pulled the blanket to her chin, and turned on the television. She fell asleep listening to a daytime talk show and dreamed of Gavin pulling her from the water, and of his lips on hers. Even if it was just CPR, she'd still felt his lips. And then the dream changed to a happy future where she and Gavin walked through downtown Charleston hand in hand. Until a dark shadow approached from behind and swung. Her head exploded in pain, and on a gasp, Ellery's eyes shot open.

4

"Ellery St. John is her name," Ryan told Gavin two hours later. Gavin had finished giving a round of tetanus shots and sewing up a couple cuts for people injured while cleaning up debris. "She lives in a condo on Rutledge Avenue. I emailed pictures of her condo that Nash pulled off social media. Also, Tibbie is Mrs. Elijah F. Cummings."

"Elijah Cummings's wife. How does she know someone as powerful as her? She's one of the grand dames of society here."

"They have the penthouse in her condo building. Or I should say, *their* building, as they own it all and turned it into condos ten years ago. They downsized, giving their mansion to their eldest son when he and his wife had their second child and moved into the penthouse in their building," Ryan told him. Nash never left a stone unturned. "Ellery works as the art director at the Mimi Hollis Art Gallery. Last night she was in charge of an exhibit for a Mark Vosslinger. So far, she has not been reported missing."

"So, she doesn't live with anyone then?" Gavin asked.

"Stop holding your breath. She's single. At least on her

social media account it appears to be so. Her last boyfriend was two months ago. Some society guy named Atherton Hawthorne. Looks like they dated for a little under a year. After the break-up, Nash noted there was an increase of Ellery's name in the papers for her job. She's been working nonstop. Today's paper had rave reviews for the exhibit she put on last night. She's launched this Mark guy to artistic stardom."

Gavin thought about all Ryan had told him, but it didn't add up. "Then who would want to kill her? No angry boyfriend, she's well liked, and she's good at her job."

"I wouldn't say the boyfriend was angry, but he wanted her back. Ellery had deleted all his pictures from social media, but he left them on his profile with her tagged. That's how I found him. He's also been actively commenting on her pictures and posts. Further, he was at the gallery exhibit. He says he was there to support Ellery. Nash did find some one-star reviews of the gallery aimed at Ellery. Mostly from men who didn't appreciate not receiving Ellery's *full attention* and a couple of artists upset Ellery didn't select their work to show. I sent those to you as well."

"Thanks a lot. And thank Nash for me too."

"No problem. Call anytime."

Gavin hung up with his cousin and opened his email. He printed off the information and then locked it in the desk. He wanted to give Ellery time to remember things on her own. He'd slowly leave clues for her to remember if she'd not regained more memories by the morning. Maybe leave the picture of her apartment on his kitchen table among pictures of other apartments for rent just to see if she remembered her home.

"Gavin?"

Gavin looked up from his desk as Sadie walked in. "Yes?"

"Sheriff Fox just called. A big alligator was spotted in the alley between the Daughters of Shadows Landing and Gil's Grub 'n' Gas. Gator's coming in from the marsh to try to catch it, but apparently one of Lydia's kids is trapped on top of a dumpster and is bleeding. Don't know if the kid was bit or if it was from climbing up to safety," Sadie told him. "The sheriff asked if you could meet him there in fifteen minutes. He's afraid there's going to be injuries when Gator tries to remove the alligator."

"Thanks, Sadie. I know it's your time to leave for the day, but would you mind staying long enough to see if I'll need help in surgery?"

"Sure thing. Um, where did that woman go? She's not in the patient rooms and she never came out to the lobby to pay."

"She's not a paying patient. She's a friend of mine."

A smile bloomed on Sadie's pretty face. "A *girl*friend?" she asked, wiggling her eyebrows. "About time!"

Gavin just chuckled and shook his head. "Yes, she is a girl and she is a friend, but she's nothing more." He grabbed his bag and ignored the crestfallen look on Sadie's face.

"We'll just see about that." She grinned as she closed the door.

Gavin hurried, gathering supplies, and strode into the living room. Ellery was up watching some talk show before the local news came on. "I have to go out. There's an alligator incident in town. I'll be back as soon as I can."

Ellery's stomach rumbled, and she laughed. "Sorry, I do love fried gator, and I'm starving."

Gavin pursed his lips in thought. "Do you think you're up for an outing? You can wait in the car while we handle the alligator, and then we can grab dinner at Stomping Grounds after. But only if you're up for it."

Ellery's stomach rumbled even louder. "I am feeling much better after the nap. I'd like to try at least, but I don't have anything to wear."

"I can help with that. He walked over to the wall in the hallway and pressed a button. "Sadie, can you come to the living room, please?"

"Oh, no," Ellery said, shaking her head. "I don't want—"

"Yes, Gavin?" Sadie said as if she'd run through the office as fast as possible. She took in Ellery sitting on the couch and smiled even wider.

"Sadie, this is my friend, Ellery. Ellery, this is my nurse and receptionist, Sadie."

Sadie pushed past him and took a seat on the couch next to a very skeptical looking Ellery and shook her hand. "It is so great to meet you. Don't you think we have the hunkiest doctor around?"

"Sadie," Gavin groaned, but it didn't stop her.

"We all think he's so wonderful, but he never takes the time to date much. But now you're here! He needs a good woman to take care of him, and I can tell you're just that woman!"

ELLERY BLINKED RAPIDLY as Sadie talked a mile a minute. She looked as if she belonged in a bikini shoot on the beach with her blonde hair and tanned skin, and Ellery was ashamed to admit she might have thought badly about her when she first saw her because she was jealous of the girl's looks. She didn't quite know how she could become jealous over the possibility of Gavin being with Sadie after only a couple of conversations, but she was. And instead of giving Sadie a chance, she'd written her off. But now she sat there nice as could be, hoping Gavin and she were a couple.

"Sadie." Gavin groaned as Sadie began to talk of all the things they could do for a date night.

"Well, we are going to someplace called Stomping Grounds," Ellery said, her energy being buoyed by this bundle of happiness sitting next to her.

"Oh my gosh! Date night after some alligator wrangling. How romantic!"

"Sadie." Gavin sounded as if he were dying. "Please, take a breath. I asked you here to help Ellery. Do you have any clothes she could borrow until I can take her to Bless Your Scarf for something new?"

"Of course!" Sadie jumped up, but then paused. "Where are your clothes?"

Ellery's heart began to pound as she looked frantically to Gavin. She didn't know what to say.

"Ellery wasn't expecting to spend the night and with the flooded roads she only has this one outfit that is still drying after being caught in the storm, which is where she was hurt. Took a nasty fall."

Ellery just nodded. "You poor thing! But I'm glad you're able to stay longer. I have a spare outfit in my locker. I'll be right back."

"Sorry," Gavin said as soon as Sadie was out of the room. "I should have known better than to think Sadie wouldn't ask a ton of questions. Unfortunately, we're a very friendly small town here so everyone will be asking you these questions. I can pick up dinner for you if you'd like."

Ellery thought about it for a moment, but the panic she'd initially felt lessened. Shadows Landing wasn't a hotbed of the who's who from Charleston. "No, I would like to go out. I think we can handle it like we have and all will be good."

"Here you go!" Sadie called out as she rushed back into the living room. "I have a jean skirt, a T-shirt, and flip-flops."

"Thank you," Ellery said with a grin. Sadie had a heart of gold, as her mother used to say. And just like that, Ellery smiled even larger. Gavin had been right, she was remembering more and more. Soon she'd remember why she was hit on the head and how she ended up in the water.

"Have fun you two. Call me and let me know if you need me to get the surgery room ready." Sadie gave a little finger wave and practically bounded back out.

"Let me show you to the guest room, and you can get changed there." Gavin reached out for her, and Ellery put her hand in his. His fingers were long, his palm wide, and his hand seemed to engulf hers. It radiated heat and something more. There was something that caused her heart to beat a little faster as he led her upstairs and into a room decorated in pale blue with white trim and furniture. The bed had a mountain of pillows and a coral comforter that looked perfect for curling up in. "I hate to rush you, but we need to be there in ten minutes."

"No problem," Ellery said, turning her back to him as he left the room. She changed quickly, happy to see the clothes fit better than expected. The top was maybe a size too small, but it wasn't bad.

Ellery flung open the door, and when she stepped out she saw Gavin standing in the middle of the room at the end of the hall. The white trimmed doorframe outlined him. He had on jeans, boots, and was stripped from the waist up. He didn't see her standing there as she took in the rippled muscles along his side and down to where his jeans sat low on his hips. He raised his arms into a T-shirt and turned slightly toward her as he pulled it over his head. Her eyes traveled down a well-sculpted chest and over the flat plain of his abdomen carved with muscle. He reminded her of a work of art. David, Doryphoros, and Discobolus. All sculptures that captured the male body's beauty.

"Ellery?"

Ellery didn't realize her eyes had dropped, and she'd zoned out. Something was on the tip of her memory, trying to push through. At least this time her head no longer hurt.

"I feel as if I'm trying to remember something."

Gavin rushed forward, taking her hand in his once again as he began to walk down the stairs. "That's great. Don't force it. What were you doing when it came to you?"

Ellery flushed red. There was no way she was going to tell him she was staring at the sexiest body she'd seen in real life. "I remembered seeing some ancient statues in person. I must have traveled to Europe at some point."

Gavin opened the garage door and tossed his medical bag into the small backseat of his convertible. He hurried around and opened the door for her. "I bet you'll remember more and more as time goes on."

5

Ellery hoped more memories would come back. She was tired of having these blank spots in her head. Maybe taking her mind off it would help. "Tell me about Shadows Landing," she said as Gavin backed out of the garage and onto a residential street. His was the first house on his side of the street. She took in the palmettos, the grass slightly mixed with sand, the smell of the river and pluff mud at low tide. Some may wrinkle their nose at the strong odor of the slippery, vacuum-like mud exposed in and around the spartina grasses as the tide went out, but Ellery always thought it smelled like home.

"This is Palmetto Drive. On my side of the street, the houses are either older or historic homes that back up to the Shadows River, which is an offshoot of Cooper River. Next to me is Shadows Park and the marina." Ellery looked behind her at the old large houses with verandas running the length of the houses and probably more in the back overlooking the river.

"Across from me are the newer houses. My cousin Ridge lives in a big new house he built on the opposite end of the street. And then our cousin Ryker, who lives in Charleston during the week, has a historical house across the street from Ridge and next to the Bell Landing Plantation on the end of Palmetto Drive. My sister, Harper, lives in that house," he said, pointing to a new small cottage-style house. "And see, the next block is Main Street. That's why Harper bought that house. The side of her lot backs up to the back lots of the businesses on Main Street, including her bar."

"So she can just walk to and from work?" Ellery asked as they turned right onto Main Street and parked in front of the crowded Gil's Grub 'n' Gas.

"Yes, and with her hours it makes me feel good she doesn't have far to go alone."

"She's not married?" Ellery asked.

Gavin reached behind him and grabbed his bag. "No. None of us are. My cousins in Keeneston have started to get married as you saw this morning, but the trend hasn't hit us here yet."

Ellery opened her door and got out, holding onto the door for support, but was pleasantly surprised to find herself feeling pretty steady. "I don't think I have a boyfriend. But at this point, I'm not sure of much."

"That's good to know," a slow voice drawled.

Ellery turned to find a man in a dark brown button-up sheriff's uniform tucked into a pair of hip hugging jeans and a tan cowboy hat on his head. His eyes were hidden behind mirrored aviator glasses, but there was no mistaking the sharp intellect hidden behind his slow words. His chiseled face was a work of art that caused more statues to run through her mind. That had to mean something.

"Granger," Gavin said, holding out his hand to the sheriff. When Ellery had thought of the sheriff she'd imagined someone with white hair, a potbelly, and a big mustache, not someone in his thirties and built like a star football player. "This is my friend, Ellery. Ellery, our sheriff, Granger Fox."

Ellery held out her hand and shook Granger's. His handshake was firm and controlled. Everything about him was controlled, as if he had a side trying to break free from his calm demeanor. "Nice to met you."

"Have we met before? You look really familiar."

Ellery shook her head and absently reached for Gavin. His hand slid around hers for support. "I don't think so."

"I see Gator hasn't gotten here yet. Want to show me the situation?" Gavin asked, eagerly changing the subject.

Granger looked at Ellery one last time and touched the tip of his hat with his finger. "Ma'am," he said before turning toward Gavin. "Lydia is dangling over the roof, talking to her kid. It's her sixth kid who found the gator. Can't remember all their names. Lydia was getting gas when the kids apparently couldn't keep their hands to themselves in the minivan. Door opened and kids went scattering. Lydia heard a scream and came running to the entrance of the alleyway only to meet face to face with the gator. The kid had managed to not see the ten-foot gator in his run from his siblings, but as soon as he heard the hiss, he screamed and jumped onto the dumpster."

Ellery followed behind them as they went into the alley. There was a large piece of plywood forming a gate across the alley, trapping the gator inside. Ellery looked back and saw a kid no more than five or six sitting on top of the dumpster playing a video game. He looked completely unconcerned about the large alligator waiting at the bottom of the dumpster. A woman, who couldn't be more than twenty-eight years old, lay on the roof of the gas station, leaning over talking to her son who was ignoring her.

"How many times have I told you not to run from the car? Lyle, listen to me or I will take away video games for a month."

"Mom," the kid whined as he rolled his eyes and went back to playing his game.

"Your father is going to hear about this," she said, and a second later the video game was turned off. "You'll be grounded for a week if you don't get eaten by this alligator."

"But Lindsey punched me in the arm, and Leah threw slime at me," Lyle complained. Ellery looked around and found a herd of children in the gas station picking on each other.

"She has seven kids?" Ellery whispered as she counted them all up.

"Her husband is in the military. Every time he comes home on leave she gets pregnant. Had her first one at twenty-one. That would be Landry Jr. He's ten now. Then there's one a year after that. Landry Jr., Lacy, Levi, Leah, Lindsey, Lyle, and Leo. I've delivered the last five."

"That's amazing. I want to look like that now, and she's a couple years older than me with seven kids." Ellery looked at the tall and trim woman in a camisole top and short jean shorts, dangling off the roof lecturing five-year-old Lyle.

"Okay, you hoodlums, who wants a snack?" an older man with dark brown skin, a shaved head, and an apron asked as he walked across the street with a tray filled with food. The kids at the gas station stopped squabbling and immediately ran to greet the man.

"Thank you, Mr. Darius. Kids, thank Mr. Darius," Lydia called out as a chorus of thanks rang out from the kids as they descended on the man in his late fifties like a pack of wild animals. When they ran away with food in hand, the man's platter was empty. "My purse is on the front seat, just get what I owe you for the dinner."

"Today is on me," the man called out. "And I saved one for Lyle when he's free."

"Thank you Mr. D!" the young voice yelled from the alley.

Darius headed over toward her as Gavin began talking to Lyle and asking him to show him the cut he got. "Ma'am," he said to her, and he nodded his shiny shaved head. Ellery took a deep breath. He smelled of barbeque and it made her mouth water.

"Oh my gosh, you smelled so good".

He chuckled. "So, you here with the doc?"

"Yes," Ellery said, holding out her hand. "I'm his friend, Ellery."

"Darius Foster. Owner and main cook at the Pink Pig BBQ right there across the street." Ellery turned around and saw the rotating giant pink pig on top of the building. Pink Pig BBQ was emblazoned on a sign in the parking lot and across the front plate-glass windows.

"It smells so good," she said, her stomach suddenly rumbling.

"Well, let me get you a sandwich to welcome you to Shadows Landing." Darius smiled.

"Not so fast, Darius. This woman will be wanting real BBQ. The kind smoked over wood for ten hours to give you the best juicy smoky taste around. Much better than your coal cooked pig."

Ellery turned to see a man equal in age to Darius, but everything else was polar opposite. Where Darius was tall and muscular, this guy was short and heavy. Where Darius had dark skin, this man was rocking a farmer's tan under his shirtless overalls. And where Darius had a shaved head, this man had a full head of white hair partially hidden under a bandana. He also had a full beard that would make him an excellent Santa Claus at Christmas.

"Earl, you know that slop you call barbecue can't compare with my work of gastro art. The flavor bursts in your mouth with every bite." Darius winked at her.

The other man held out his hand. "Earl Taylor. Owner and cook of the Lowcountry Smokehouse. And I wouldn't feed Darius's barbeque to a Clemson fan! Why don't you and the doc stop by and have a free meal on me to taste real barbeque?"

"She will not be going anywhere with you," Darius said with a grin. "She thinks I smell good. And if she thinks that, she's going to die on the spot when she tastes my cookin'."

"Because it'll kill her! A beautiful woman like you should only have the best, and my barbeque is the best around," Earl said smugly as Ellery's head turned back and forth between the men bickering as if they were two of Lydia's children.

"We'll have to settle this debate another time, gentlemen," Gavin said with a smile on his face as he shook both men's hands. "Here comes Gator. We already have plans for a quick meal at Stomping Grounds."

"He's going all fancy," Earl muttered.

"Trying to impress her, I'm sure," Darius agreed as Ellery watched a dented pickup truck, covered with so much mud she couldn't tell the make, model, or even color of it, pull to a stop.

The truck bed was covered in metal wiring, creating a big cage. Inside the cage was a big wooden coffin looking box with numerous air holes drilled on the top. A large man somewhere between twenty and forty years old hefted himself from the truck. He was over six feet, had a beard that put Earl's to shame, and wore thigh high waders over his jeans. His shirt was like the truck, undeterminable under all the mud. Unlike Earl, he was solid muscle. He could have been a linebacker in the NFL the way he was built.

"Thanks for coming, Gator," Granger said, holding out his hand and shaking Gator's.

"What've you got?" Gator asked as he looked into the ally. "Bubba, that you?"

The gator opened his mouth and hissed.

"Yup, that's him. You can tell, he's missing a tooth. A tooth that I happened to have right here," Gator said patting his necklace.

"Is that the one I dug out of your arm last year?" Gavin asked.

"You betcha. Every time it storms, Bubba likes to go explorin'. Last hurricane he was on the back porch of the Bell plantation. Now he's coming into town for little tropical storms. Ridge had me come get him last month when he found him in his pool. I'll get my things, but I'll need some help with Bubba. He's a little over five hundred pounds and still growing."

Ellery knew alligators. She was from Charleston after all, and there were gators up and down the coast. However, she'd never seen one so close and had never watched as people merely shrugged their shoulders and took off any loose articles of clothing as they headed to capture Bubba. And Bubba looked like he couldn't wait. She would have sworn the gator smiled in anticipation of the battle to come.

Gator pulled the wooden box from the back of the truck, and Granger helped him carry it closer to the alley. Then Gator pulled out some electrical tape, rope, and two hand towels as the men all lined up behind him.

"You're not going in there, are you?" Ellery whispered as she grabbed Gavin's hand.

"Of course I am. Worried about me?" He smirked, and Ellery really hoped she didn't have a boyfriend because right now Gavin seemed to be wiggling his way into her heart. Or at least her panties—she wished.

"Yes. That's a huge alligator. You could get hurt," Ellery said fearfully.

"Gator knows what he's doing. Besides he'll need five people to pick Bubba up, and I won't clear you for that kind of activity yet." He winked at her as he handed her his medical bag. "I'll be right back for that. If anyone starts bleeding, you can patch them up."

"That's not funny," Ellery called out as Gavin joined Gator, Granger, Earl, Darius, and a guy coming from the gas station she guessed was Gil since it was written in blue script above a picture of a worm on a hook.

"Landry," Gator called out and the eldest boy disengaged from a fight with two of his siblings.

"Yes, sir?" the lanky ten-year-old asked as he ran toward them.

"I want you to pull that wooden gate away enough for us to get inside and then close it. We don't want Bubba bustin' out. As soon as we got Bubba, I want you to pull it all the way open."

"Yes, sir," Landry said with excitement as he moved to grab the wood plank set up across the alleyway.

"Okay, Landry. Open it up."

Ellery nervously clutched the medical bag as Bubba hissed louder and snapped while Gator led the group into the alley.

"Don't worry, they've done this a hundred times or more."

Ellery turned and looked down at a woman a couple years younger than herself. And even though she was petite, her curves weren't. The rainforest green sundress matched her eyes and showed off her hourglass figure. Her long brown hair was pulled into a high ponytail and there was dry paint on her slim fingers.

"Tinsley Faulkner, I'm Gavin's youngest cousin."

"Ellery. Your cousin is . . . a friend?"

Tinsley laughed as they watched Bubba track Gator with his eyes. "Friend, is that what you call it? I've already heard from Sadie you spent the night with Gavin."

Ellery's mouth fell open. People were already talking about her? And with Gavin? Okay, that part wasn't bad, but did they think she was a big city floozy? "Gavin helped me last night when I was stuck in the storm. That's all."

Tinsley shrugged a smooth and tanned shoulder. "Too bad. Gavin's a great guy."

"Well, I didn't say I wasn't interested," Ellery defended, and Tinsley laughed again.

Ellery watched as Gil distracted Bubba, then all of a sudden the big man leapt. Bubba tried to snap his head around as Gator lay on his back with his hands pressing down behind the alligator's head. Ellery was pretty sure she'd gasped out loud and now realized she had also grabbed Tinsley's hand and squeezed it tight as Gavin and the rest of the men pinned the alligator down with their bodies.

"Towel," Gator said calmly as Gil tossed the towel over Bubba's face. As soon as Bubba's eyes were covered, Gator grabbed his jaws and pulled the gator's head up toward his face. He tucked the jaws of the massive alligator under his chin and faster than any cowboy roped Bubba's jaws closed and used the electrical tape to keep the towel over Bubba's eyes.

"Okay Landry, take down the gate," Gator called out as the men repositioned themselves to pick up Bubba.

"Come on, let's get the box closer. It's easier for them to carry the box than Bubba."

"You know Bubba?" Ellery asked. Tinsley and Landry pushed the heavy wooden box into the alley as the men grunted and picked up Bubba.

"Sure. He was in Harper's, that's Gavin's sister, front yard one day when I pulled in. Bubba didn't let me get out of the car, and when I tried to drive away he bit my tire. Gator and Harper and some of her neighbors rescued me.

Tinsley and Ellery hopped back as soon as the men drew near. "Gil, open the box, will ya?" Gator called out. Gil ran over, pulled off the lid, and took out a bag of screws and a power drill.

The men's faces were red as they worked to awkwardly carry the five hundred pound alligator and set him in the box. As soon as he was in, Gavin grabbed his bag, sent her a wink, and headed straight for Lyle.

"Sure, friends you call it." Tinsley gave Ellery a look that left Ellery grinning. If only she could remember who she was and whether or not she was married or had a boyfriend. Until then she couldn't reciprocate Gavin's flirtations.

Gator closed the box and all the men were back to lift it into the back of the pickup. "You need help?" Gil asked.

"Nah. Turtle can help me when I get him to the swamp. Thanks for your help."

"Send me your invoice," Granger told him, shaking Gator's hand.

The men began to disburse as Tinsley and Ellery watched Gavin patch up Lyle, and Lydia made her way off the roof of the Grab 'n' Gas and ran to her son. Meanwhile, the others had started a water war with the squeegees used to clean windshields.

"Hey," Tinsley yelled at them. "Put those back and go get a juice box from my fridge. Don't forget to get one for Lyle."

The kids ran by them, crossed the street, and turned into an old building with a sign hanging that simply read "Art Gallery." Ellery felt her breath hitch as she was drawn to the gallery. "This is your place?" she asked over her shoulder.

Tinsley turned and caught up with her. "Yes. I just opened it. I'm kinda new at this gallery thing, but my family convinced me to show off my work. If it was up to me, I'd still be hiding in the woods painting. Do you like art?"

"I love it," Ellery said as they crossed the street and headed up the old cobbled sidewalk to her gallery. Ellery was about to open the door when the herd of kids raced out with juice boxes. Ellery stepped inside and gasped. It was as if she'd been pelted with memories. "I work in a gallery," she said on a whisper as she visualized herself last night in the black dress placing a sold sticker next to a painting. She closed her eyes and tried to remember more. The faces were all a blur, but the art . . . the art she could see.

"You do?" Tinsley asked. "I admit there are quite a few galleries I haven't been to. Which one do you work at? I wonder if I know it."

"Excuse me," Gavin interrupted. "Are you ready to go eat?"

Ellery could only nod because she felt like crying. She couldn't remember the name of the gallery, but she knew something with certainty. She worked at one.

"It was so great meeting you. Please, stop by anytime to talk art," Tinsley said, walking with them toward the door.

"Tinsley," Ellery said suddenly, "you painted the beautiful art in Gavin's house."

"That's right. Funny you've been there long enough to notice that. Have a nice date." Then Tinsley turned and headed back into the gallery as she pulled out her phone.

"The family will be descending," Gavin muttered. "She's telling them all I have a new girlfriend."

"Well, I learned I work in an art gallery. Now if I can remember if I have a boyfriend, then—" Ellery stopped suddenly and almost covered her mouth with her hand.

6

"Then what?" Gavin asked as casually as he could. He didn't want to admit to himself how badly he wanted to hear her answer. He didn't know why this woman had gotten under his skin. He couldn't stop thinking about her. On top of that, knowing she didn't have a boyfriend made it very hard not to be too forward.

"Um, then we'd know if this was really a date. Not that it is. I'm sure you're only feeding me out of obligation." Ellery was talking a mile a minute, and he knew she was embarrassed.

He reached for her hand and slid his fingers through hers as they began to walk again. "It's a date, Ellery."

Gavin enjoyed seeing her blush as they walked by the church. He pulled her to a stop and looked back to where Bubba was caught. "Across the street you saw the Daughters of Shadows Landing, it was one of the buildings Bubba was trapped between. Then next to that is Harper's bar. And if you haven't remembered where you live by tomorrow, then I'll take you to Bless Your Scarf so you can get some clothes."

"Main Street is lovely. It's so historic," she said as she

gazed past the antique shop and at Stomping Grounds at the end of the street.

"It was settled in 1690 by rice farmers. Main Street was built by pirates in the 1700s. There was an old tavern that burned down in 1770, a hotel, which is now part of the courthouse, and small houses belonging to the pirates. Over time, they became rich from their smuggling, and by the late 1700s and early 1800s, these buildings were all built and here they still stand. They've been converted into businesses now."

Ellery turned and looked at the tall church steeple. "I'm surprised they built a church if they were pirates."

"Churches were sanctuaries. If the law ever showed up, they'd hightail it into the church. Now it's a real church, but the reverend likes to remind everyone that the church will always be a sanctuary to those in need, since we don't have too many pirates anymore."

Gavin looked at the white church with the tall steeple covered in dark gray shingles. Light through the stained glass windows would be creating a breathtaking view inside the historic church.

"The reverend didn't care that pirates were using it to hide out?"

"See those stained glass windows? How do you think a little church in the middle of nowhere could afford those? They still use the gold chalice for communion. A chalice that looks shockingly similar to one the Spanish say went missing when a boat of theirs disappeared in 1793," Gavin said with a smile. He loved all the old tales of Shadows Landing.

"Really?"

"Really. Shadows Landing got its name because it was perfect to come in under the shadows to unload their stolen goods. The dock down at the marina has been there since they settled the area. The water is tricky and only those who knew the depths could navigate it with those big ships. So they'd wait until nightfall and slip past Charleston. Anyone who pursued them would get stuck as the pirates escaped up to Shadows Landing. They'd unload and wait for high tide to navigate their boats to the offshoot that runs behind Main Street," he said, pointing behind the church. "The boats would then be hidden if anyone made their way up Shadows River."

Gavin and Ellery began walking past the courthouse and the sheriff's department. Ellery sniffed the air and sighed with pleasure. "That's the Lowcountry Smokehouse," he said, pointing to the pit smoked BBQ restaurant across South Cypress Lane. Main Street began at Palmetto Drive and ended on Cypress. If they'd turn left they could take South Cypress into Charleston. If they turned right they'd pass a law office, a beauty salon, and a couple of small shops before coming across some smaller houses built in the 1930s through 1950s. His cousin Wade, who was in the Coast Guard, lived there. About a mile up from Wade was their friend Edie. Past that was the school and then the road turned into North Cypress and led out to the country where Tinsley and Trent, Wade's brother, lived.

"It smells so good. I'll have to try them both out before I leave. Well, I assume I'll eventually remember enough to leave. It's not like I can live with you forever." Again her face turned pink, and Gavin was gentlemen enough to not comment on the idea of her living with him, especially in the same bed. Since he'd seen her in the hallway dressed in Sadie's borrowed clothes, he had to admit, he'd thought about it more than once.

"Well then, date number two can be barbeque," Gavin

said as they crossed the street to Stomping Grounds. People packed the booths and outdoor tables at Lowcountry Smokehouse, Stomping Grounds, and Pink Pig. Music played from their back patios and the small town was alive with laughter, fun, and friendship. For as small of a community as Shadows Landing was, they had a lot of people come from the surrounding towns to eat their famous barbeque. But Shadows Bar was the local hangout. Since there were no hotels, the tourists usually left after dinner and then the restaurants and shops would close and everyone would gather at Harper's for a couple drinks.

"Sounds good," Ellery said with a blush on her cheeks and a smile on her lips.

Gavin opened the door and ushered her in. Locals got first dibs on tables, and the waitress led them to the last available one. Televisions played the news on silent. During football or basketball season, sports were the only thing on, but summer was lean for sports so they were left with the local news.

"We have a shrimp boil tonight," the waitress said as she handed them their menus.

"That sounds great," Ellery said as her stomach rumbled again.

"We'll have that then. Thanks, Mary Jane." Gavin handed the waitress the menus back. Two mason jars of sweet tea were placed in front of them, then it was just the two of them.

"I'm so excited," Ellery said, leaning toward him. "I remember I work in an art gallery. Now I wonder which one? And I wonder what I'll remember next?" she asked with a large grin on her face. He was glad to see her regaining some memories.

"How are you feeling? Are you worn out from the walk?"

"A little, but I'm starving. I might climb over you to grab some of that guy's dinner," she said with a giggle as she looked at the giant plate of food at the table behind them.

"That's good. Your body is healing."

Ellery nodded her head as she looked at the coastal decorations and pictures of locals that hung on the walls. "So, do you have a large family?"

"Not overly large, although it's recently gotten bigger. I told you about my sister, Harper, who owns the bar. Then you met my cousin Tinsley. Tinsley's brother is Ridge. He's a builder. Then there's Wade and Trent. Wade is in the Coast Guard, and Trent makes stunning furniture. Last is Ryker. He's the one who only lives here on the weekends. He runs a shipping company in Charleston."

"Faulkner Shipping? That's your cousin?" Ellery asked and then shook her head. "How do I remember that and not my last name?"

"Memories are strange things, you never know when something will pop back up. But, yes, that's my cousin. You know him?" Gavin asked hopefully.

"I don't think so. But I know he's always in the Charleston Social Magazine. They ran a profile on him recently."

"That's right," Gavin said, impressed she recalled that. The improvement in her memory was growing by the minute.

"Here you go, doc. And doc's friend," Mary Jane said with curiosity as she laid down newspaper before picking up a big pot and pouring out the shrimp, corn on the cob chunks, smoked sausage, and chunks of potatoes.

"Mary Jane, this is my friend, Ellery. Ellery, this is Mary Jane."

"It's nice to meet you," Ellery said, even though Gavin

could see her hand sneaking toward a plump shrimp. "Does everyone know everyone in Shadows Landing?" she asked when Mary Jane left. Ellery popped the shrimp into her mouth and groaned with delight.

"Yeah. We're a very small town. It was annoying when I was growing up, but now that I'm older, I really appreciate it. They're very supportive of each other and welcomed me and my practice with open arms, even though many of them have known me since I was born."

"Do your parents live here?"

Gavin shook his head. "My parents, Jason and Jessica, along with my cousins' parents, Brian and Amy, Paul and Kim, and Robert and Angela, all moved to Florida upon retirement. They bought a small hotel on the beach and are running it together. Although, I think they mostly go fishing."

Gavin went to ask Ellery a question, but she was staring over his shoulder as if she'd seen a ghost. Gavin turned around and saw a picture of an old man and woman on the television.

"Tibbie," Ellery said softly. "I remember her! She's my neighbor." Gavin smiled as Ellery's eyes went wide.

"Mary Jane, turn it up please," Gavin called out.

Mary Jane nodded and lifted a remote from the bar and turned the volume up.

"Mr. and Mrs. Elijah F. Cummings are asking for the public's help. Their friend and neighbor has been missing since the hurricane," the reporter said.

"Miss St. John?" Gavin heard Granger ask from behind him.

"Yes?" Ellery answered automatically as she turned her head from the television before jumping up from her seat.

"That's me! I'm Ellery St. John!" She threw her hands around Gavin's neck and kissed his cheek.

"Miss St. John is five foot seven with golden blonde hair and blue eyes. If anyone has seen her, please call the police at—" the reporter said as the phone number was flashed across the screen along with her picture.

"Miss St. John," Granger said again, stopping at the table, "we need to talk. Privately."

Gavin looked around then and noticed people were watching them. "Mary Jane, a to-go box, please."

"Coming right up."

"Miss St. John, why don't you come with me and Gavin can follow?" Granger suggested, holding out his hand for her to take.

"I'm not a criminal, am I?" Ellery asked, nervously.

"Granger, what's going on?" Gavin asked as he dropped his voice.

"Not here," Granger said under his breath as he smiled. "Poor girl can't take a vacation without her friends worrying about her," Granger said loud enough for the diners to hear. "Let's go call them so no one is worried anymore."

But that didn't fool Gavin. Something was wrong—very wrong. And as Granger escorted Ellery from the diner and across the street to the sheriff's department, he just hoped what Ellery had asked wasn't true.

7

"Do I need a lawyer?" Ellery asked as Granger Fox led her across the street. She was sure if the locals hadn't been gossiping about her being with Gavin, being escorted by the good-looking sheriff after she appeared on the news was sure to send tongues wagging.

"I don't know. Something is going on though, and we need to get to the bottom of it. That starts with you and me having a little chat." Even through the southern drawl, the tightness in his voice crept through.

Dread filled her as he opened the door to the courthouse and lead her down the hall before turning right into the sheriff's department. There was a tall counter five feet inside, dividing the small lobby from the back of the department. A receptionist sat behind the desk. She was in her fifties with her hair, probably a red at some point but had lightened with age, pulled up into a bun.

"Brenda Baker, Ellery St. John," Granger said as Brenda buzzed them into the back through the locked door on the far side of the counter.

"Hi, sugar. Boy, this is a real mess. I sure hope you're not a killer. You look too sweet to be one," Brenda said in her deep southern accent.

"A killer? I'm not a killer!" Ellery gasped as she whispered, "At least I don't remember being one."

"Brenda," Granger said with disapproval, "have Kord meet us in interrogation. Also, show Gavin in when he arrives."

"Yes, sir," Brenda said, sending Ellery a wink. Well, at least the receptionist didn't think she was a murderer.

Granger walked her down the small hall. There were two offices in the back, one with Sheriff Granger Fox and one with Deputy Kordell King written beside the door. Between them and the front desk were rows of filing cabinets, a couple of messy desks, a large oval table for meetings, and a dry-erase board set up on wheels. Currently there was a MISSING printout taped onto it with her picture front and center. Granger walked into the room at the back of the office space and flicked on the light. There was a small table, big enough to fit two people on each side. The carpet was worn and looked as if it had seen better days. The light was harsh, and it caused her head to ache as she covered her eyes with her hand to shield them from the bright glare.

"Could you turn down the lights?" Ellery asked as she cringed.

"Why? Do they make you uncomfortable?" Granger asked, leaning against what she guessed was a two-way mirror.

"I have a concussion and the lights are making my symptoms worse," she said as the pain became stronger.

"Take a seat," he ordered a second before the door opened and a young, maybe in his mid-twenties, deputy came in. His smooth dark brown skin lay over muscled arms. At least that's all she saw as she kept her head down to battle the lights.

"Miss St. John was about to tell us how she got a concussion," Granger said to the man. Ellery saw him cross his arms over his broad chest. The deputy had a flat stomach under his uniform. What, did they all play wide receiver in college? They were built for speed and strength for sure. He took a seat across from her, and his face finally came into view. His black hair was trimmed short, almost to his scalp, with perfect trim lines as if the barber used a ruler when he shaved it. His lips were full and his face angled. He was incredibly handsome, and by the little smirk he had right now, he knew it.

"Miss?" Ellery asked, keeping her eyes down to lessen the painful glare of the lights. "So, I'm not married?"

She heard the momentary pause. "No, you're not married, ma'am," Deputy King said. His voice was strong, yet warm. He wasn't scaring her like Granger was. He was obviously the good cop in this scenario. "Did you think you were?"

"I didn't know," Ellery finally admitted.

There was a knock at the door, and when it opened Ellery saw Gavin's feet step into the room. "Dammit, Granger, Ellery has a concussion. Turn down those lights or we're leaving right now."

"She was just going to tell us how she got that concussion, and then I will," Granger said with steel to his voice. He was a completely different man from the guy she'd met while wrangling Bubba the alligator. He'd been relaxed, kind, and gentlemanly. This Granger was all business.

"Now or I'm calling her an attorney." Gavin pulled out his phone and Granger turned down the lights. Relief rushed through her as the sharp pain lessened to a dull ache. "Thank you. Why don't you tell us what's going on so we can help. Otherwise we won't be saying a word."

Gavin sat next to her and grabbed her hand for support —support she desperately needed. "They think I killed someone. I couldn't do that, could I?" Ellery whispered, but Deputy King leaned forward, and she was sure he heard her.

"You don't know?" Deputy King asked with a raised eyebrow.

"Who do you think she killed? All I saw on the news were her elderly neighbors and good friends, the Cummings, reporting her missing," Gavin said, keeping his hand tight on hers.

"Tell me about the concussion, and I'll tell you about the report I got from Charleston," Granger said, keeping his arms crossed. He looked relaxed, leaning against the mirror, but Ellery knew he was nothing of the kind.

"Ellery?" Gavin whispered as he asked for her permission to share what he knew.

"Go ahead and tell him. I would hope I'm not that kind of person," Ellery told him as she began to bounce her knee nervously.

"I found Ellery clinging to a log at three in the morning when I went to secure my boat. She remembered her first name, but not her last. She remembered she was from Charleston, but not her address. There was an open wound on her head a couple inches behind her ear and she was barely breathing. I preformed CPR until she cleared herself of water. Then I sewed up her head injury. She spent the night and most of the morning throwing up water. After sleeping and rehydrating, she started to remember more as the swelling went down. I'd classify it as intermediate memory loss brought on by retrograde amnesia. However, the layman's term I'd say is Swiss cheese amnesia. It's why she can remember some things, but not others."

"What else are you remembering?" Granger asked.

"I walked into Tinsley's art gallery and remembered I worked at one. I can't remember which one. Then when you said my last name, I instantly knew it was mine. And when I saw a picture of Tibbie on the television I remembered her and my condo on Rutledge."

"Can I see this alleged injury?" Granger asked with disbelief clear in his voice.

"Sure," she said, patting the back of her head. "Gavin, can you show them? I haven't actually seen it."

"What's the last thing you remember?" Deputy King asked as he and Granger walked behind her. Gavin parted her hair and then there was silence as they saw the swollen wound.

"I think someone hit me with a bat. I had this dream where I was looking into a car window as I was grabbing for the door handle, and I saw something arc behind me and then pain and darkness."

Granger and Deputy King whispered to each other and then she felt fingers on her head pushing hair away. "It doesn't look like a bat. Why did you think it was?" Granger asked.

"I thought it could be a bat, but I don't actually remember seeing it. I remember thinking it looked like whoever was behind me was swinging a bat, so I assumed it was one. You know how ball players hold their bats up high over their shoulder and then swing? That's what I saw. I think."

"Do you know how you got in the water?" Deputy King asked as he walked back around and took a seat at the table.

"No. I'm sorry." And Ellery was. She'd like nothing more

than to remember everything. "Now that I've answered that, can you tell me why you think I killed someone and who you think I killed?"

Granger opened a file on the table and slid it toward her. There was a picture of a man glaring at the camera next to a painting. A painting she remembered putting a sold sign next to. "Do you know this man?"

Ellery's head hurt, and she put her fingers to her temples and massaged the pain. She looked at the picture but couldn't keep her eyes on the man. Instead, she focused on the painting. "I remember putting a sold sign in front of that painting."

"What about the man?" Granger didn't seem as impressed as she was about her remembering the painting.

Ellery shook her head. "It's like a black pit. I look at him and my memory just goes completely black like my head is floating through an abyss. Everything recent seems like that. Two years ago, great, I can tell you about my birthday party with my friends or the time I got sunburned on Isle of Palms during spring break, but yesterday? Last week? Even six months ago, I got nothing."

"How long have you worked at—" Deputy King started to say, but Gavin cut him off.

"She needs to remember on her own." Gavin turned to her and smiled gently as he squeezed her hand. "Where is the last place you remember working?"

"I worked at Greta Waters Art Gallery on Fifth Avenue in New York City. I earned my undergrad degree at College of Charleston and then my master's in New York City. My goal was always to come back to Charleston. Then two years ago I moved back, rented an apartment, and began applying for local jobs. While I was applying I worked for private collectors. That's how I know Tibbie and Elijah. I found some paintings for them, and in return they moved me up the list to get a condo in their building."

"You started your current job a year ago," Granger said, looking at a printout. "Are you saying you have short term memory loss?"

"That's what I am saying," Gavin said with a hard voice. Ellery squeezed his hand in thanks for sticking up for her.

"But you're having dreams of being hit and of selling this painting," Deputy Kind stated more than asked, and Ellery nodded her answer.

"It's common when dealing with memory loss. It'll either come back slowly in dreams or when she smells or sees something or all the sudden," Gavin explained.

Granger looked to Gavin, and Ellery saw his lips thin as he thought. "Gavin, can I see you outside?"

Gavin looked to her and Ellery smiled as best she could. Right now she was scared to death. "It's okay," she said reassuringly, even though letting go of Gavin's hand was the very last thing she wanted to do.

Gavin gave her hand one last squeeze before getting up and walking out the door with Granger. Ellery looked across the table to Deputy King. "Tell it to me straight. Did I kill someone, Deputy King?"

8

"It doesn't look good for her," Granger said as Gavin took a seat in Granger's office. "We need her to remember in order to clear her name. I see her now, talk to her now, and she doesn't strike me as a murderer. Especially with that head wound. That's not a slip and fall or a self-inflicted wound. That was a kill shot that she somehow managed to survive, but Charleston police don't see it like that. They want her, and I have to turn her over."

"Who do they think she killed?" Gavin asked as he ran his hand over his face and let out a lungful of air.

"He was a pretty famous local artist by the name of Mark Vosslinger. Last night, Ellery put on a huge exhibit of his work. The Coast Guard found his body this morning in the bay."

"Why do they think Ellery killed him?" Gavin asked.

"I need more information. Charleston was very tight lipped, but they did say her car was found at his house. Is there any way you can speed up her memory?"

"I can try," Gavin said with resolve. "I need all the pictures you can get from social media. Pictures of her work place, pictures of the art, pictures of anything that looks important to her, and pictures of her with this Mark guy. We have to be careful not to plant false memories but to encourage the recall of old ones. If this doesn't work, I can call a friend of mine in Charleston who does hypnosis. That can help with amnesia brought on by traumatic events, which I think is what caused this memory loss."

Granger motioned for Gavin to come around the desk. "What should I print off?" Gavin scanned the social media accounts and began to point.

"YOUR CAR WAS FOUND at this man's house. Do you think you were in a relationship with him?"

Ellery sighed as she really looked at the picture. "I mean, I get this nagging feeling I should know him, but it's the painting I remember. It's like I can see it right here in front of me. Down to the brush strokes."

"Do you own a boat, Miss St. John?"

"I don't think so. I know I like going to the beaches on Isle of Palms and Sullivan's Island. I know I can swim. I was on my high school swim team and I can surf. I even have three boards. But I don't remember a boat."

It felt good to work her brain. She'd been putting it off because of the pain, but the more of these memories she could remember, the more excited she got. "Ask me more questions."

"Okay," Deputy King said, leaning forward. "Have you ever been so mad you could kill someone?"

"Magnolia Tyford my sophomore year of college. She was my roommate and slept with anyone and everyone, all the while locking me out of my room."

"What did you do to her, if you didn't kill her?" Deputy King asked.

"I'm not allergic to poison ivy, but she was. I got some and smeared it on her sheets so she was miserable for the sorority cotillion." Ellery paused and bit her lip. "Okay, and I might have grabbed a couple harmless king snakes and put them in our room too. I was going to put them back because she was scared to death of snakes, but as I was bending over to grab one from under the bed, here came Magnolia with another guy. She literally yanked me off the ground and shoved me out the door."

Ellery saw Deputy King fighting not to smile. "King snakes are harmless, did she know that?"

"No, but I did. But that's the maddest I've gotten in my whole life. It's just bad manners to keep kicking your roommate out every night. So, I cracked the door and peeked in as Magnolia did her best porn star imitation. It wasn't pretty. She kept flinging her hair around and smacking him in the face as she made this strange noise that resembled a cross between a goat and a chimpanzee."

Deputy King bit his lip to stop from laughing, but Ellery couldn't help but smile. She doubted Gavin made goat noises in bed. He probably would whisper something sexy that would have her throwing herself at him.

"Do you think Magnolia could have hit you?"

Ellery shook her head. "I don't think so. Last I heard she'd moved back to Savannah and was married to a plastic surgeon. She moved out of the sorority house that night because of the snakes, and I really didn't see her much after that."

The door opened and Ellery watched as Granger and Gavin came in. Dammit. Now she couldn't stop thinking about what kind of noises he'd make during sex and more importantly, what kind of noises he'd have her making.

"Ellery?" Gavin asked for what she thought may have been the second or third time. She might have trouble remembering little details about her past, such as where she worked, but her mind had no trouble coming up with all kinds of images of Gavin with his muscles flexed as he pumped into her.

"Yes!" Ellery tried to smooth over her shout and swallowed hard with a mix of embarrassment and heart pounding thoughts she was trying to hide.

"I thought I could show you some pictures to see if they jog your memory," Gavin said with a look that sent her mind running down the dirty path of him naked again, wearing only the little smirk on his face. It was as if he knew what she was thinking.

"Sure. Anything to help me remember who did this to me."

Gavin put down three pictures and her mind instantly recalled when they were taken. "My condo!" she said excitedly as she picked up the pictures and told them all about her little home and how she got it.

"What about this place?"

Gavin put down a picture of an art gallery. The old sign read Mimi Hollis Art Gallery. It was as if her mind was chugging through mud. It was slow, hard to get moving, but as Gavin put down the interior pictures the gears picked up speed. "It's familiar, but I can't really say for sure," she said with disappointment. "These paintings though, I remember them."

"Anything from these pictures?" Granger asked as Gavin laid out more photos. One was of a perky brunette who couldn't be more than twenty-two. Another was an older man in a preppy suit. Another image was of the brooding man they'd shown her before. More and more photos of the three people, of the street outside the gallery they'd shown her, and then photos of her smiling with these people were placed in front of her. She shook her head as she looked at them. "I don't remember—" But then her eyes kept going to the background where paintings, sketches, and statues caught her eye. "That's my favorite. It's a Karlsburg. See how he used the shadows to act as a whole new painting within a painting. It's so clever."

Gavin and Granger looked at each other and in seconds a computer was placed in front of her with the pictures of all the paintings currently on sale at the art gallery. "You remember through art. Tell us about each painting," Gavin told her as he pulled up the first painting.

There was no "aha" moment—some of her memories were simply there. With each painting, she was able to tell them more and more about the art, the artist, and why she loved them. She remembered her time in college and her art classes. She remembered every painting that had touched her soul. The only thing she couldn't recall were the names of the people she worked with and where she worked. "Oh, these are the Mark Vosslinger collection," Ellery said with a sigh. They were simply gorgeous. "He's going to be huge . . . wait." Her mind clicked, and she lunged for the photos they'd brought in earlier. She shoved them around the desk until she came to the one she was looking for. "This is Mark! He's the artist of these paintings. I remember."

Granger shared a look with Gavin and then turned the computer to pull up social media pictures from the exhibit yesterday. "That's right. That's the artist, Mark Vosslinger. Did you know him well?"

"Not really. I talked to him some when he brought his

artwork in." Ellery stopped and looked up with surprise. "I work at an art gallery. Wait, do I work at this Mimi Hollis Gallery?"

"How much do you now remember from last night?" Gavin asked, avoiding answering her question.

"I remember hanging all these pictures and deciding which should be featured at the prime spots in the gallery," Ellery said before biting on her lip as she tried to push the mud from her mind. She'd have better luck wading through the pluff mud. "Why do I remember the art, but not the people? How can I remember hanging the pictures but can't remember the gallery where I work or who I work with?"

"What about these photos?" Granger asked as he turned the computer back around to her, again trying not to give her any answers.

Ellery flipped through them. "I remember this," she said, pointing to her putting a sold sticker by a painting. "The rest . . . I see them as if they're other people. I know that's me. I probably know the people in the pictures, but I have no memory of them being taken or what we were talking about, or who those people are. It's as if it's not me in them."

"What's your most recent memory?" Gavin asked.

"Thinking you were kissing me," Ellery answered absently as she was still staring at the photos.

"Kissing you? I'm pretty sure I would have remembered that," Gavin said with a grin that had her blushing.

"I thought you were kissing me, but it turned out to be CPR."

Deputy King snorted and tried to cover it by coughing.

"Traumatic amnesia. Luckily it appears that most of your retrograde is getting better through art memories. We think your injury occurred not too long after these photos,"

Gavin told her. "What would you do after the exhibit was over? Just your best guess based on your past history."

Ellery suddenly felt cold. She shivered, but her eyes were too glazed to see the concern on the men's faces. "I would have cleaned up and closed the gallery." Her body went from shivering to shaking as the image of a dark raining night came over her. Her heart beat in fear as she reached for her car. She saw the reflection of an arm raising and then . . .

"Ellery!" Gavin yelled as he wrapped her tight in his arms.

Ellery took in a shuddering breath as she buried her head in his chest and tried to force herself not to cry. Her whole body shook with fear. There was something dark and dangerous in Charleston and her mind was hiding it from her.

"I remember being hit. It was the same as in my dream. It was raining, and it was dark out. But I felt fear. I felt panic. And then I saw the arm raise, and I knew I was dead." Ellery began to take deep breaths. "I can't go back to Charleston. There's someone there who wants me dead."

Ellery collapsed into Gavin's strength as she let him hold her. His warmth slowed her shaking, and his arms tight around her calmed her breathing. "Wait," she said, pulling away. "If I'm the person who should be dead, then who did you all think I killed?"

"Mark Vosslinger's body washed up in Charleston this morning," Granger told her seriously. She knew he was watching her closely to gauge her reaction, but she didn't need to fake the shock she felt.

"Mark is dead?" She gasped. "How? And why do the police think I did it?"

"I don't know how. They didn't release that information

on the bulletin. But you are a suspect. Your car was found at Mark's house."

"That doesn't make sense. Mark hated people coming over to his house. I've actually never been to his home. I offered to come pick up a painting once and he bit my head off. It was his creative space, and he didn't want the stench of business to come near it. Those were his exact words." The memory from that encounter when she'd called Mark and offered to pick up the work was suddenly clear as day, but when she tried to think about what happened to her, it was as if there was a brick wall preventing her mind from accessing it.

"I have to call the police, Ellery," Granger said as he unfolded his arms and stood up straight.

Fear and panic raced through her body so hard she physically shook. "No!" Ellery cried.

"I'm sorry," Granger said, walking from the room, but leaving the door open.

"Please, they'll kill me!"

"Who will kill you?" Granger asked, stopping at the door and turning around.

"I don't know," Ellery admitted as tears began to stream down her face. "I just know I can't go back there. Someone wants me dead."

"Then the police will protect you. I'll be right back."

Ellery clung to Gavin as he tried to soothe her. "Kord, there has to be something you can do," Gavin almost begged the deputy.

"I'm sorry, Gavin. But this isn't my call. She's wanted for questioning."

GRANGER STRODE BACK in five minutes later as he talked on

his cell phone. Ellery looked up and saw that his jaw was tight, and he was staring right at her. He lifted his finger to his lips to indicate they needed to be quiet and then put the phone on speaker before gently setting it on the table.

"So, you believe the suspect hit the victim over the head with a blunt object? Is that what he died of?"

"I can't confirm that, Sheriff Fox, but I can't deny it either, if you get my drift. That woman is dangerous. Orders are coming down that she's armed, and if you see her, it's shoot to kill if necessary."

Gavin slipped his hand over her mouth right when Ellery would have gasped.

"So, have you seen her?"

Ellery held her breath as she waited for Granger to answer the question.

"No, sir. I called to get more information because I thought I'd seen her, but like you told me a moment ago, this St. John woman has a small tan birthmark on the back of her calf and I'm looking at this woman in my custody right now and she doesn't have it." Ellery's hand subconsciously moved down her leg to cover the small tan mark on the back of her calf. "Sounds like you got your hands full down there. It takes someone important to get that kind of pressure put on you."

"You got that right," the police officer snorted. "Thanks for checking in, Fox. Let me know if you see our girl."

"Will do," Granger said, keeping his eyes locked on Ellery as he hung up. Everyone sat quietly for a moment. Ellery held her breath waiting for Granger to arrest her. "Well, it appears you've gotten yourself into one hell of a mess, Miss St. John."

"Please, don't send me back."

"I won't. It's too much of a coincidence that Mark was

killed with what sounds like the same weapon someone hit you with, and you were both found in the water. What you missed of the conversation was a discussion where I learned there were no other suspects. They want you and only you for this crime. The problem is there is no evidence, besides your car being at Mark's house, to link you to the crime."

"It doesn't sound like they want to arrest her. It sounds like they are hoping she'll run, and they'll be able to shoot," Gavin said as Kord nodded in agreement.

"Miss St. John, I believe you're being set up, and I'm wondering why." Granger crossed his arms over his chest again.

"I am too." Ellery sighed with frustration. The answer was in her head. She just needed to figure out how to unlock it.

9

_____

Gavin held open the sheriff's office door for Ellery as she walked outside, lost in thought. The humidity enveloped them like a hot wet blanket as they quietly walked down the street toward his car. Gavin wanted to say something supportive, but finding out someone had wanted to kill her made for awkward conversation. However, in the end, he didn't need to say anything.

Ellery walked close to him, her shoulder bumping his before she casually laid her head there for a brief moment. In that one second, Gavin felt his heart race and her body relax. He looked at her as they walked slowly down the sidewalk. Did he dare touch her? His body cried for the contact, but his mind told him not to push it. In the end, he held his breath and wrapped his arm around her waist. His hand sat lightly on the curve of her hip as they walked.

Gavin waited for Ellery to move away or tell him not to touch her like a boyfriend would, but instead, she leaned into him. The side of her body pressed against his, and they walked in silence the rest of the way to his car.

"I don't know where to go," Ellery finally said as she

stood next to his car. She was staring at it as if the car would answer her.

"You'll stay here, with me. I'll keep you safe." Gavin had never felt this primal urge to protect before but it was there, along with some other primal feelings.

"You don't even know me. Why put yourself in danger?" Ellery asked as he opened the door for her.

"Because I want to know you," Gavin said simply. A ghost of a smile came over her face as she watched him walk around the car and get in.

"I want to get to know you too."

In that moment, Gavin felt as if he were the luckiest man in the world. He turned and smiled at her before making his way back to his house. "Tomorrow we'll go shopping. I don't think it's a good idea to go back to your condo."

"I agree. Right now just the thought of going back to Charleston chills me to the bone."

Gavin opened the door to the house, and she stepped through and froze. Gavin walked into her back, not expecting her to stop so quickly, sending Ellery stumbling forward a couple steps. Gavin's hands grabbed her to help steady her as he heard a woman speak.

"So you do have a girlfriend?"

"Harper. What are you doing here?" Gavin asked his sister, who stood in the small mudroom with her arms crossed over her chest and a glare in her eyes.

"I was here this morning, and you failed to mention you had a woman staying here. Then Tinsley called to say how wonderful your new girlfriend was. You've never hidden a woman from me before, so the only conclusion I can reach is that she's a no-good gold digger, and you knew I'd call her out on it."

Gavin felt Ellery tense in front of him as he put his hand

on her shoulder and glared at his very over-protective younger sister. He was supposed to be the protective bigger brother, but so far, Harper had run off way more girlfriends than he had boyfriends.

"It's sad that's how your mind works," Ellery said softly but with steel to her voice. "You think the worst of people before you look for the joy they can bring."

"I do not," Harper protested but then stopped when she saw Gavin nod. "I'm looking out for my brother. My brother who is too kind-hearted for his own good."

"Really, Harp, you treat me as if I'm completely incapable of dating," Gavin said with a roll of his eyes. "When it's you with the horrid track record."

"Me? At least I know the guys I date are bad and will be short term. You think the best of everyone and they weasel their way into your life. Gavin, buy me a new dress. Gavin, buy me jewelry. Gavin, buy me—"

"I get it," Gavin said coldly. He didn't like to think of himself as better than anyone else, but he was very successful. Where his cousin Ryker wore his success as a shield deflecting anyone he deemed not worth his time, Gavin had gone in the opposite direction and tried to show everyone he was the same old Gavin who'd biked around town as a kid. It just happened to lead to some women wanting his money, even if it was nothing compared to Ryker's wealth. But he was still considered a big catch. The town's only doctor held some prestige, and some women wanted that more than they wanted him.

"So," Harper said, staring daggers at Ellery, "what do you want?"

"To not die," Ellery answered.

Gavin squeezed her shoulder again and pulled her against him. "I won't let you die."

Harper's face fell. "Oh my gosh! You're dying? I'm so sorry. I thought you were using my brother like so many of the women here have done."

"I'm not dying. Someone is trying to kill me, and your brother saved me."

Harper's mouth fell open in surprise as she looked to Gavin to see if it were true. Gavin nodded and Harper rushed forward. "We won't let anyone hurt you, right Gavin?"

Gavin rolled his eyes as Harper threw her arms around Ellery, pushing him out of the way. "Who is trying to kill you? How did Gavin save you? You know, wait a second. The family should be here so you don't have to repeat it."

"Harp—" Gavin warned, but it was too late. Harper had already sent the first text. He felt his phone vibrate in his pocket. Then vibrate again and again and again.

"They'll be here in thirty minutes. Tinsley is bringing dessert. Ridge is bringing whiskey. Wade said he has some beer he can bring. Oh, and Trent is bringing chips and dip," Harper said as she read the texts.

"Harper. We're not dating," Gavin hissed. His sister looked up at them and then shrugged.

"I like her then. It's rare to find a woman who isn't auditioning for the role of wife. But if you're not dating now, you will be. I see that look at the bar every night."

"WHAT LOOK?" Ellery asked as conflicting feelings raced through her. Right now she was a little hurt at Gavin's pissed off declaration they weren't dating, yet relieved to have support during this time. She definitely felt something for Gavin, but right then wasn't the time to act on it.

"Lust," Harper said, reaching for her hand. "What can I do to help you?"

Ellery was afraid she was going to have whiplash from the one-eighty Harper just pulled. First she was practically threatening Ellery, then just like that, Harper was her friend. She had thought about what a catch Gavin was, and she couldn't deny Harper's statement. She was feeling lust for Gavin, but she didn't want to be just another woman wanting something from him.

"Actually, there is," Ellery said as Harper pulled her along into the living room.

"What is it?" Harper asked, sitting down on the loveseat with Ellery, which forced Gavin to take a seat across from them. Ellery didn't know why he looked so annoyed. After all, he did just tell Harper they weren't dating.

"I need clothes, and I can't go back to my house and get them because someone is trying to kill me."

Harper eyed her up and down. "I don't think my clothes will fit, but my friend has a whole ton of stuff she gave me to take to the abused women's shelter in the next town. It's in my car. Why don't you look through it and see if any fit. Then when this bad person is caught and you're no longer in danger, I'll donate the clothes."

"Thank you. Do you think your friend will mind?" Ellery hoped not. Harper's body was straighter. It was clear she was strong from lifting kegs and cases of liquor. Her arms were sculpted, her breasts were probably a full B cup while Ellery's were a size larger, but the main difference was Harper's narrow waist.

"Not at all. She wanted them to help someone in need, and you fit the bill. I'll go get them. Try not to make out while I'm gone."

"Harper," Gavin groaned, but the first thing Ellery

thought of when Harper left was just that. What would his lips feel like if he was kissing instead of performing CPR? Every time his hand touched her, she felt her skin heat underneath his touch. "I'm sorry about my sister. She's a bit blunt. It's how she keeps everyone in line at the bar each night."

"It's sweet that she worries about you."

"I worry about her. She's constantly having a date or two with these men who are no good for her. And the one time I have a woman at my house she dares accuse me—"

"Of dating," Ellery said, not wanting to hear herself talked about as if she were a bad influence.

Gavin grinned as he moved from his chair to the couch. "I thought we already had a date. The police interrogation was awfully romantic."

Ellery blushed. "You're right, you did say it was a date."

"And if I wanted a second date?" Gavin asked as his voice lowered.

"I'd say yes," Ellery whispered back as the front door opened.

"Seriously? You two are practically going at it on the couch," Harper said with a roll of her eyes. "Wade's pulling up now."

"Sitting on the couch together isn't going at it," Gavin said with a roll of his own eyes as he adjusted his pants when Harper wasn't looking.

"Whatever. You want to and that's what matters. Anyway, here are the clothes, Ellery. Do you think they'll fit?"

Ellery reached into the bag and pulled out some cute southern boutique styled clothes in sizes ten and twelve. "They should be perfect," she said, holding up a cute blousy top and a swirly floral print skirt that would hit her mid thigh. "Thank you so much."

"No problem," Harper told her as the front door opened and a tall man with dark brown hair and forest green eyes walked in. His hair was shorn short against his head, and his shoulders looked as if he'd have to turn them to get into the door. He was tall and broad shouldered with a muscled chest that tapered down to a flat stomach. "Wade, this is Ellery, Gavin's possible girlfriend. Someone's trying to kill her."

Wade raised one eyebrow in question as he looked to Gavin and then Ellery. He held out his hand. "Nice to meet you, ma'am."

"Nice to meet you too. You look exhausted."

Wade shoved his six-pack of beer into Gavin's hands and mustered up a smile. "I'm in the Coast Guard and just got off after twenty-four hours straight of rescues. Are you the injured woman Gavin called me about?"

"I was injured, and I am a woman, so that's a strong possibility."

"This is her," Gavin said, walking back into the living room after putting the beer in the fridge.

"Interesting."

"What's interesting is the fact that you bailed on poker night."

Ellery looked toward the door and saw a man about an inch shorter than Wade with eyes the same color green as a field of grass. He was in worn jeans and his chocolate brown hair was shoved back from his lightly stubbled face.

"Trent, this is Ellery. Ellery, our cousin Trent," Harper called out as she grabbed the chips and dip from him and set them on the coffee table. "Trent makes furniture. Like this table." Harper held out her hands as if she were a hand model.

"It's beautiful. You made this?" Ellery asked.

Trent shook her hand and nodded. "Thank you. It's nice to meet you, Ellery. What's this about being in trouble?"

"Wait until Ryker gets his ass over here." Harper turned to Ellery once again, clearly loving her role as organizer. "I saw him pulling up."

Ellery turned and smiled at Tinsley, who walked in carrying a plate of cookies. Her long hair was pulled into a ponytail, and she'd changed into coral shorts and a white T-shirt. Where Harper was tall, around five foot eight, and strong, Tinsley was petite and curvy. Not saying she wasn't strong, but unlike Harper's athletic body, Tinsley's was softer in an elegant way. Everything about Tinsley from her soft voice to her dancing eyes made you want to hug her.

"Tinsley!" Ellery said happily as she jumped up and did just that. Wade snagged the cookies, and Ellery hugged the little artist. "It's good to see you again."

"But not under these circumstances. I thought everything was going well and you two were a happy new couple, but to hear you're in danger?" Tinsley put her hand to her heart. "I can't stand it. Not after what happened to sweet Edie."

"Who's Edie?" Ellery asked as she and Tinsley sat down.

"She's a friend of the family," Tinsley explained. "Her husband was killed on a mission. He was a SEAL. And then the person who killed the whole team kidnapped her to get to her brother, the lone survivor who could tell the world what really happened. They stole her from my house. I still have nightmares, and I know Edie does too."

Ellery's heart dropped. Someone came to Shadows Landing and kidnapped a friend of theirs. Was Ellery putting them in the same situation?

"What is so damn important that I had to speed from Charleston to get here?" A deep voice rumbled through her chest. Ellery turned around and would have been shocked if she hadn't already seen pictures of Ryker Faulkner in local magazines. His ice green eyes pierced her as his six foot four inch muscled body strode predatorily into the house. His hair was such a dark brown it could have been the same black as his suit. His face was etched into a frown, even though the angles of his face were sexy enough to have angels leaping from heaven to have a chance with him.

"Ryker, meet Ellery—" Gavin started but was cut off by his cousin.

"St. John. Yes, I know," Ryker said, his eyes seeming to see inside of her. Ellery gave an involuntary shiver.

"You know me?"

"You were in the Charleston Social, promoting some exhibit this past month for the Mimi Hollis Gallery. Look, if you're here for money, you have to go through the application process like everyone else."

Ellery's eyes went from wide to narrow. He thought she'd pull something like this just to get some money for the gallery? "Bless your heart, you sure are a conceited jerk. My momma taught me better manners than that, but obviously yours did not. Someone is trying to kill me, and Harper sent out the text before we could stop her since she thinks Gavin and I are dating, which we aren't. Well, unless you count a meal that was cut short by a sheriff's interrogation as a date, and if you count CPR as a first kiss."

Ellery's hands were on her hips, and she was in a full tizzy as she refused to back down from Charleston's most influential up-and-comer. She was taken aback when instead of a cutting remark, Ryker grinned. It wasn't a full smile, but the change completely transformed him from uptight and controlled to panty melting. His whole face softened, and it was then she realized there was a whole lot more to Ryker Faulkner than the controlled demeanor he presented.

"Well, since you're not dating my cousin, I take it you're available?"

She wanted to sputter, but southern ladies did not sputter. They handled even the toughest of men with aplomb. So, instead of staring open-mouthed at him, she smiled. "How sweet of you. See, you can be nice."

Gavin slipped his arm around Ellery's waist. "And she's already dating me—interrogation or not."

Ellery turned her smile to Gavin. So, he was really interested in her. "That I am. But I appreciate you being here because, if you don't mind, I really think I could use your help," she said to Ryker, who now looked amused as he poured a glass of whiskey.

"So, now that we're all here, why don't you tell us what's going on?" Harper said, taking a seat next to Tinsley as everyone found their spots in the living room. Ellery took a deep breath and slipped her hand into Gavin's as she began as far back as she could remember.

10

"Wow, who would want to kill you and Mark?" Harper looked between Gavin and Ellery.

"We don't know, but it has to be someone powerful enough to put pressure on the police force," Gavin told his family.

"What about that ex-boyfriend of yours? At least, I'm assuming he's an ex since you're kind of dating my cousin. However, that's not the word around Charleston," Ryker said from where he lounged back in a leather chair with one perfectly suit-clad leg crossed over his other leg. His black dress shoe didn't even bounce from where it rested on the opposite knee as he sipped his drink.

"Ex-boyfriend?" Ellery asked. The memory of a broken heart seemed elusive, yet there. She tried to grab it then it was gone. And while the memory of working at the gallery wasn't all the way back, she was remembering more about the gallery. Not the people in it, but of the actual gallery itself.

"Yeah, you and—" Ryker began to say before Gavin cut him off.

"She needs to remember as much as she can on her own," Gavin explained, and Ellery decided to let it go. When she stopped trying to remember, she found she actually did remember things.

"You are up on all the gossip. Goodness. Do you belong to a charity league?" Ellery asked even as she smiled to herself imagining Ryker in a roomful of powerful southern mommas deciding on flowers for an event. Everyone in Charleston knew the town was run not by the politicians and business leaders but by the charitable women of the town. They wielded more power behind their colorful sundresses and scarves than the governor of the state.

"It's not gossip. It's knowledge."

Gavin snickered. "Don't tell me you watch those reality shows based in Charleston too."

"Knowledge is power." Ryker's face slipped into a chilly mask that dared anyone to argue against him.

Ellery took pity on him. "I remember a broken heart but not a boyfriend. Or in this case, ex-boyfriend."

"Could he have been mad enough to kill over the breakup?" Tinsley asked.

"Not many people say no to your ex," Ryker told them as he tried to stay vague. "He's from a very old and powerful family."

"But it turned out all right," Tinsley said with a kind smile. "Because if you hadn't broken up with whoever he is, you wouldn't have met Gavin, and Gavin would never break a woman's heart."

Bless her heart, Tinsley was always looking for the good.

"If she can stay alive," Ridge muttered and then cringed when he realized he'd said it loud enough for everyone to hear. "Sorry."

"No, it's true. Someone wants me dead." Ellery sighed and took the tumbler of whiskey Harper handed her.

"What does Granger think?" Tinsley asked of the sheriff.

"He doesn't know, but he knows he's not turning Ellery over to Charleston police," Gavin said. As if speaking his name, Gavin's phone rang and Granger's number popped up on it. "Granger, what's the matter?"

"Sorry, sweetheart. I'll be home late. I have an officer from Charleston here at work, and I have to run him over to someone's home real quick."

"What?" Gavin asked as he almost pulled the phone away to stare at it.

"Now, don't be mad, sweetheart. It won't take long. This officer needs to check on someone real fast. See you soon."

Gavin hung up and looked wide-eyed at the roomful of people. "Granger has a Charleston officer with him. They're coming to check on Ellery."

The room was silent except for Ellery's gasp. "They'll know it's me by my birthmark," she said, turning her leg so the room could see the small tan mark.

"I can take care of that," Tinsley said, leaping up and grabbing her purse. "Sadie probably has some more things in her locker. Harper, grab them and a pair of scissors, then meet us upstairs."

Ellery wasn't given a chance as the petite powerhouse grabbed her and hauled her upstairs faster than Ellery thought possible. She was shoved onto the chair as Tinsley dropped to her knees and lifted Ellery's leg. "This should cover without a problem," she told Ellery as she dumped her purse and pulled out all her makeup. In minutes the birthmark was gone.

"Wow. It's like it never existed," Ellery commented.

"Now we need to make you look completely different," Tinsley ordered.

"How do you know about all this?" Ellery asked.

"I'm an artist, and what is makeup but paint for the skin?" Tinsley asked rhetorically as Harper raced up the stairs.

"I got some bright red lipstick, some makeup, and a bright pineapple print scarf."

"Great," Tinsley said as she ordered Ellery to close her eyes. Ellery felt brushes running over her skin and hair as Tinsley ordered Harper around. She sat still as her heart pounded. Her mind tingled as if it were trying to pull open a door to her memories, but the door wouldn't budge.

"There, what do you think?" Tinsley asked as she stepped away so Ellery could look in the mirror. Her hair had been quickly cut into a sleek shoulder length bob that made the angles of her face stick out. The scarf had been tied around the top of her head so only some of her hair hung out the back. The parts showing looked brown instead of blonde. Then there was her face. It looked almost gaunt in the sharp angles Tinsley had somehow created. Then with the use of eye shadow, her bright sky blue eyes suddenly looked much darker. Ellery scrunched her nose. She had freckles!

"I don't look anything like myself. How did you do that?"

"Sorry about cutting your hair, but blunt edges change the look of your face, which I contoured with makeup. Since we didn't have time to dye your hair, I covered the brightest blonde streaks with the brown mascara. And then the freckles are just eye shadow, so, whatever you do, don't touch your face or they may smear."

There was a knock at the door and Ellery looked with panic at the two women. "Don't worry. We've got you,"

Harper said, grabbing her hand and running from the room. They tore down the stairs, and Harper practically flung Ellery onto the couch as the men stared at them. There was another knock at the door, and Gavin finally shook his head, gave Ellery a thumbs up, and went to answer it.

"Granger," Gavin said happily. "You decided to join us after all. That's great, but I hope your girl isn't going to be mad. Didn't you have a date with her tonight?" he asked about Granger's made up girlfriend.

"She's going to be mad all right. This is Officer Hurst from Charleston. He needs to see your visitor to make sure she's not a missing woman."

Ellery heard Gavin laugh again. "Missing? She's not missing. She's right here. Has been since she arrived from Keeneston. We told you this already."

"And who exactly is she?" Ellery heard the officer ask. Shoot, they hadn't come up with a name yet.

"Come on, Gavin. It's your turn," Ridge barked. "Either Granger is in or out."

Ellery's attention snapped back to the Faulkner family as five cards were shoved in her hand. Beer, whiskey, chips, and now cards. It looked as if this had been a planned game night.

"He's out," Gavin said, opening the door. "Come on in."

Ellery didn't even know what game they were supposed to be playing as she tried to casually take a bite of a chip as she watched the men come into the room. Granger's eyes flashed in surprise but then quickly went back to annoyed.

"See, she's not the woman in the poster," Granger said, pointing to Ellery.

The officer looked to be around forty years old. He was in a uniform, so he wasn't a detective, which was good.

Detectives tended to look more closely. "What's your name?" he demanded.

"Emma Johnson," Ellery stammered as she looked back and forth between them. "Why?"

"Can I see some identification, ma'am?" the officer asked sharply.

"About that," Ellery stammered. "I kinda dropped my purse in the ocean." Which was the truth, maybe.

"It was my fault. Emma wanted to see the container ships, and we were walking on the gangway when one of the workers slammed into her. I decided to catch her instead of her purse," Ryker said with a shrug as he sipped at his whiskey, looking completely in control. "I think I made the right call, don't you?"

If only Ellery felt that way. Her heart was racing. Her breath was shallow. Her palms were sweating.

"Sorry if I don't just take your word for it, sir," the officer responded.

"Ryker." Ryker narrowed his eyes at the officer and suddenly the temperature in the room dropped ten degrees. "Ryker Faulkner. Both the governor and the mayor take my word. So does the police commissioner for that matter, so maybe you might want to rethink that statement."

"Sorry, Mr. Faulkner," the officer said nervously. Ryker had quite the reputation as a cutthroat businessman, and apparently he wielded power outside of his shipping business as well. "I need a way to identify her so I can tell my superiors she isn't Ellery St. John."

"Would the word of an FBI agent work?" Gavin suggested. "We can call your friend from home, Ryan Parker."

Ellery blinked at him and then nodded. "Sure. Let's call Ryan and Sienna. Although I'm afraid we'll wake the baby."

The officer was busy on his phone apparently looking up Ryan Parker. "Is he the head of the Lexington FBI office?"

"Yes, sir," Ellery answered, hoping that was correct.

The officer let out a sigh. "That'll work. But I'll also need to look at your legs."

"Excuse me?" Harper snapped. "What purpose would that serve, you perv?"

The officer blushed pink as Gavin called Ryan. Ellery saw him speak quietly into the phone as the officer tried to calm Harper. "The missing woman has a birthmark on her calf. That's all."

Harper looked to where Gavin gave a small nod of his head, and Ellery realized Harper had bought Gavin enough time to tell Ryan to cover for them. Ellery shrugged, stood up, and turned around, giving the officer a nice view of her legs. "I assume you don't need me to pull up my skirt."

"No, ma'am. Thank you. Sorry to bother you. Now if I can just get confirmation of your identity I can leave you alone."

"See what trouble you caused, Ryker? You should have let me fall overboard." Ellery teased Ryker as he looked as if he'd grin again. His lip twitched but didn't smile.

"What kind of gentleman would I be if I let that happen?"

"I wasn't aware you were a gentleman," Ellery shot back as Harper snorted.

"Touché," Ryker said, his lips finally curving up into something of a predatory smirk. "I think I owe you dinner to make up for it."

"Officer, here's Agent Ryan Parker," Gavin said, handing the video call to the officer as he glared at Ryker who only smiled wider.

"What can I do for you, officer?" Ryan asked.

"I'm on a missing persons case, and I've been asked to check the identity of Mr. Faulkner's woman friend here, but she doesn't have an ID. Apparently it was dropped overboard when she was boarding a boat."

"Woman friend? Are you talking about Emma?" Ryan asked, and Ellery almost sighed with relief. She didn't know Ryan Parker, but she felt as if she owed him a hug.

"Yes. Can you identify her?"

"Sure. Bring her to the phone."

Ellery heard the command and got up to meet the officer. She saw her face on the small screen and Ryan's on the main part of the phone. Sienna was behind Ryan with the baby sleeping in her arms.

"Hey, Emma!" she called out and Ellery smiled.

"Hello, Ryan. Sienna. How's little Ash?" Ellery asked.

"Thankfully asleep. You know how he is at night," Sienna responded completely ignoring the officer.

"So, you can both identify this woman?" the officer asked.

"Yes. That's Emma Johnson of Keeneston. The sheriff's office is closed right now, but I can probably get them to fax you something in the morning if you really need it."

The officer shook his head. "No, that's all right. I have your name down. Can my boss call you if there's any questions?"

"Sure thing. See you when you get home, Emma."

"Don't do anything I wouldn't do," Sienna winked before the phone hung up.

"I'm sorry to have bothered you. Thank you for your time."

"Of course. I'm sorry you didn't find the person missing. Is her family looking for her?" Ellery asked.

"No. She doesn't have any family left. But her neighbors

and her boyfriend are looking for her."

Ellery wanted to scream. Why couldn't she remember? But instead she just nodded. "That's so sad. I hope you find her."

"Thank you. I'll be in touch if I need anything else. Sorry to bother y'all tonight."

Ellery sat back down as Gavin walked them out. An FBI agent had just lied for her. She'd known this guy for less than twenty-four hours and his family was protecting her. And now she had people actually looking for her. The door closed and Ellery finally slumped against the couch. "I should leave. Go someplace they'll never find me and—"

"And hide for the rest of your life?" Wade asked, shaking his head. "You're right where you need to be."

"An FBI agent just lied for me. Won't he get into trouble? Won't you all get in trouble?"

"Let's not worry about that right now," Gavin said, taking a seat next to her. "Let's keep you safe and work on getting your memory back. If we can prove you're not Mark's murderer, we'll probably only get in a little bit of trouble."

He smiled at her, but all Ellery could feel was fear. It was as if something was reaching out for her, but she didn't know what it was.

"Wade and Gavin are right. Stay here. I'll see if I can find anything out from the ex-boyfriend," Ryker said, tossing back his whiskey and standing up.

Gavin's phone pinged and he looked at it. "Ryan wants to talk to Granger and you sometime soon. He's thinking the FBI may need to get involved if this is a police corruption issue."

"Really?" Ellery asked hopefully.

"Yeah, but it won't be immediate. Ryan will need to talk to the right people and make sure they're not part of it."

"Oh." Ellery hadn't thought about that. Now she began to second-guess herself. All these people were looking for her. Did she really do this? Just what happened to her after the party?

"I can't tell you not to worry," Tinsley said softly. "But know you're not alone. I'm sorry you don't have any family left. We're here for you anytime you need us."

Ellery looked around and saw the group nodding. Even Ryker nodded. "I'll let you know if I find anything out."

"You know, my nana used to say if you wanted to know anything that was happening in town you went to brunch at The Hartford," Ellery told Ryker with a grin. The Hartford was a stuffy club where society dames gossiped, and the men played golf or went shooting on the extensive property. "I'm assuming you're a member."

"Of course I am. It's where all the real deals in Charleston are made. But your nana was right." Ellery would have sworn she saw Ryker cringe before he looked to Gavin. "And you really like this one?"

Ellery's mouth dropped open, and she was about to rip into him, but she held back because she really wanted to hear Gavin's answer.

"I do."

Ryker let out a long breath. "You two owe me. I'll talk to you in a couple of days." And then he was gone.

The room was quiet until Trent laughed. "I'm imagining Ryker surrounded by all those middle-aged matrons for Sunday dinner. They're going to eat him alive."

Ellery laughed right along with everyone else, but her heart wasn't in it. Her heart was currently occupied with the sexy doctor who was looking at her as if he wanted to kiss her. And maybe this time it wouldn't be in order to resuscitate her.

The pounding on the office door woke Gavin at six in the morning. The sky was starting to lighten as the first rays of the rising sun broke through the horizon. Gavin hadn't been sleeping much. He'd had a fitful night as he thought about the woman in the room next to his. A woman he hadn't known long yet felt he had known forever.

At the sound of the pounding, Gavin's emergency instincts took over. He leapt from bed, pulling on clothes, and raced from the room and down the stairs. The woman who'd kept him awake last night in his thoughts called out after him, "Is everything okay?"

"Clinic emergency at this hour on a Sunday," Gavin said, not bothering to slow down. He was the only doctor in twenty miles, so it could be anything from a broken bone to a cut to a heart attack. If it wasn't something he could handle, he'd try to stabilize the patient for the ambulance or helicopter.

"I'll help," Ellery said, racing down the stairs after him.

Gavin pushed through the door from his house into his office and then into the small lobby as the pounding and ringing of the bell continued. Gavin unlocked the door, flung it open, and found Turtle buck naked, holding a young snapping turtle over his crotch.

"Save me doc!" Turtle yelled as he pushed his way into the clinic. Turtle was Gator's younger cousin. He was skinny as a pole with mud brown hair cut short on top with not quite a rat-tail and not quite a mullet, but some cross of the two that hung down to his shoulder blades. It was a mullet tail. Or rat mullet. Either way it was redneck couture.

"What happened?" Gavin asked as he flung the surgery room door open. Neither of them paid much attention to Ellery following close behind.

"A turtle bit my ding-dong! What does it look like?" Turtle cried as he held onto the shell of the small snapping turtle.

"Ellery, there's a large metal bowl in the cabinet. Fill it was water, please," Gavin ordered, not looking at her as he bent to examine the turtle latched onto Turtle's little turtle. "It's a young snapper. You're lucky. He's only three inches or so, probably not quite a year old."

"It doesn't feel lucky!" Turtle snapped as Gavin grabbed the metal bowl from Ellery's hands and began looking frantically around the office.

"An adult could have bitten your penis off," Gavin said calmly. He gathered his gloves, gauze, and the other supplies he would need to clean the wound.

Turtle used one hand to hold the turtle and the other to hold the metal bowl as he lunged for the reflex hammer. Before Gavin could stop him he was holding the bowl over the turtle and his penis while banging away on the bowl with the reflex hammer.

"What the hell are you doing?" Gavin yelled over the

racket of metal bowl being hammered on as if Turtle had suddenly joined a heavy metal band.

"My granny always said if a snapper latched onto you make loud noises to get it off."

Gavin grabbed the hammer and the bowl before Turtle did any more damage. "Old wives' tale, Turtle. Just like the time she told you if you brush your teeth more than once a week you'll wear the enamel off. Or that time she told you if you had sex standing up the girl wouldn't get pregnant. Or the time she told you if you swallowed a watermelon seed a watermelon would grow in your stomach."

Gavin handed the bowl back to Ellery who was struggling not to laugh. She turned and busied herself filling it with water as Turtle's brow creased in thought. "Maybe you're right. I guess I should run anything medical by you first. Does that mean my teeth won't be fall out by chewing gum?"

"No, your teeth won't fall out. But they will if you don't brush them daily." Gavin put on his gloves and leaned forward. "It appears he's latched onto your foreskin. How do you feel about being circumcised?"

Turtle went white as Ellery brought him the large bowl of water. "Let's just see what kind of damage there is." Gavin held the bowl up to the turtle and submerged the actual turtle and Turtle's little turtle in the water. "Just hold still and relax." Turtle shot him the finger. Gavin couldn't blame him. It had to be hard to relax with a snapper hanging from your manhood.

"So, you're Gator's cousin?" Ellery asked, trying to distract him. Turtle nodded. "Does that mean you handle turtles like Gator does with alligators?"

"No. Why would you think that?"

Gavin tried not to laugh as Ellery looked at him totally confused. "Then is Turtle your real name?"

"Nah, it's a nickname I got in high school."

"Does it have anything to do with a turtle?" Ellery asked.

Turtle caught his breath on a sob and looked at the ceiling. "It has to do with my little turtle. It likes to come out of its shell to wave at my lady friends. But I might have to get a new name if I get the tip snipped."

Gavin saw the minute Ellery realized Turtle was a nickname for his uncircumcised penis and blushed red. She sputtered, trying to think of something supportive to say.

"If anything it'll make it look bigger. No more hiding for that turtle," she finally said. "They'll have to call you Big Turtle. Or maybe Tortoise."

"Really?" Turtle asked as the turtle let go, and Gavin quickly pulled the bowl away from Turtle and handed it to Ellery. "Empty this off the dock, will ya?" Ellery rushed away, carrying the turtle in the bowl as Gavin got down to business. "I can try to stitch it or I can cut it off—your call. If I stitch it, it'll pull some and won't look good. I also don't know how painful it'll be for you when you get an erection. You're missing quite a chunk of skin."

Turtle collapsed onto the exam table holding the gauze to his penis and cried, "I just wanted to take a morning swim in the creek. I guess the turtle saw my goods dangling and thought it was food."

"I've read research that circumcised men last longer in bed," Gavin reassured.

"Cut it off," Turtle said suddenly and decisively. "Maybe then I can find a woman."

Gavin shook his head. He didn't know if it would help or not, but he was guessing a good workout routine to bulk up a little and showers inside instead of in creeks might go a long way to helping Turtle get a date. Right now, he smelled of pluff mud, and that was not a nice cologne.

ELLERY NAVIGATED her way around the kitchen after releasing the small turtle. She looked in the cabinets and took out two plates before moving to the refrigerator and finding some eggs and bacon. She wanted to make breakfast for Gavin while he attended to Turtle. It was the least she could do since he let her stay at his place, feeding and clothing her.

She'd never thought of herself as the medical type, but she really enjoyed seeing Gavin in action. It made her realize how much more than the art world was out there. She'd been living and breathing art since her freshman year of college. She had friends, sure, but the more she met Gavin's family, the more she realized they weren't true friends. They were friends brought together by generations of debutante balls and marriages. They had a way of making a large world seem small, and Ellery had never taken the time to step out of that small circle. It felt as if she knew so many people, but she'd begun to realize she didn't know them at all, just like they didn't know her at all.

"Penile emergency is over." Gavin sighed as he walked into the kitchen and sniffed the air. "Smells great. Thank goodness you didn't cook sausage links. I think my turtle is already suffering sympathy pains."

"Do you want me to kiss it and make it better?" Ellery said saucily before realizing what she'd just said. What was it about Gavin that made her feel so comfortable to blurt out all kinds of things her grandmother would have said were unladylike?

"Yes, please," Gavin answered instantly.

Ellery laughed off the awkward moment even though her mind was squarely inside Gavin's pants. "Here's some breakfast. I thought you might be hungry."

"Starved. Why don't we take it outside and have a picnic on the dock?"

"Sounds great," Ellery said with a smile. She picked up the food and carried it down the backyard and to the end of the dock. Gavin laid out a blanket and set the plates down. "I miss this." She took a deep breath.

"Bacon or the picnic?" Gavin asked as he filled her plate with food and set it down in front of her.

"Relaxing. I haven't done it in so long. I've always been pushing myself to climb the art gallery ladder and sell more, impress more, get better artists . . . It's nice to feel the breeze on my face and enjoy a meal with a handsome man."

And it was nice. Gavin told her stories of his family and of being a doctor in the small town. He'd been offered a big shot job in Charleston, but he'd always wanted to come home.

"Even after your parents moved to Florida?"

"Yes, my cousins are like siblings to me, and this hometown is just that—home. I know everyone here. I've traded stitches for fresh cobbler. I've brought babies into the world and patched up their skinned knees as they've grown into little kids. I've held the hands of people I've known my whole life as they passed away. This is my town, my family. It's where I belong."

"Have you ever thought of moving to Keeneston?"

Gavin shook his head. "I actually just met them this past year. I hate to speak ill of the dead, but my great-grandmother was not very nice. She told my grandparents that their sister, Marcy, wanted nothing to do with them. So,

I grew up knowing I had family out there, but nothing else. I met my cousin, Layne, at a medical conference in Charleston when I needed help with my best friend, Walker. You'll meet his sister, Edie, soon."

"Oh, the one who was kidnapped, right?"

Gavin nodded. "Right. Layne helped Walker after he was injured. She's a physical therapist. It was when I met Layne that we realized we'd both been lied to for many years. Great-Grandma told my family Marcy wanted nothing to do with them while telling Marcy we didn't want to have anything to do with her. It caused a generational split until I met Layne, and we figured out what had happened. When she married Walker, the whole family, including my grandfather and great-uncle, went to Keeneston to meet them. We've been growing close ever since."

"That's horrible but wonderful at the same time. I wish I had family to turn to like you do. My grandmother raised me, and she passed away five years ago."

Ellery leaned back and closed her eyes as the sun fell on her face and she listened to Gavin's family stories then shared some of her own.

"Oh shoot," Gavin said, suddenly jumping up. "I lost track of time."

"Do you need to be somewhere?" Ellery asked and started picking up the plates.

"Church. You don't miss church in Shadows Landing. Reverend Winston will show up at your door to see if you're sick and then you end up feeling as if you were caught skipping school. Plus there's the whole barbeque thing."

Ellery chased Gavin uphill toward the house. "What whole barbeque thing?"

"Sundays are for townies only. Earl and Darius have a cook off. The person with the most votes gets that week's prime advertisement spot in the paper and online. Do you have a hat to wear? Never mind. I'll call Tinsley. She'll meet us there," Gavin called out as he raced upstairs. "Hurry and get ready. Wear your best dress." And then his door slammed, and Ellery stood huffing and puffing from the sprint uphill, inside, and upstairs.

Now, she was a good southern woman who knew how to dress for church, but a hat? Why did she need a hat? Ellery shook it off as she dumped the bag of clothes Harper let her borrow and got dressed.

12

"Here you go, Ellery," Tinsley said, handing the work of art that was a hat to Ellery as Gavin practically propelled them inside the thick wooden doors of the church.

"Thank you. This is beautiful."

"My Aunt Paige in Keeneston makes them. I bought a ton when I was up there last time. As you'll see, the men may have a barbeque competition, but the women—"

Tinsley didn't need to finish for Ellery saw it. Hats were everywhere. Bright, colorful, large, small, feathered, or . . . was that an alligator head? Every woman there had on an anything-but-normal hat, and everyone was crammed as close as they could get to the front of the church. This was definitely not like her church where everyone competed for the last row.

Trent waved them over to a pew right in the middle of the church. Gavin slid in and then Ellery, followed by Tinsley. Harper leaned forward and glared. "Do you know how hard it was to save these seats? What took you so long?"

"Emergency patient."

Trent snorted. "Turtle made it here thirty minutes ago.

He's in the front row telling everyone about his new pleasure providing penis."

Wade leaned forward and whispered. "He won't stop talking about it. He's saying he's like Spiderman. He was bitten but came out bigger and better than before."

Ellery and the rest of the Faulkners were trying not to laugh loudly in the historic church. Bells began to ring and everyone quieted down. Ellery took a moment to look at the stained glass windows casting colorful rays of light on the congregants. The doors opened on each side of the altar as a diverse group comprised of all different races, sexes, and ages filed in wearing white choral robes. Each robe had a different color sash running down each side of the zipper, turning the large group into its own rainbow of color.

A young boy, his skin dark brown and his soft looking raven hair sticking up in a stylish pompadour, stepped forward with a curly red headed boy whose fair face was covered in freckles. You could hear a pin drop as everyone waited for the two boys to sing. They opened their mouths and sang to Jesus as the back doors opened and the reverend appeared. Everyone stood, some swayed with the music, some held their hands up to God, and others shook the reverend's hand as he made his way down the aisle.

Ellery couldn't take her eyes from the choir as they began to slowly join in with the boys who couldn't be older than twelve until she heard, "You're new. Welcome."

Ellery turned and found the reverend looking right at her as he shook Tinsley's hand. He was in his forties, his smooth umber skin was a warm dark yellow-brown. His almond shaped eyes were smiling as he reached his hand for hers.

"Reverend Floyd Winston. Thank you for joining us this morning."

"Ellery St. John. I'm happy to be here."

Reverend Winston smiled, and it warmed her. There were times you just knew someone was kind, and that was the reverend. His clipper cut hair had soft coils on top before it was shaved down at the sides, which made him appear even more approachable. He wore a white robe, but the trim was made up of colorful pieces from all the different colors of the choir.

"You are always welcome here, Miss St. John. Think of it as your sanctuary."

And then he was moving on to the rest of the parishioners. Reverend Winston made it to the altar right as the chorus finished their song. He shook hands with the two young singers and bowed his thanks to the choir before turning to the congregation.

"Today I want to talk about our history, for we learn from it and we grow from it. Please be seated." Ellery sat as the reverend began walking slowly across the altar, looking at each member of the church. "Shadows Landing was a place of sin."

Some members shook their heads in shame. Some nodded in agreement.

"But it was always a place of Jesus. Even sinners can love Jesus and have a home here."

Someone shouted, "Amen" and Ellery couldn't tear her gaze from the reverend as he continued to speak. "This church was built from sin and therefore we will never turn anyone away who seeks her sanctuary, sinner or not."

There was that word again. Sanctuary.

"Inside our hallowed walls you can find safety. Safety for your soul and your person. No one can come into our church to remove a person seeking solace. To this day, in the Shadows Landing ordinances, those in need of sanctuary are safe the moment they pass through those doors. We may not have pirates in Shadows Landing anymore, but that doesn't mean there aren't those who need the protection of our Lord."

"Amen," the crowd said with passion.

"And it's not just in this church that we find sanctuary. It's this town. A town founded to protect pirates now protects each other. When Miss Ellen needed a new hip, who took her in?"

"We did!" the church cried out.

"When Miss Lydia's husband is deployed, who helps take care of her children while we pray for his safe return?"

"We do!"

"When Mr. Gator lost his pinky to that alligator, who helped him heal?"

"We did!"

The reverend nodded his head, and his walking sped up. He was using his arms now as he talked, and people were beginning to stand up. "And when a woman is unjustly accused of a crime, where can she turn?"

Ellery froze halfway up to her feet. Was he talking about her?

"To us!"

"Amen!" the reverend shouted as the choir launched into a stirring song about a sinner's redemption. Although, she really wasn't quite sure if she was a sinner or not. Either way, she'd take the protection they were offering her.

"Reverend Winston knows everything that's going on," Gavin whispered as people sang. It didn't matter if they were off key, they sang with their whole hearts.

"But they'll turn me over to the Charleston police if they find out I'm wanted," Ellery said as she had to lean against Gavin and whisper into his ear.

"The reverend has just deemed that you will be safe. The town will take you in and protect you. And as I told you before and Rev just said, the church is a sanctuary. If worse comes to worst, you come here. The police can't drag you out. You may think you're alone, but you're not."

Ellery stood still as the music surrounded her. People were dancing where they stood, people were praying, people were singing, but she was not. She stood still, staring at the large cross, wondering if that was really true. She'd never felt so alone and yet so surrounded by love. She was troubled, rectifying the conflicting feelings. The music died down and the reverend walked right to her.

"Ladies and gentlemen, I want to welcome Miss Ellery— a true symbol of strength. Dr. Faulkner found Miss Ellery unconscious in the water in the middle of the night and brought her back from death's door."

"Hallelujah!" the chorus sang and Ellery almost jumped with surprise.

"Miss Ellery is battling amnesia but is regaining more of her memory every day."

"Hallelujah!" Now the whole congregation joined in.

"But the devil is at work. Someone tried to kill Miss Ellery, and they haven't been caught yet. Instead they're using their powers of evil to frame Miss Ellery for murder."

The congregation gasped. Someone cried out, and one of Lydia's seven kids said "cool."

"But we won't let the devil go unpunished because we will vanquish the shadows with our love."

"Hallelujah!" the crowd called out even louder than before as the choir launched into another gospel song about protecting a weak lamb from the wolves.

"I know people, Miss Ellery," Reverend Winston said as the others around them sang. "And I know you have a good heart. You will always be welcome here. Please, let me know if I can do anything for you. Sheriff Fox told me of your struggle, and the women's group has put together a bag of necessities for you. They'll drop it off at Dr. Faulkner's house after lunch."

Ellery's hand rose to her heart at the thoughtfulness. "Thank you," she said, grasping his hand. "Thank you so much."

"People tell me I'm easy to talk to. I'm happy to sit and hear your story if you ever feel like telling it. Be blessed, Miss Ellery."

The rest of the service passed quickly, and before she knew it the church was filled with the smell of barbeque. The two choirboys followed the man and woman holding communion only the boys were each holding a giant platter of barbeque. The reverend blessed the gold chalice and then the bread representing the body of Christ before saying a blessing over the two plates of barbeque.

"After you take communion," Gavin whispered, handing her a five dollar bill, "you take the offering of barbeque from each platter and put your donation to the church in the box of the barbeque you like the most. The one that raises the most money is deemed the winner. The money stays with the church, but the advertising goes to the winner. Then be ready because things get a little dangerous after that."

"Dangerous, how?"

But communion had started and their row was standing. Ellery followed Tinsley through the procession, received communion, and then the boys solemnly handed her a piece of barbeque from each plate and Ellery felt like dropping to her knees in prayer because nothing had ever tasted so good before.

IN SHORT ORDER the money was counted and Pink Pig won by forty-two dollars. Ellery noticed as Reverend Winston was giving his closing remarks people were starting to crouch in sprinters starting position. Purses were in hand. Hats were being pinned down. Butts were on the edge of the pews.

"Go in peace," Reverend Winston said, and they were off. The doors were flung open. People were dashing down the aisle. A little old lady hit someone with a cane and tripped them before jumping over them.

"Come on!" Tinsley said, dragging Ellery out of the pew and shoving her way past an older lady with feathers from her hat blinding her as she tried to run down the aisle.

"What's going on?" Ellery yelled as Gavin pushed her from behind to hurry them along. Wade jumped pews and shot out the door with Harper hot on his heels.

"There's limited room at the Pink Pig and Lowcountry Smokehouse. You don't want to be on the waitlist. It'll take forever!" Gavin yelled up to her. "Go Tinsley! We'll meet you there!"

Tinsley took off. She was tiny and used it to her advantage, weaving in and out of people as they funneled out the doors and down the stairs. An old man jumped the curb in a Rascal scooter and gunned it down the street. It shot off going at least twenty-five miles per hour as he passed the people sprinting down the street.

"That's Mr. Gann. He used to build dirt cars for racing, but now that he's ninety he tinkers with his scooter," Gavin called out as they hurried down the stairs right as Mr. Gann shot the finger to a man in a motorized wheelchair.

"And that's Mr. Knoll. He had a competing race team. Dirt track racing is pretty big here."

"Run Quad!" a large man with deep brown skin and a shaved head yelled. "Five seconds! Faster!"

"That's Terrance Clemmons III and his son, Terrance the IV. Everyone calls the son Quad and his father, Terry. Quad is a sophomore in high school and a big shot basketball player. Terry's been coaching him since Quad was able to hold a ball. He's constantly training Quad, and it's paying off. Every month we have a new division one coach showing up in town to talk to him about playing in college. Plus he usually gets a good spot in line."

"He's so tall," Ellery called over her shoulder as she weaved her way through the crowd, taking elbows to her sides and stomps to her feet.

"The flat top adds another three inches, but he's six foot eight and still growing."

Quad flew past Wade and jumped into the line gathering at the door to Pink Pig. "Last week Lowcountry Smokehouse won, so I'm not surprised Darius won this week. The two usually trade wins. There, Wade and Harper are in line and Tinsley's not that far behind."

Gavin slowed Ellery to a fast walk. "How many people can fit?"

"Only about half the congregation can get seats at both places. Otherwise you're on the waitlist, and it could take anywhere from thirty minutes to three hours to get your seat."

"Why not go home?" Ellery asked as Gavin grabbed her hand to lead her up to where Trent had now joined Wade, Tinsley, and Harper. Ryker was strutting down the sidewalk. He didn't run.

"It's tradition. Everything closes on Sunday except these two restaurants that are only open for brunch. At two in the afternoon, the whole downtown is closed. Everyone goes fishing or boating or the social committees host bake sales, quilt sales, and so on."

"Ellery, a moment," Ryker said, stopping next to them in line. "I went out last night and ran into your ex-boyfriend at the yacht club bar with some of his friends. He is telling everyone you and he are a couple and he's worried sick about you."

Ellery felt her eyes go wide in shock and hurt. "How can I not remember? I would think I would remember him, but all I feel is annoyance."

Ryker gave a sympathetic shrug. "For what it's worth, I don't think anyone is buying it. When your ex went to hit on the cocktail waitress, his friends called him pathetic. What I got from this is first, he's a loser, and second, his friends aren't real friends. I found the whole thing very fake. Fake girlfriend for appearances and fake friends because of money and connections. As you know, appearances are everything."

"So, we're not dating?" Ellery asked as she felt her breath rush out in relief.

"I couldn't get a straight answer. If you aren't, he will do anything he can to keep up the appearance that you are together. I don't know why he'd do that, but I don't trust him."

It sounded like a warning and Ellery supposed it could be. Maybe her ex liked the appearance of a doting boyfriend of a missing woman for the attention.

"Thank you," Ellery said, her spirits somewhat lowered. She hated the idea of a man telling everyone they were together and playing the dutiful and loving boyfriend to the press if that wasn't true. "I appreciate you helping me out."

With a nod of his head in acknowledgment of her thanks, Ryker turned to his family and began to chat as

Gavin wrapped his arm around her. "It'll be okay. Don't worry about him. Who you are is what matters, not what he says you are."

Ellery rested her head against his shoulder and thought about it. Trying to remember who her ex was was a distraction. She needed to push the distraction away so she could focus on the real issue of narrowing down who wanted her dead.

"Hi, y'all," a pretty woman with shining chestnut brown hair and electric blue eyes said as she joined the family. Tinsley leaned forward and kissed her cheek before Harper pulled her in for a hug. Each of the men proceeded to kiss her cheek, including the cold and immovable Ryker, who Ellery was beginning to think wasn't so very cold. "Gavin, I heard you've had quite an interesting past couple of days."

Gavin slung his arm around the woman's shoulder and pulled her against his side as he smiled at her. Ellery swallowed hard. She felt it and knew exactly what it was—jealousy. And when the woman put her arm around Gavin's waist as if it belonged there, Ellery had to admit she was not thinking very ladylike thoughts about the woman right then. And that stopped her mid-breath. She'd never been the jealous type. Gavin wasn't hers, but right now she wanted him to be. In the midst of this nightmare, she'd found the man of her dreams, and his name was Gavin. Her heart began to stutter as she looked at him. Really looked at him. Not his sexy body, but who Gavin was. Someone who took care of those in need, someone who risked it all to rescue her, someone who loved his family, someone who cared deeply, and someone who she trusted. And in this moment she realized Gavin was someone she was falling in love with.

13

Gavin pulled Edie to his side and kissed the top of her head. Her eyes were still sad from the death of her husband, but she was working hard at building a life back in her hometown of Shadows Landing.

"Edie," Gavin said, drawing her attention from something Harper was saying, "I want you to meet a friend of mine." Gavin saw it then, the way Ellery's full lips thinned slightly. Something was the matter.

Gavin reached for Ellery, and while she didn't pull away she seemed rigid. "Ellery, this is Edie Greene."

"Wecker," Edie corrected. "Well, Greene and Wecker. Growing up it was Greene, but I got married." She shook her head and held out her hand to Ellery. "Sorry, I'm new to this widow thing. I just changed my name to Greene-Wecker. It was supposed to be a symbol of me moving on and being a strong independent woman, but it just feels like me playing dress up."

"Nice to meet you," Ellery said, relaxing and giving a gentle smile to Edie. "I'm sorry about your husband."

"Thank you. After he died I moved back here and

bought my parents' old house. With Trent and Ridge's help, and of course Tinsley's with her artist's eye, I've slowly been updating it. Are you new to Shadows Landing?"

"I floated by and didn't want to leave," Ellery tried to joke, but all it did was cause an image of Ellery almost drowning to come into Gavin's mind. They were supposed to go boating today, but Gavin didn't think she was ready to go out on a boat. And if he were honest, he wasn't either.

"Oh my gosh, you're the woman Reverend Winston was talking about. I know exactly what you're going through. I'm so sorry." Edie reached out and hugged Ellery as the waitress, Tamika, Darius's teenage granddaughter, called them to their table.

Edie grabbed Ellery's hand as they followed Tamika to the large rectangular table. Everyone shuffled in and grabbed a seat, and Gavin found himself across from Ellery, who was seated between Edie and Ridge. There was no menu on Sunday. There was only the church special. Barbeque, mac and cheese, collard greens cooked in bacon fat, and sweet tea.

Everyone talked at once as they leaned over each other or talked across the table. There were shouts of laughter, teasing, and stories told as Gavin watched Ellery. She relaxed into herself and soon was part of the family. Gavin felt like a fool, but he couldn't keep his eyes off her. When she smiled he felt it all the way to his soul.

"Stop staring like a lovesick teenager," Ryker whispered with an elbow to the ribs. Gavin grunted as Trent leaned over from his other side.

"But Ryker, he's in love," Trent said dramatically.

"I'm not in love," Gavin hissed, but it even sounded false to his ears. While he may not be completely in love, there was no denying he was well on his way there. There was something about Ellery that seemed to draw him to her.

"Right," Ryker said. It would have been accented with a roll of his eyes, but Ryker didn't roll his eyes.

"You're infatuated. You can't stop looking at her. Not that I blame you. She's beautiful, nice, fun to talk to." Trent stopped and then grinned. "I mean, if you're not into her, I'll take her."

"I already called dibs," Ryker said.

Gavin snapped his head toward his cousins and glared. "The hell you both will." Trent tossed back his head and laughed.

"Told you so." Even Ryker grinned as he shook his head at Gavin. "Shoot me if I ever turn into a lovesick puppy."

While his mind hadn't wrapped itself around falling for Ellery, his heart was running toward love with all it had. The way it beat faster when she looked at him was only one of the hints he was falling for the last person he should—a woman who didn't live in Shadows Landing, a woman who was wanted for murder, a woman with amnesia, a woman who might be his patient. Yeah, his mind knew this wasn't a good idea, but it wasn't only his heart telling him it was a good idea as he slid the napkin over his lap. He'd gotten more erections in the last two days than in the entire past year. And dammit, that meant Ryker was right. He was a lovesick teenager again.

"Gavin!"

"What?" He looked at Ridge who had snapped his name.

"You didn't hear me the first five times I said your name. What were you thinking about?" Ridge asked with a mischievous smile that had Ryker and Trent snickering.

"Today."

"That's what we were just talking about. I was asking Ellery if you two were going to join us on the river."

He looked at Ellery and saw the worry in the fine lines around her eyes and lips. "No. I think we're going to take it easy. Ellery is still recuperating from her injury."

She smiled her thanks at him and Gavin felt like a superhero. "I am getting tired. But how about you all stopping by afterwards for dinner? I make really good burgers."

"I wish, but I have to get back to Charleston. Someone wants me to meet with society matrons," Ryker said, winking at Ellery. "Rain check?"

"Absolutely. We could all get together on Friday," Ellery said with a smile and Gavin felt it again—the way his heart constricted. She wasn't rushing off to get home. She may not realize it, but she was making plans for the future.

"Friday is perfect," Harper told them. "We can have dinner and then head over to the bar for a couple of drinks."

"Shameless ploy to get us to spend money in order for you to make money," Ridge teased as Harper stuck her tongue out at him.

"I was going to say they're on the house, but not for you anymore," Harper teased back.

The table laughed again as Harper and Ridge continued to tease each other. The food arrived, and Gavin found himself more relaxed and happier than he'd been in a long time. It was like he discovered a piece of him that had been missing when he hadn't even known it was missing. He did now though.

THEY SPENT two hours at Pink Pig before they all headed out onto the sidewalk. Gavin slipped his arm around Ellery's waist as if it belonged there. He held his breath for a moment until he realized she wasn't going to move away and then the nerves turned to pride as he escorted her down the street to his car. "Thank you for coming with me today."

"It was so much fun. I just adore your family."

"Yeah, they're pretty great. I'm sorry if you wanted to go boating."

Ellery shook her head as Gavin started the short drive home. "No. Honestly, I was a little nervous to get on a boat. Somewhere in my head I think there's a bad memory there."

"It would explain how you ended up in the water."

"That's what I'm afraid of." Ellery wrapped her arms around her chest and hugged herself as Gavin pulled into his garage and turned off the car. He hopped out and ran around to open her door as an SUV pulled into the driveway right behind him. It looked like the chauffeured SUV Ryker sometimes rode in.

Gavin had his arm around Ellery's waist as they walked slowly to the edge of the garage. Another car pulled up on the other side of the street as two ladies from church got out of it. However, the huge man getting out of the SUV was not from church. He was dressed in a suit with black sunglasses covering part of his thick square face.

"Can I help you?" Gavin said, stepping protectively between the man and Ellery.

"I'm here to give Miss St. John a ride back to her family."

"You must be mistaken. This is a friend of the family, Emma Johnson."

The man moved forward quickly and Gavin held his ground. Ellery screamed. He heard the women shouting, but he couldn't look because the man had decided he would go through Gavin instead of around him.

"Get inside!" Gavin ordered as the large man shoved

Gavin and pulled out what looked to be a gun. Ellery and Gavin froze. Gavin stepped slowly to the side to place his body in front of Ellery's. "What do you want?"

"Miss St. John's presence is required back in Charleston."

"And I told you, you have the wrong person. I've known Emma most of my life. She's from Kentucky, not Charleston."

"You might be able to fool—" *Thunk.* A plate of cookies was thrown through the air like a Frisbee before hitting the man on the back of the head.

"You don't be holding a gun on someone on Sunday!" Ruby Lewis yelled as she and Winnie Peel, the co-chairs of the church's women's league, raced across the street. Well, race wasn't exactly the right word. Hobbled was probably better since they were around eighty years old and complete opposites in every way except for the hobbling.

Ruby was the exact picture of a sweet rounded grandmother who spent her afternoons baking treats for all the kids in the neighborhood. Her reddish brown skin was now wrinkled, but she always had a smile and a piece of candy stuck in her bra. And there was lots of room in her bra. She was all boobs, belly, and butt and every kid in Shadows Landing loved to get hugs from her because then they got a treat. Winnie on the other hand was just as sweet but in a more fragile way. Her pale skin resembled wrinkled paper, as she no longer went out in the sun much. She couldn't weigh more than a hundred pounds and slightly resembled a chicken with her sagging skin around her neck and beak-like nose. She may be small, but she was mighty. She ran the church like a well-oiled machine, and no one second-guessed her.

"The Lord will strike you down, so help me God!" Miss

Ruby declared as the bright blue feathers from her church hat bounced in her face as she charged toward them.

"Or I will, bless your heart. Don't you know how rude that is? Don't you have anything better to do? You need a job. That's what you need, young man," Miss Winnie lectured as the rim of her large hot pink floppy sunhat fell forward into her face. But that didn't stop her, she just used her cane as a way to feel her way up the driveway.

The man holding the gun stared as his mouth partially dropped open, and Gavin took advantage of the distraction. He lunged forward and grabbed the gun. "Get out of here!" he yelled to Ellery as he and the man struggled. Another man stepped from the back of the SUV and startled Miss Winnie, who bashed him over the head with her cane.

Gavin felt the cold metal of the gun absorbing the heat from his hand as it dug into his palm. He tried to force the barrel to point away from him, but right now if the man pulled the trigger he would be in serious trouble. Gavin's arms flexed, thankful for all the surgeries, baby deliveries, and boating he'd done that made him rather strong. He used one hand to try to twist the gun from the man's hand and the other to prevent the man from pulling the trigger. When it looked as if he was going to lose the battle, Gavin lowered his shoulder and rammed it into the man, sending him stumbling back and right into Miss Ruby.

"You should be ashamed of yourself!" Miss Ruby yelled as she grabbed the man by the earlobe and pulled. The man gave a surprised squawk as Miss Ruby yanked him backward. In surprise, he loosened his grip on the gun, and Gavin was able to twist it out of his hand. He didn't do much hunting like so many around there did, but that didn't mean he didn't know how to use a gun.

Gavin pointed it steadily at the two men. The big one

was still being berated by Miss Ruby, the feathers on her hat bobbing in his face, while the second man was rubbing his head from where Miss Winnie bonked him with her cane.

"Miss Winnie, can you please call Granger," Gavin asked politely.

Miss Winnie hobbled over to him and patted his cheek. "You're such a good boy. I'll be back in two shakes of a lamb's tail."

He heard someone running in the house and knew it wasn't Winnie. Ellery stormed from the garage with a boating paddle held up as if it were a bat. "Who are you?" she demanded.

"We're just doing our job. We were hired to find you," the large man answered after Miss Ruby twisted his ear.

"But I'm not lost, and I'm not this Ellery person! Who hired you?" Ellery yelled as she raised the paddle threateningly.

The man clenched his jaw when Miss Ruby twisted his ear harder. All of a sudden, the man who had been leaning against the open back door after the cane to his head moved his arm. Taser prongs shot out and into Miss Ruby's bottom. The old woman's eyes went wide as she dropped her grasp on square-face and shook. The feathers of her hat danced, and Gavin saw the moment she was going down.

"Dammit," he muttered under his breath as he lunged forward to catch Miss Ruby instead of keeping the gun pointed at the men.

As he caught over two hundred pounds of grandma, the two men leapt back in the SUV and tore down the driveway. Gavin heard the paddle drop, and then Ellery was there helping him slowly set Miss Ruby down on the driveway.

"Oh, you poor thing! What can I do?" Ellery asked, turning to Gavin.

Miss Ruby shook her head and blinked her eyes. "Well, I haven't had a tingle like that since the sixties."

Sirens reached them as Miss Winnie tottered outside. "What in tarnation happened to you?"

"I got a tingle in my butt," Miss Ruby told her old friend.

"Lucky you. I haven't had one of those since the sixties."

Gavin tried not to laugh, but Ellery's snickers made him lose it.

"What happened in Shadows Landing in the sixties?" he asked as he tried to calm his chuckles.

"Civil Rights protests," Miss Ruby told him. "The school was segregated, but then one day it wasn't. The local leaders all came together two days before back-to-school and agreed we were going to stop bussing students to Charleston since we didn't have a black school here. Protests broke out in front of the school."

"But then the church ladies' league came and handed out brownies to everyone," Miss Winnie said, picking up the story. "And I should point out that there were quite a few of us who had already crossed racial lines, so to say. There was only a small group that opposed it, but they were very vocal."

Miss Ruby nodded, her feathers bouncing. "That's right. Winnie and I were already friends from youth group. But those few protesters had evil hearts."

"Sure did. But then the ladies passed out these brownies to both sides of the protest," Miss Winnie told them. "The next thing we knew, we were arm in arm singing gospel songs."

"And it gave us a tingle," Miss Ruby added.

"Quite the tingle," Miss Winnie agreed.

"After that we all got naked and jumped in the river together," Miss Ruby said matter of factly.

"Yeah, hard to spew hate when you're naked in the river with your ding-a-ling floating up. Turned into one heck of a party," Miss Winnie remembered.

"Those church ladies just kept feeding us and we kept partying. Next thing we knew it was two days later, the school was open, the kids had already started, and no problems had come up. Everyone kinda looked at each other naked in the river as we tingled on our inner tubes and agreed everything was groovy. Not to say there haven't been some tensions every now and then, but we work through it. We're too small of a town to be divided. Instead we chose to work together," Miss Ruby told them as she finally reached for Gavin's hand. "Now help me up. I have a craving for those special brownies."

Gavin and Ellery bent and hauled Ruby to her feet as the two sheriff's SUVs slid to a stop in front of the house.

"What happened?" Granger asked, already leaping from the SUV.

"Someone tried to take this sweet young girl," Miss Winnie said with a thump of her cane.

"And I got a tingle in my bottom," Miss Ruby added. Granger stopped mid stride, and Kord covered his mouth with his hand in order to hide the smile.

"They stunned Miss Ruby," Gavin clarified, "on the bottom."

Kord snorted and covered it with a cough. "I'm so sorry, Miss Ruby. Let me drive you home after all this excitement. I'll make sure your car gets delivered to you."

"Do you happen to have your great-grandmother's brownie recipe?" Miss Ruby asked as she took Kord's arm.

Kord led Miss Ruby to his car, and Gavin saw Miss Ruby pointing to her car. A second later, Kord strode up to the house with bags of clothes in each hand. "From the church," he said, handing them to Ellery.

"Thank you," Ellery said, taking the bags from him.

"May I escort you home too?" Kord asked Miss Winnie as he held out his elbow for her to take.

"Depends. Can I play with your siren?"

"Do I get some apple pie?" Kord asked back as Miss Winnie tweaked his cheek.

"Of course you do. Such a good boy."

"Then you can play with my siren anytime."

Gavin would have sworn he heard Miss Winnie mutter, "Don't I wish," under her breath as Kord escorted her to the SUV where Miss Ruby was already sitting.

Granger was shaking his head as he watched Kord drive off with Miss Winnie playing with the controls to the siren. "Let's go inside and you can tell me what happened."

Gavin reached out and took Ellery's hand in his. This was suddenly much more than a theory that someone was after her. Her memories may not have been back, but her instinct that someone had hurt her must be true if they were willing to kidnap her to get her back to Charleston.

14

Ellery didn't know whether to laugh or cry when she recounted what had happened. Luckily Gavin told most of it, and she just bit the inside of her lip to stop all emotion because right now she needed to think and not be distracted by Miss Ruby's ear tugging antics.

"Are you sure they weren't police?" Granger asked again.

"I'm positive. They didn't identify themselves as such, they weren't in uniform, and in fact they reminded me of personal security."

"Someone powerful was pulling the strings, at least that's the impression I got from Officer Hurst. I'm afraid my call to report you triggered this whole mess, even when I denied it was you. I'm guessing since nobody has been found and then when Officer Hurst couldn't give them more information on Ellery versus Emma, they hired private security instead of the police to handle this," Granger said as he looked deep in thought. Ellery could see him thinking through all the possibilities. This had to be a tough case for a small town sheriff, but he didn't seem overwhelmed.

"Have you seen a case like this before?" Ellery asked.

Granger nodded. "I skipped college and went into the Army. Did a tour and got a job as a cop in Washington DC. I saw a lot of things like this. Everyone backstabbing everyone, either through blackmail or murder. I left after a couple of years and moved back to my hometown and ran for sheriff. I had wanted the quiet life, but Shadows Landing is never quiet. Gators on the loose, fist fights over barbeque, and don't get me started on the craft fair."

"What should I do? Will I be safe anywhere?" Ellery asked, feeling all hope slipping away.

"You need to remember who hit you," Granger told her, not bothering to beat around the bush.

Gavin put his arm around her and pulled her to his side. She looked up at his face etched in worry. "I think it's time we go back to Charleston."

Panic clawed at her. Her heart beat so strongly she was afraid it would stop. Her throat was constricting, and her lungs didn't seem to be working. Fear was pulling her into the darkness as black spots became larger and larger until she couldn't even see Granger standing in front of her.

"Ellery!" Gavin barked, the demand in his voice bringing her back from the darkness. "It's okay. We won't get out of the car. I've heard being completely relaxed and thinking of other things and, on the opposite side, retracing your last steps, can both work to jog your memory."

"Let's try relaxing first," she managed to say as she clung to Gavin. His strength, his warmth seemed to ground her.

"Okay," Gavin said slowly as if trying to reassure her. "We'll try that first."

"You might want to consider staying somewhere else," Granger told them. "It appears they know she's here or at least think it could be her. They'll be back."

"What about your patients?" Ellery asked. Not only was

her life turned upside down, but now she was turning Gavin's upside down too.

"No one should be stopping by tonight, but I can leave a note to call Sadie if they need anything. We can stay at the Bell Landing Plantation. They have two rooms they use for bed and breakfast stays when they feel like it," Gavin told her. "We'll do it for tonight and see if we can take your mind off of things."

A night at a plantation with Gavin? Sounded like heaven, but the way her heart was beating she didn't know if relaxing was quite the right word for it. "I don't want to put them in danger."

Granger shook his head. "They will protect you better than I could. Shooting is not a hobby for them, it's an obsession. Clark and Suze Bell host duck hunts every year, and then there are the multiple trophies for skeet shooting they both have from the time they were children all the way up to this past year's senior division win."

"Are Gage and Maggie in town?" Gavin asked before turning to Ellery and telling her they were the Bell's two grown children.

"Yes. Gage arrived this afternoon and Maggie a couple days ago. She's under the weather so she wasn't at church," Granger said as if there had to be an excuse not to be at church. Well, there probably did in this town.

"Last time I talked to Clark he thought they might be moving back to the plantation now that they're out of college and settling down with jobs in the family business," Gavin said to Granger as Ellery felt completely lost in this family catch up.

"But that's four people now I could be putting in harm's way. I don't want them Tasered in the ass or worse, shot, all because I'm there."

Granger turned a serious face to her. "Gage is named after a twelve gauge shotgun shell and Maggie's full name is Magnum Bell. She won a silver medal in the last Olympics for trap shooting. While Gage didn't get an Olympic medal, he's won his fair share of national competitions and was on the Olympic team."

Okay, that did make her feel a little bit better. "As long as they're not in danger, I'll stay there tonight."

"Great. Then tomorrow after I see my patients we can go to Charleston if we need to. I'll call Clark and Suze while you go through the things Ruby and Winnie brought and put together a bag for the night."

Ellery thought Gavin would come inside with her, but he made no move to follow her. Instead he turned his back to her and began to talk quietly to Granger. Ellery decided whatever it was, he obviously didn't want her to know about it, which only made her worry more. Guys should know the time to protect a woman's delicate sensibilities was over. As Ellery lifted the bags and walked past the door to Gavin's office, she thought about that. She wasn't a hunter. She wasn't even a regular shooter. She knew how to wield a paintbrush. But she also knew how to wield a scalpel when she was making sculptures.

She dropped the bags and looked toward the garage door as if she were doing something wrong. When no one opened the door, she quietly snuck into Gavin's office and into the surgery room. In seconds, she found scalpels and quickly took one before sneaking back out.

Upstairs, she dumped the clothes she'd been given and laid out the clothes she wanted to take with her. There were a pair of jeans that fit, a couple of sundresses, a pair of sneakers, sandals, and cowboy boots that all fit, but when it came to undergarments, that was another story all together.

As in, there were none. Necessities made up a toothbrush, toothpaste, tons of hairspray, two types of hairbrushes, deodorant, and a complete Mary Kay makeup kit.

Well, she'd wash her bra and panties in the sink tonight and leave them out to dry overnight. Then she'd ask Harper or Tinsley to pick up some if she couldn't get them herself. Now, for something to sleep in. Ellery rifled through the rest of the bag until she saw it. "Mother of pearl," she whispered, holding it up. Thank goodness she had her own room.

ELLERY STARED in wonder as Gavin drove up the Spanish oak lined driveway. They drove straight on the tan graveled road for half a mile before the moss covered trees stopped and the space opened into a large circular drive with a massive fountain in the middle lined up perfectly with the center of the large rectangular plantation house. The brick was painted white and consisted of a ground floor in case of flooding and then three additional stories of covered verandas running the entire length of the house and most likely wrapping all the way around it. At the center of the house, two staircases curved upward and met at a landing before leading to the front door on the first floor.

As Gavin pulled into a small parking area off to the side of the house, the front door opened as a man and woman, both in their fifties and both wearing tan slacks and loafers came to stand on the veranda.

"That's Clark and Suze Bell, owners of Bell Landing Plantation. It's been in Clark's family for generations and will be passed down to their eldest child, Gage, someday," Gavin told her as he turned off the car.

"Let Timmins get that, Dr. Faulkner!" Suze called out as they went to grab their bags. A man in navy slacks and a white polo with the outline of the house over the left breast pocket greeted them.

"Hi, Timmins. How are you doing?" Gavin shook the man's hand. He looked to be a couple years younger than she was with a head full of blonds, browns, and even a slight trace of red in his long hair currently tied back in a bun she'd kill for. She could never get her messy buns so, well, messy.

"Sometimes I can't even. This adulting thing is hard AF. But then I was slaying it on the board out at Sullivan's Island yesterday, and I thought I'm totally living my best life, ya know?" He grabbed the two bags and started walking toward the house.

Ellery blinked as she tried to make sense of it, but then Gavin slipped his arm around her and introduced him. "Timmins, this is Ellery. Ellery, this is Timmins. He's the new house manager." Gavin lowered his lips to her ear and whispered, "Timmins only speaks millennial." Ellery had to choke down her laughter as they climbed the stairs.

"Timmins, could you put their bags in their room please and then bring them some champagne?" Suze asked as she reached out her hands for Gavin. Her perfect blonde chin-length bob didn't dare frizz in the humidity as she kissed Gavin's cheek and then turned to her. "I am so glad you two could join us on your romantic date. You were lucky we had the one room left."

One room? Ellery looked at the house and blinked. There had to be at least ten bedrooms. What did she mean there was only one room left?

"Maggie didn't tell me her sorority sisters were visiting for a couple of days. But, lucky you, that meant the Sumter Suite is available." The picture of southern elegance turned to Ellery and reached for her hand. "You are going to have the most romantic night. I'm Suze Bell and this is my husband, Clark. Your room is in the opposite wing from where our daughter and her friends are. You'll be quite alone, and you'll find a special treat I left for you both on the balcony."

Ellery shook hands with Clark as he wrapped his arm back around his wife and smiled at them both. "Timmins will put your bags in your room, and he'll bring dinner at seven. Until then, enjoy the pool, walk the gardens, go for a horseback ride, or just rest in your room with a book. If you need anything at all, don't hesitate to ask."

"Thank you, Mr. and Mrs. Bell."

"Oh, please call us Suze and Clark," she said as she patted Ellery's hand. "Now, you two have a good time."

Timmins showed them to their room and Ellery wanted to jump onto the bed and squeal. It was a king-sized four-poster bed. A large overstuffed couch sat in front of a fireplace. There was a claw-footed tub in the marble bathroom along with an all glass shower with six shower jets and a rainfall showerhead. When they pushed open the French doors, they discovered their own private paradise on the balcony. On the left side, Suze had a hammock put up, overlooking the gardens that sloped down to the river. On the right was a dinner table all set up for a private dinner for two.

"This is beautiful," Ellery said with awe, but Gavin must have heard the inevitable *but* coming from her.

"I'll sleep on the couch. You can have the bed."

Ellery looked at the massive bed and then to the couch. She'd fit perfectly on it, but he might be cramped. But when she looked back at the bed she wasn't picturing herself alone in it. Especially when Gavin stripped off his shirt and pulled out a pair of swim trunks. "Do you feel like a swim? They also have a hot tub."

"I, uh, wasn't supplied with a bathing suit."

"No problem. Maggie's sure to have one you can borrow." Gavin moved to the phone and made the call. A couple minutes later there was a knock on the door. Gavin answered it, and a beautiful blonde bombshell let out a squeal and threw herself into Gavin's arms.

"It is so good to see you!"

"You too," Gavin said as he swung her around then set her on her feet. "Meet Ellery. Ellery, this is Maggie Bell."

"Oh my gosh!" Maggie smacked Gavin's bare stomach. Right on Ellery's favorite rippled muscle of his six-pack. "You didn't tell me your girlfriend is so pretty." And then Ellery was enveloped in a hug. This was the Olympic shooter? She figured someone named after ammunition would be tough looking, but Maggie was all soft curves. Instead of being dressed in camo as Ellery pictured, Maggie had on a cute short jungle green and hot pink paisley dress that highlighted her green eyes and long strawberry blonde hair. She also didn't appear to be under the weather—the fibber. It only made Ellery like her more.

"I am so glad I brought the blue bikini for you. It's going to match your eyes perfectly. Now, you two have fun! Call me if you need anything else." And with a wink, Maggie was off like a whirlwind, leaving behind a blue bikini dangling from Ellery's hands. A very tiny blue bikini.

15

Gavin tried to play it cool, but it was hard, in more ways than one, when Ellery walked from the bathroom in a tiny bikini the same blue as her eyes. Her breasts were barely contained in the small triangles and her legs were on full display, but it was the soft curve of her hips, the smoothness of her stomach, and the way her butt looked when she bent to pick up a towel that had his mouth going dry.

Relax. He needed her to relax so she could possibly remember who was after her. This was not a seduction. This was . . . she bent over to rub lotion on her legs, and the eyeful of breasts sent all good intentions out the window. After all, orgasms were relaxing.

THEY SPENT the day strolling through the gardens, swimming in the huge pool overlooking the river, and sometimes just lying quietly in the sun together. They laughed, they played, they flirted, and they had fun. Ellery was smart, didn't back down when she had her own opinion, but she also listened to his thoughts. She teased and made him laugh. He could talk to her about medical things without her eyes glazing over, and similarly, her love for art had made him want to know all about it. With her explaining it, it came to life instead of put him to sleep like it did in school.

"Maggie sent some chilled champagne," Timmins said with a wide smile as he set two glasses on the small table between their lounge chairs. "You and your bae are total relationship goals. I gotta bounce. My job never ends," he said with a huff.

"What's a bae?" Gavin asked, watching Timmins's man bun bounce as he walked back to the house.

Ellery giggled as she sipped the champagne. "You can't be that old. Aren't you still a millennial?"

"I'm thirty-four. I claim Oregon Trail generation."

"What?" Ellery laughed outright. "There is no Oregon Trail generation."

"There should be. It's the greatest generation ever. We grew up playing the Oregon Trail game in grade school when computers first appeared in the schools. You young'uns wouldn't understand," Gavin teased.

Ellery giggled again, then her eyes darkened. He saw them trail over his body and felt like throwing her over his shoulder and running for their bedroom. "Well, you look pretty good for an old man."

"Old? I'll show you old." Gavin leapt up and scooped Ellery in his arms as she laughed hard. He carried her to the deep end and tossed her in. Ellery splashed down into the water and came up laughing.

ELLERY WAS HAVING FUN. She couldn't remember the last time she laughed so hard. Well, that wasn't saying much since she wasn't sure exactly how much she didn't remember of her life for the past couple of years. She remembered college, graduation, and everything before then. Well, at least she thought she did.

She blinked the water from her eyes and looked at Gavin who was grinning at her. His body was warmed by the sun. The small smattering of dark chest hair only made him look hotter. Well, the six pack and that V along his hips didn't hurt either.

"Pretty good for an old man," Ellery called out. "Too bad you're too old to catch me."

Ellery took off swimming as she heard Gavin splash into the water. She didn't try very hard to get away, and in seconds his arms were wrapped around her. His skin slid along hers, and it made her want him even more. Her chest heaved, something she only thought happened in historical romances, but she was breathing so quickly with desire that her chest was actually heaving, and she wanted nothing more than his hands on her.

Gavin spun her in his arms until they faced each other and pulled her close enough that her nipples brushed against his chest. She might have moaned but was unsure if she'd done it in her head or out loud. Ellery encircled his neck with her arms to bring herself closer to him. All day she'd fallen a little more for Gavin until she was completely head over heels for this man. A man who respected her, listened to her, and laughed with her. And one she was sure would be a loyal and caring boyfriend instead of a selfish one.

"Well, you caught me. Now what are you going to do with me?" Ellery asked, her voice dropping as she tried to calm her rapidly beating heart.

His eyes dropped to her lips as the hands at her waist

tightened and pulled her against him. "I'm going to claim my prize."

Ellery hoped that meant he was going to kiss her—a real kiss and not CPR this time. Her heartbeat sped up with every inch Gavin's lips got closer to hers as he bent his head. Ellery tilted her head, offering her lips, and Gavin took what she offered. His warm and wet lips claimed hers, and his hands slid from the side of her waist until he'd wrapped his arms around her. Instinctively, Ellery lifted her legs around his waist as Gavin pulled her closer.

She felt the tip of his tongue run along her lip and opened her mouth for him. Ellery loved the way Gavin gripped her as he carried her to the edge of the pool. His lips never left hers, and in that moment she could see Gavin as a pirate from the old days, plundering everything she had to give and demanding more. While his touch was gentle, his kiss was anything but. Heat pooled in her belly as he pushed her against the side of the pool, anchoring her to him as he pushed his hips forward and took all she had to give.

Ellery heated all over from his hardness pressed against her. Desperate to feel more of him, she dropped her hands from his neck and ran them over his pecs and down the ridges of his abs. Her fingers toyed with the waistband of his swim trunks, but suddenly Gavin broke the kiss. He was breathing hard, his eyes glowed, and his lips were slightly swollen. Ellery imagined that's what she looked like as well.

"As much as I would love to continue right now, I can't do so in a pool where people could easily see us. I want you all to myself. And some things are hard to do underwater that I very much want to do to you."

Ellery's heart was pounding as Gavin placed a slow

sweet kiss on her lips. "We have all the time in the world," he whispered to her when she tried to deepen the kiss.

Ellery didn't want to remind him they didn't, in fact, have all the time in the world since someone was trying to kill her.

GAVIN TOOK a deep breath as he waited for Ellery to finish getting ready. Timmins had set up dinner on the balcony a moment before. He'd given Gavin a wink, and Gavin had felt like groaning. They had been seen. Thank goodness it was only Timmins.

Over the sound of Ellery's hair dryer, Gavin heard a knock on the door. Someone was ignoring the privacy sign. He walked across the suite and opened the door, but it wasn't Timmins. It was Gage. Gage Bell had graduated from college then went to get his master's. He spent every summer working for his father and was now back in Shadows Landing for good.

"Gage, I heard you were back," Gavin said, shaking Gage's hand. At twenty-six, Gage stood a little over six feet and took after his father with his light brown hair and his blue-green eyes.

"I am. I'm going to start full time at the family business," Gage said with a smile. "But I brought you something."

"Me?" Gavin asked with surprise as he looked down at a glossy white bag with the plantation logo on it and stuffed with bright pink tissue paper.

"Yeah. After your display in the pool I thought you'd like it."

Gavin would have blushed if he was that sort of person, but medical school stopped any blushing. He pulled out the pink tissue and reached into the bag. "Condoms," he said, shaking his head as Gage grinned. "Great, thank you."

"You're welcome." Gage winked as he turned away. "It's great seeing you. We'll catch up soon. Have fun!"

Gavin shut the door and looked at the condoms. It had been the only thing preventing him from contemplating sex with Ellery, but now . . . Shit, now he had no excuse to not think about it as a real possibility. Especially after their show in the pool. And it wasn't like he worried about sex with women before, but with Ellery he somehow knew it would be more.

The sound of the hair dryer turned off, and before Gavin could leap across the bed to stash the gift in the nightstand, the bathroom door opened and Ellery strode out in a pretty sundress. "What's that?"

Gavin shoved the condoms behind his back. "Nothing. Gage just stopped by to say hi."

"Oh, too bad I wasn't ready. I'd like to see if he's as nice as Maggie." Ellery made her way into the room. Gavin turned as she moved, making sure to keep his front to her as he tried to slide over to the nightstand.

"He is very nice. I'm glad he's moving back to Shadows Landing. Why don't you pour the wine? It's out on the balcony."

Ellery looked at him and he knew she was suspicious, but she didn't push it. "Okay," she said slowly with a false smile. As soon as she was out of the room Gavin dove across the bed, yanked open the nightstand drawer, and shoved the condoms inside.

"Gotcha!" Ellery cried, leaping back inside.

Gavin slid his hand under the side of his face and pretended to be stretched out along the bed. "Yes?"

Ellery looked at him posed on the bed. "What are you doing?"

"Just lying here, why?"

She shook her head. "Fine. Don't tell me. Wine is ready and dinner smells delicious."

Gavin gave a fake stretch and bounced out of bed. "Then, may I escort you to dinner?" He gave a small bow and offered her his arm. Ellery laughed and all was right once again.

16

"That was so delicious," Ellery said, setting down her fork. "Thank you for this. It's been the most perfect day."

Gavin reached across the small table and placed his hand over hers. "I think so too. Ellery, I—" Ellery leaned forward, cutting him off. She didn't want talks of tomorrow. She didn't want reality to set in. She was living a dream and as such, she was going to complete it her way.

It wasn't exactly as smooth as she imagined in her head. In her head she leaned forward, Gavin leaned forward, and they kissed over the romantic glow of the candle. Reality was one hand hit the side of her plate, sending food scraps tumbling and almost breaking the plate as the wine glass tipped over, staining the white tablecloth with the deep red Malbec wine. But she wasn't one to give up. Maybe Gavin wouldn't notice? So she pressed on, leaned forward, and stared into his eyes. She saw her own desire reflected there.

"Ellery."

"Yes. Oh yes, Gavin. You know what I want. What I need," she practically begged as her eyes closed, and she tilted her lips. Her body flushed with heat as the spilled wine was forgotten and ideas of climbing over the table and into Gavin's lap took over.

"Ellery!" Gavin cried again.

"I'm so hot for you right now," Ellery admitted. "Kiss me or I might explode."

Ellery puckered her lips as her body burned. That was, until cold water splashed on her. Ice cubes went down the front of her dress as water dripped off her face and down her chest. Her eyes shot open as she sputtered to talk.

"You were on fire," Gavin said with a cringe.

"I told you I was, and you literally gave me a cold shower." Ellery threw her napkin at him in a huff. Her nose wrinkled and she sniffed again. "What's that smell?"

Gavin was fighting not to smile. "Why are you laughing?" she asked as she crossed her arms over her. "What the hell?" Ellery looked down at where she'd crossed her arms to find the ruffle of her sundress was crispy.

"As I said, you were on fire. Literally as well as figuratively."

Ellery groaned as she covered her face with her hands. "I was trying to be smooth so you'd make love to me. In one of my favorite movies they kiss over the candles on a cake, and it was so romantic. I guess that's why it's a movie. No one would be stupid enough to do that in real life. They were probably fake candles in the movie."

"I'm not a southern gentleman for nothing," Gavin said, picking up the table and moving it aside. "It's bred into me to chivalrously give my lady anything she desires."

Ellery's blush was as red as the wine she'd spilled. She hadn't meant to admit she wanted nothing more than a night with Gavin to keep this dream going. She'd just been flustered, and it had popped out, but now he had moved the table and before she knew it she was up in his arms.

"I better get you out of those wet clothes. I wouldn't want you to get a cold."

Ellery wound her arms around his neck as she laughed. "So corny."

"Yes, but it sounded considerate, right? Which is more romantic than telling you I've been thinking of nothing but slowly stripping that dress from your shoulders to free your breasts for my mouth before pulling it from your body and feasting on you."

Ellery was suddenly short of breath as she glanced down to make sure the heat she was feeling wasn't her back on fire. She gulped as Gavin carried her into the suite. "No," she said breathlessly, "that sounds better than the corny line."

"Really?" Gavin grinned and made her want to rip her clothes off because slowly stripping sounded like a bad idea at the moment. "Then would you like to know how hard I am and how badly I want to slide into you over and over again until you're screaming my name?"

Ellery nodded. She was breathing so quickly she didn't think she'd be able to manage words as he set her on the bed. Ellery reached for the hem of her dress to quickly pull it off, but Gavin stopped her. "I did say slowly, right?"

Again, Ellery nodded as her heart beat loudly in her ears. Gavin took his time pulling off his shirt before climbing onto the bed and lying next to her. He rested on his side, propping up his head with his hand. Ellery raised her hand to his chest and felt his heart under her palm as he leaned down to kiss her. Every time they kissed it seemed to get better and better. This time Gavin was slow as his lips parted hers and his tongue ventured inside. Ellery melted into the kiss as one of Gavin's fingers ran from her cheek, down her neck, over her collarbone, and slowly dragged the thin spaghetti strap of her dress off her shoulder.

Ellery moaned into his mouth and felt the breeze from the open French doors blow across her exposed nipple a second before a strong and sure hand closed around it. Gavin's thumb played it to a peak as his hand explored her. Her whole body was on fire as Gavin shifted over her. He held himself up on his elbows and as his one hand continued its playing, the other began the light trail down her neck, across her collar bone, and slowly dragged the other strap from her shoulder.

"You're so beautiful," Gavin whispered reverently. Ellery opened her eyes to see him dip his head toward her breast. Her fingers speared his hair as his tongue drew a slow, titillating circle around her nipple before he was slowly pushing her dress down over her stomach. With each inch of skin exposed, Gavin's mouth made sure to kiss, lick, or nibble it.

By the time Gavin pulled her dress and panties from her body, Ellery wasn't sure she'd be able to speak. Her body had never been so relaxed yet so wired at the same time. Her hips moved on their own, her breathing was quick and shallow, and she was burning hotter than when she'd been on fire.

Gavin stood and stepped out of his pants. Ellery's eyes traveled across his chest, down the rippled muscles, and . . . Ellery gulped as she looked down to make sure the bed wasn't on fire. Nope, all good.

Ellery felt the bed dip as Gavin began to crawl back up her body, making sure to hit every sensitive spot along the way. Ellery was seconds from grabbing him, flipping him, and having her wicked way with him before he finally made it back up to her face for a searing kiss.

"Do you want this? I can stop if you want me to," he

asked as he looked into her eyes and brushed a strand of hair from her face.

"Don't you dare. But we do need—"

"Condoms," they said together. Gavin rolled off her, and she took advantage and scrambled for her nightstand.

"Here," they both said as they came back to each other.

"Where'd those come from?" they said at the same time as each looked at the condom box in the other's hands.

"Gage brought these when you were getting ready," Gavin told her.

"Maggie brought these when you were in the shower," Ellery said and began to laugh. Her laughter stopped when she saw Gavin's eyes heating with lust as he watched her breasts sway with her laughter. Soon she matched the intensity in his green eyes as he raced to slip a condom on.

Gavin lowered her onto the bed, and she felt his weight on her. It was warm, hard, loving, and safe. Her heart was in his hands. And then she lost herself in Gavin, knowing she'd remember this forever.

GAVIN WRAPPED his arm around Ellery as he pulled her to his side. Her head was resting in the crook of his shoulder, and her hand was splayed on his chest. He should have told her he was falling in love with her, but his brain was not working properly from the mind-blowing sex they'd just had.

Ellery's breathing slowed and fell into a steady rhythm as he stroked her hair. "I'll keep you safe. Always," Gavin swore before drifting off to sleep with the woman of his dreams, in quite possibly the ugliest nightdress he'd ever seen, wrapped in his arms.

17

Charleston, Last Friday Night...

ELLERY DUCKED into the back of the Mimi Hollis Art Gallery, located on the very popular and historic Meeting Street in downtown Charleston, South Carolina and did a little celebratory dance.

In fact, the historic three-story brick house turned art gallery had once belonged to Mimi's grandmother who had left it to her when she died in 1904. That was when Mimi, or Mary Hollis as her name really was, turned it into an art gallery. In turn, Mimi died and left it to her grandson, who left it to his son, Hollis Thomas Coldwell, who was Ellery's boss—a boss Ellery had just impressed.

In Charleston, your past always meant something. "Who are your people?" is more important than "Where did you go to college?" Something Ellery learned when she'd been applying for the art director job. The Coldwell and Hollis families had been in Charleston for ten generations. The St. Johns had been there for six. In fact, Ellery got the job at the

Mimi Hollis Art Gallery because her great-grandmother and Hollis's grandmother had both been on the Garden Gates Historical Society Gala Committee some eighty years ago.

Ellery danced in a little circle as she fist pumped the air. Tonight she'd just sold four Mark Vosslinger paintings. Mark himself wasn't her favorite person, bless his heart, but his artwork was outstanding. Hollis had discovered Mark selling his paintings in the open-air Charleston City Market three years ago. But after tonight, Mark was way bigger than any market and even Charleston, for that matter. And Mark and the Mimi Hollis Art Gallery were going to be famous. Hello job security.

Ellery straightened her black sheath dress and fixed the loose champagne blonde hairs that the summer humidity had let escape from the sloppy ballerina bun sitting on the top of her head.

"You look beautiful."

Ellery gasped and spun to the back door. "Atherton! What are you doing here?" she asked her ex-boyfriend. Atherton Hawthorne was the epitome of old money. His ancestor was the first governor of the area. Hawthornes had been in the city since before Charles Town became Charleston. Their money built downtown, their plantation began the whole city's trade with the north, and their opinion had led South Carolina to vote in favor of independence.

"I've missed you, Ellery."

"And I told you it's over," Ellery hissed. Atherton was gorgeous in his custom tuxedo. His light brown hair was liberally highlighted with blonde streaks from his time outside. He was always running, surfing, or hunting with the "it" crowd of Charleston's playboys. And he knew he was handsome. He paid a lot of money for his sexy smile, his tailored clothes, and his very sexy sports car. He had a condo downtown overlooking the city that was bigger than most houses. His parents had a mansion on East Battery—the old and very elite row of houses overlooking Charleston Harbor. And the family plantation outside of town had been handed down for twelve plus generations. But none of that mattered when Ellery had caught him in bed with a socialite named Bitsy.

Bitsy's platinum blonde hair had still been up in a fancy style from the charity event Ellery couldn't go to because she'd been hosting an evening with a local artist. She had decided to surprise Atherton and found Bitsy in nothing but a pair of expensive cowboy boots and her pearls, bouncing away on top of Atherton.

Bitsy had been thrilled, Atherton had been astounded that Ellery would actually break up with him, and Ellery had been spitting mad. So she'd reverted to generations of southern manners as a cold smile had broken out on her face. "Bitsy, darling," she'd said as the twenty-one year old bimbo turned in faux shock. "What would your mother say, knowing you were bouncing around in bed with your cowboy boots on? Where are your manners?"

Bitsy had gasped. Atherton had tossed Bitsy from him, giving Ellery a view of his shrinking erection. And Ellery had grabbed her clothes from the closet as Atherton told her all the reasons she couldn't leave him.

That had been two months ago. Ellery wouldn't say she'd moved on, but she was definitely over Atherton. Her heart had been mended with a couple shots of whiskey, and she'd never looked back. Only, Atherton had been popping up all over town. He couldn't get over the fact she'd left him. And then two weeks ago, he'd walked into the local bar she frequented and punched the man she'd been talking with. A man who was a tourist simply asking for directions to a nearby restaurant. And now he was at her big gallery exhibit... uninvited.

"It's not over. You're just being dramatic. I was with Bitsy to show her some moves since she was a virgin. It was educational. I told you that. It didn't mean anything. It was only a favor for an old friend." Atherton's frown turned back into a smile as Ellery blinked at his stupidity. "This is your big night. You should have the handsomest man in Charleston on your arm."

Ellery blinked at him then shook her head. "Get out, Atherton. You're not my date."

His smile slipped again as he took a menacing step forward. "Who is? You better not be here with that artist. He's so far beneath us."

"I'm here alone, Atherton. I know you don't understand this, but I'm working. And we're over. Now get out." Ellery slammed her hands against his muscled chest and pushed all six feet of him out from behind the curtain separating the show floor from the back room.

Taking a deep breath to compose herself, Ellery stepped from the back into the perfectly lit gallery. The old brick walls were exposed and the hardwood floor was polished, allowing the generations of scrapes and dents to show.

With a wide smile, Ellery stopped next to where Hollis stood tall, talking to some of the Charleston elite while Mark stood near the bar in the back, angrily tossing back whiskey. Mark had perfected his persona of the brooding artist.

"Excuse me, Mr. Coldwell," Ellery said with a professional smile to the men and women who were dropping seventy-five thousand dollars or more on each painting. "But I need to put this up."

Hollis saw the sticky SOLD tag Ellery put on the brick next to the painting and nodded. "Great job, Ellery," he said in his slow as molasses southern voice. "Mrs. Tandy was just saying she would be back to look at the Charleston gate piece."

Ellery wanted to do a little dance again as she made the appropriate response to one of Charleston's grand dames dressed in a bright blue tunic with a bright pink, yellow, orange, and purple design and white silk pants. Color was in for Charleston and not only on the houses.

Ellery had been working there for a little over a year, and under her direction several local artists had been launched to success. Tonight had been all hers. The marketing, the organization of the exhibit, the exclusive guest list, and the idea to include several invites to galleries in New York, London, and Paris.

After placing the sold card next to the landscape, Ellery ignored Atherton as he walked around the gallery. She moved in the opposite direction of him as he made his rounds, and she said her goodbyes to the guests beginning to leave for the night. There was talk of a tropical storm hitting late that night, which in Charleston only meant you made sure to stock up on cocktails. However, it prevented people from staying later than normal. Anything less than a major hurricane was an excuse to drink.

SOON THE GALLERY EMPTIED, even Atherton, who was throwing a drinking party for the storm that night, had left with the others. Ellery handed a check to both the bartender and the caterer. Tables were removed, money was secured, and she was ready to head home. Hollis locked the front door and turned to her with a huge smile. He was in his late forties, had perfectly cut light brown hair lightly peppered with some gray, and was stylish in his tan linen suit with a pale pink dress shirt and a purple bow tie with brightly colored pineapples on it.

"You should be very proud of yourself. Tonight was a smashing success."

"Thank you, Mr. Coldwell," Ellery said, picking up her purse from the backroom.

"Let me walk you out." Hollis opened the back door for her then locked it as they entered the small parking area in the back of the gallery. At one time it had probably been a grand secret garden. "Now, I don't want to see you back here until Monday. You deserve these two days off."

Ellery unlocked her sedan with her key fob, and Hollis opened the door for her. "Thank you. I'm going to sleep through all of it." She laughed as she climbed in.

"Stay safe and enjoy yourself. I'll probably drop by Monday afternoon to see if Mrs. Tandy came in."

"Okay. Have a nice rest of the weekend, Mr. Coldwell."

Hollis closed her car door and strode over to his luxury sports car as Ellery put her bag away and waited for Hollis to leave before carefully backing out and driving down Meeting Street, turning onto Queen Street. Even though it was close to midnight people were still enjoying the nightlife downtown. Ellery dodged horse drawn carriages and ghost tours as she made her way to her small one-bedroom condo on Rutledge Avenue overlooking Colonial Lake Park. Her condo building had been a huge historic house owned by the sweet Tibbie and Elijah Cummings before it was divided up. Her whole condo had probably been someone's bedroom in the eighteen hundreds, but all 750 square feet were hers now.

Ellery parked in her parking space and opened the

lobby doors. She looked at the small bank of post boxes until she found the one for Apartment 7 and inserted her key. The front door opened and old Miss Tibbie, really known as Mrs. Elijah F. Cummings, came in with her small Yorkshire terrier dog in her arms. Miss Tibbie and Mr. Elijah had the four-bedroom, twenty-five hundred square foot penthouse. Tibbie never went by her real name of Tabitha. Instead she insisted on being called Tibbie, but good southern manners never allowed you to call an elder solely by their first name, so Tibbie became Miss Tibbie. Even her dog had to be called Miss. Manners never went out of style in Charleston. Similarly neither did seersucker suits.

"Oh, the wind is really picking up," Miss Tibbie said, setting Miss Muffy, her small lap dog, down on the marble floor. "How did the art show go tonight?"

"Really well, thank you, Miss Tibbie." Ellery smiled kindly at the older woman who had become her very good friend over this past year.

"Well, I'm glad you're in for the night. I heard the storm has been upgraded to a category one hurricane. We'll get our skirt blown up, but no slap on the ass." Ellery grinned at the eighty-year-old woman who headed for the elevator. "Are you coming up?"

"I'm just checking my mail. I'll be up in a minute. Good night, Miss Tibbie. Please tell Mr. Elijah hello as well."

"I will. He'll be delighted your show went well. Stop by in the morning to tell us about it." The old, heavy metal doors to the elevator closed as Ellery turned to pull out her mail. She looked out the front door and saw the neighbors down the street putting up their storm windows. "Damn," she muttered as she shoved her mail into her purse and headed back outside. She should have rolled them down at the gallery before she left, but she hadn't checked the weather forecast because she was too eager to get home. It had been plausible deniability. But now there was no denying a storm was coming, and she needed to protect the gallery.

The wind was picking up, but if she hurried she could roll the metal storm shutters over the gallery windows and be tucked into bed reading when the storm hit. There might be some flooding, but Charleston knew the drill. Ellery started her car, turned onto the street, and headed for the gallery.

"Ellery!" she heard her name being yelled far off in the distance. Through the fog of her dream, her name reached her and yanked her from the darkness. Ellery's eyes popped open, but instead of a person swinging something at her in the rain, she saw Gavin's worried face above her with her hands being held gently, yet securely, in his own. "What's going on?"

"You're safe. We're at the Bell Landing Plantation. You were having a bad dream. You began crying out for help. Can you remember what you dreamed?"

Gavin was calm and his voice steady. That grounded her as she drew a separation between her dream and the real world. She was in a well-appointed suite instead of outside in the rain. Sunlight peeked through the white plantation shutters instead of the darkness from the night in her dreams. "I remembered some of what happened," she told him, scooting up the bed so she could lean against the headboard. She hugged the blanket to her as if it would protect her as she recounted her dream with a mixture of excitement and dread.

"So, you were heading back to the gallery. Was anyone there?"

"I don't know. The last thing I remember is driving out of my condo parking lot. And then my dream jumped to me running. But, the parking lot behind the gallery has those cobblestones from my dream. Could I have made it back to the gallery and been attacked there?"

Gavin nodded. "It's a possibility. There wasn't much time between when you left the gallery and when you returned. Was anyone still at the gallery when you left?"

Ellery shook her head. "No. If my dream is correct, Hollis walked me to my car and left. It took me a minute to get everything put away in my car and I saw him leave. We were the last two at the gallery."

Gavin sat against the headboard and patted his bare chest. Ellery didn't speak as she wriggled over to him and rested her head against the warmth of his chest. His arm came around and anchored her as her mind raced. She listened to the steady beat of his heart and let her mind go back to the dream. Safely in his arms, she relived the dream in a wakened trance.

"Gavin, I think that's what really happened. It feels so real. Can I see the pictures from the gallery you showed me at the police station?"

Gavin leaned over, grabbed his phone, and pulled up the art gallery's social media posts from the night of Mark's exhibit. Ellery leaned against him as he pulled up the first photo. Excitement filled her. "I remember this! She bought the small painting of King Street for twenty thousand dollars. She said it was perfect for her bathroom."

Ellery took in the photo and was transported back to the gallery. The warmth of the night, the feeling in the air that rain was on the way. The way the lights made the artwork glow. The sounds of talking, laughing, and glasses being filled with champagne. She was there. And so was Hollis, Mark, Atherton, and the sales assistant, Blair. Hollis mingled with the who's who of Charleston's elite. Blair assisted her and flirted with every man who took a second look at her tight little black dress. Atherton bugged Ellery. And Mark sulked. She remembered her annoyance with him. She'd put in all this work to sell his paintings, and he acted like a little boy who didn't get the toy he wanted. Except this little boy tossed back drinks instead of tears.

Gavin turned to the next photo, and she saw Atherton in the background of the photo. The photo was of Hollis and his mother, the very formidable Sylvia Coldwell. Sylvie, as her friends called her, smiled in her colorful silk suit next to her son. She was tall and willowy, and her straight, thick steel-gray hair dared not touch the top of her shoulder and was always adorned by a crystal encrusted barrette or headband of some kind. The night of the party she wore a bright turquoise suit with a white silk headband encrusted with pale pink crystals. She looked young, even with her gray hair. Hollis had let it slip that his mother visited New York City once a month to shop and get specialized facials that involved some very gross treatments, but Ellery couldn't argue with the results.

However, what was interesting about the picture wasn't Hollis and his mother. Right behind them Atherton had his hand resting on Blair's ass. Following the direction Atherton was looking, Ellery saw herself talking to a customer with her back to Atherton and his handsy action with Blair. "That asshole," Ellery grumbled.

"Hollis?" Gavin asked with interest.

"No. Atherton. I remember it all. He's definitely my ex after he cheated on me. Look, he's right behind Hollis with his hand on Blair's ass. The sad thing is no more than ten minutes before this he was begging me to come back."

She felt Gavin's body tense beneath her, and not in a pleasurable way. She looked up to find his jaw tight and his eyes hard. "I will never make that mistake again. Atherton never believed me when I told him it was over."

"He'll learn soon enough," Gavin said a little harshly before letting out a breath and relaxing. "Tell me more about the pictures."

Ellery flipped through them all, and the excitement built as she realized she remembered them all. "What do you think this means?"

"It means your retrograde amnesia is gone. The only thing you can't remember is the traumatic incident. It's called traumatic amnesia. It's your brain's way of protecting you from scary memories or because the hit you took bruised the part of your brain housing those memories. However, I believe it's more likely the case that your brain is trying to protect you."

"It was so scary my brain doesn't want to relive it?" Ellery asked.

"Basically. I believe you'll remember it when you're ready. When you have enough clues to trigger your brain into remembering or when your brain has healed enough."

Ellery thought about what Gavin said and tried to remember what happened after she began her drive to the gallery, but nothing came. It was a black pit. A pit she could see the other side of. She remembered Gavin's lips on hers. She remembered finally feeling warm again. But between leaving her condo and Gavin giving her CPR she felt like the pit would drag her into a darkness she'd never come back from. Her mind simply refused to go near it.

Ellery rested her head against Gavin as she looked

through the pictures again. When she closed in on the last picture the phone rang. Ryan's number from Keeneston popped up. "Your cousin," she said, handing the phone to Gavin and not hiding the curiosity she had.

"Ryan, what's going on?" Gavin asked, putting the phone to his ear. "Yeah, hold on."

"Ryan wants to talk to us and Granger." Gavin pulled the phone away from his ear, put it on speaker, and conferenced Granger into the call. "Okay, Ryan. We're all yours."

"Sheriff Fox, this is FBI Agent Ryan Parker. I heard you've been assisting my cousin," Ryan said by way of introduction.

"Well, when you grow up in a small town," Granger said by way of explanation.

"You protect your own because they're all your friends. Yeah, I know," Ryan said with a chuckle. "You have three old ladies armed with kitchen tools?"

"No, we have old ladies armed with the Bible and desserts."

"Close enough. We could be sister towns," Ryan said with a chuckle. "Ellery, are you on too?"

"Yes," Ellery said, too nervous to say anything else.

"Good. So, I called Peter Castle, a friend in the Charleston FBI office. He's from Kansas, but we went through training together at Quantico. He's moved around as he climbed the ranks. He's second-in-command and arrived in Charleston eight months ago," Ryan said as a way of saying this FBI agent wasn't part of the hometown crowd. Hopefully that truly meant he was impartial.

"He went to talk to his boss but was told it was a local matter, even though kidnapping and missing persons are FBI matters as well," Ryan told them, and Ellery felt her heart drop. No one was going to believe she was innocent of murdering Mark.

"The head of the FBI around here is Randy McCarthy," Sheriff Fox said, jumping into the conversation. "He's a born and raised Charlestonian."

Ellery felt her hands begin to shake. Even the FBI wouldn't help her.

"That makes sense. It's definitely not protocol and not what Castle was expecting." Ryan paused, and Ellery could practically hear him grinning. "Which is why he's on his way to meet with you before going over McCarthy's head to the Deputy Director."

Ellery assumed that was big since Granger let out a low whistle.

"He has those kinds of connections?" Granger asked.

Ryan chuckled. "No, we do. We may be a small town, but we're very well connected."

"Wait, what does all of this mean?" Ellery asked, feeling as if she was missing something.

"It means," she heard Granger say, "that they've been outmaneuvered. Whoever is after you is powerful in this area. They know all the power players in Charleston and know them well enough to have an innocent person framed for murder. But, as much as some people there like to think, Charleston is not the center of the world. Your friends went higher—all the way to Washington."

"If the authorities in Charleston can't be trusted, we'll bring in new ones. That's what Castle is doing. He's going to get permission from Washington to take over not only the missing person case but also to quietly look into a corruption case. If you didn't kill someone and they're framing you, this could bring Charleston politics to its knees. The head of the local FBI office, police, and whoever else is trying to cover this up will go down," Ryan explained.

"How can one man do that?" Ellery asked.

"Because he's now not only one man," Ryan explained. "I'm involved too, and I have many resources from my family and friends in Keeneston. Once I get a report from Castle that he has any evidence of corruption, I'll come to visit my cousins and together we'll take down the officials with our handpicked team of agents, and of course with the aid of the Shadows Landing Sheriff's Department."

"You'd do all of that for me?"

Ryan made a sound in the affirmative. "We've been estranged from the Faulkners through no fault of the families but because of our great-grandmother. We've reconnected, yes, but not once has Gavin, or any of my cousins, called asking for a favor. For him to do this means you're important enough to be considered family, and family looks after its own."

Gavin wrapped his arm back around her and pulled her against his side before placing a silent kiss on the top of her head. She wasn't alone. For the first time she felt hope.

"What do I need to do?" Ellery asked with a newfound determination for revenge. Revenge on whoever killed Mark. Revenge on whoever tried to kill her. Revenge on whoever was still trying to destroy her career, her name, and her life. It was time to stop being scared. Red hot anger seeped into her being and chased the shadows away. She was going to make them pay for what they did.

19

"Are you sure you're okay?" Gavin asked once again. He looked at a very determined Ellery sitting in his kitchen. She had a massive knife clutched in her hand so tightly her knuckles were white.

"I'm fine."

Clearly she was not fine. But having grown up with a sister, Gavin knew when a woman dropped the fine bomb he either needed to retreat or hunker down. Since said fine woman holding a large knife accompanied this fine bomb, retreat sounded like the best option.

"I have patients until noon," Gavin said, glancing at the clock. Nine. His first patient would be here already. "You know how to use the intercom and get into my rooms. Don't hesitate to do so. Okay?"

"Fine."

Damn, this was not good. A second fine. "I can stay," Gavin said as he reached for the chair.

"I said I'm fine," Ellery said. While not quite a snap, her knuckles turned whiter as they squeezed the knife, and retreat was the best course of action. He darted in and kissed her forehead before practically leaping back. "Hey. Yesterday was the best day . . . and night"—he winked—"of my life. I'll be back as soon as I can."

He made his retreat and saw her hand relax around the knife and the semblance of a smile on her face. The idea of her being worried had his protective instinct flaring to life and burning bright as he walked into his first exam room.

Sadie was busy counting supplies while his patient sat with a thermometer under her tongue and a blood pressure cuff filling up. "Doc, I can't find one scalpel," Sadie whispered. He glanced back as if he could look through the wall to Ellery.

"Don't worry about it. I know where it is." Gavin paused as Sadie wrote down the vitals. "Can you check my medical bag and make sure I have everything? Also, add in a handful of needles, a vial of insulin, and a vial of Haldol." Gavin had all the drugs running through his mind as he thought about what he might need. "And the Ketamine."

Sadie looked curiously at him. "What are you doing? Treating acute psychosis in a diabetic alligator?"

"Ketamine is helpful if I need to do emergency surgery." But then he turned to his patient, ending the conversation. "Now, let's look at this rash."

Sadie quietly left the room. While Gavin tended his patients, his mind was on ways to protect Ellery if it came to that. He might not be law enforcement, but he knew more ways to kill someone than the average person. Of course, he'd worked his whole life trying to prevent death, but if he had to kill, he would. Haldol, while used to treat psychosis, was also helpful in knocking someone out, although, it would take seven or so minutes to work. Ketamine would knock them out sooner, but Haldol lasted longer. There were pros and cons to both, but both would work if he needed someone out of the way, but not dead. Dead was where the insulin came in, or a simple injection of an air bubble into a vein or artery. There were plenty of ways to kill someone. Gavin just hoped he didn't need to use his education to do it.

ELLERY HAD CALMED down when the front door opened. This time she wasn't afraid. She silently set down her cup of coffee and wrapped her fingers tightly around the knife she had taken from the butcher block.

Without any shoes on, she padded silently toward the sound of the footsteps as they headed her way. Ellery pressed herself against the wall to the right of the entrance to the kitchen and waited. The footfalls echoed in the quiet house as they grew louder. Then she saw the shadow—a big one. A head appeared and then large shoulders as her shaking hands raised the knife to prepare to strike.

"Gav, you here?"

Ellery froze. Relief flooded her and she felt like crying as Ryker strode in. Then she lost her breath for an entirely different reason. Ryker must have seen the knife and in one swift move he had her pinned against the wall with his hand around her throat and the knife suddenly in his other hand.

"What the hell is this?" Ellery shivered as Ryker slowly lifted her so she was standing on the tiptoe of her big toe. Gone was the smirking man who'd winked at her before, and in his place was someone much more deadly.

"Thought you were them," Ellery managed to whisper.

"Gavin?" Ryker asked, not removing his eyes from hers.

"Office. Patients."

Suddenly she was free. She expected to drop to the ground, but Ryker's hands where surprisingly gentle as he supported her. He was standing close and smelled of man. It was the only way she could describe it. Ryker towered over her, and even though he'd had her pinned against the wall moments ago, Ellery felt safe that he was there. His body was a solid muscle barrier between her and the world as his hands slid slowly down her arms to hold her hands. "Did I hurt you?"

Ellery swallowed, expecting to find her throat sore, but it wasn't. "No," she said, sounding surprised.

"It was the knife. I didn't know you were on the other end of it. It's not the first time I've had one pointed at me, and I didn't appreciate it then. Although, you're considerably more attractive than the last guy who tried to stab me."

"Someone tried to stab you?"

Ryker shrugged. "It happens in my line of work."

"That's why I'm in art."

Ryker raised one eyebrow, and Ellery broke out laughing. "I guess art isn't as safe as I thought."

"I don't think I've ever laughed when someone has tried to kill me."

"I either laugh or cry," Ellery told him.

His face suddenly looked horrified. "Don't you dare cry."

Ellery finally stepped away from Ryker as the front door opened again. "Calm down. It's Wade," Ryker said, his voice soothing. "Besides, no one would be able to get through me to get to you."

"While that's incredibly sweet, you do know I love your cousin, right?"

Ryker grinned, and his whole face softened, causing her to go breathless. "Thought you did."

"Do you only flirt with taken women?" Wade asked as he walked into the kitchen.

Ryker shrugged. "It's all I have time for."

"You owe me," Wade said as seriously as he could, but he was smiling so Ellery knew it mustn't be too bad.

"For what?" Ellery asked as she was finally getting to know the personalities of Gavin's cousins. Ryker was the protector—the tough guy. But even tough guys fell in love. And Wade, with his clean-cut Coast Guard looks, came off as an easy going, party guy. But she suspected he was all business when he was on the job. She was also beginning to think his happy-go-lucky attitude was how he coped with his stressful job.

"Mr. High and Mighty got knocked down to earth by the garden committee meeting at the restaurant last night and called in reinforcements."

Ellery fought not to smile as Ryker frowned. "Were you cowed by society matrons?"

"I need to hire them," Ryker said seriously as he moved in his expensive suit to pour a cup of coffee. "But, I became successful by finding people's weaknesses and exploiting them."

"And Wade was their weakness?" Ellery asked with disbelief as she looked back and forth between the two men.

"Show her," was all Ryker said as Wade's smile grew.

Wade pulled out his phone and pulled up a photo. Ellery looked down and almost gasped out loud at a society matron's various social media sites. Wade was wearing his dress blues. His short dark hair, his deep green eyes, the way the uniform hugged his wide shoulders, and then tapered with this narrow waist . . . and don't get her started on what the pants did. No wonder one of the grandest dames of Charleston society, who had to be eighty if she were a day, was wrapped around Wade like a second skin, grinning into the camera.

"Is your hand on her ass?" Ellery asked.

Wade's smile widened. "Ryker called in the big guns for a reason."

"What did you find out?" Ellery inquired without giving a reaction to the comment.

"What didn't he find out?" Ryker snorted as he sat at the kitchen table as if it were the head of a conference desk. He commanded power in every move he made. "It was embarrassing. Your friend, Tibbie Cummings, was there. She giggled like a schoolgirl when Wade winked at her. All he had to do was mention seeing her on the news and hoped that pretty woman in the picture showed up soon and those women couldn't talk fast enough."

Ellery reached out and patted his shoulder. "Are you okay? Do you need me to flirt with you to make you feel better?"

"I'll feel a lot better about myself if you flash me," Ryker said dryly as Ellery faked smacking him against the shoulder before turning back to Wade.

"Tell me everything," she said, feeling excited. They'd learned something. She knew it. "How is Tibbie? Please tell me she isn't behind this."

Both Wade and Ryker shook their heads. "No way," Wade said. "She loves you like a granddaughter and is distraught about you missing. However, not everyone is."

Ryker nodded and picked the story up. "They forgot all about me when Wade started buying them shots. He took off an article of clothing with each shot the group took."

"What?" Ellery practically screamed with her eyes wide. "You stripped?"

"No. I'm way more subtle than that. First was the hat, second was the jacket, third was the tie, then rolling up the sleeves, then undoing the top couple of buttons. No real skin, but it got them talking. That and the shots of whiskey."

"It got them shitfaced," Ryker clarified.

"Exactly," Wade said, grinning again.

"Anyway, it worked. Hollis's mother, Sylvia Coldwell, thought you were angling to become the next Mrs. Coldwell," Wade said, pouring his own cup of coffee.

"Me? No way. I've never had an interest in Hollis, and he's never expressed any interest in me. Now, as to why Blair got the assistant job—" Ellery rolled her eyes. Hollis was old enough to be her father. "I don't know anything for sure, but she's incredibly flirty with everyone."

"That's good to know," Ryker said dryly.

Ellery rolled her eyes at him again. "Atherton already found that out. I remembered more this morning. I looked at the pictures again," she said, pausing to have Ryker pull up the social media pictures on his phone as she quickly filled them in on her memories before scrolling until she found the picture with Atherton's hand on Blair's ass. "And this was only a couple minutes after he begged me to get back together with him."

"Never liked him. Uses the wrong head to think with. It's why he's failed at everything he's tried to do and why he now works for his daddy on a really short leash," Ryker said, handing the phone to Wade.

Wade nodded. "I learned all about you and Atherton from his mother, Louisa Hawthorne, and grandmother, Beatrice Hawthorne."

"Do I want to know? I'm beginning to think only Tibbie

likes me," Ellery said with a sigh as she plopped into an empty kitchen chair.

"They have mixed feelings. Tibbie is friends with Beatrice, who likes you because of all the great things Tibbie says about you. That and I don't think she likes her daughter-in-law very much. But Louisa despises you. Although, to be fair, I think she'll despise any woman who is with her son. That is not a healthy relationship. She still sees him as this little boy to be pampered. To her, you are not good enough for him. But then again, no one is."

"Yes, she was always very cold to me," Ellery told them.

"And we found out why Atherton wants you back," Wade told her.

"Money." Ryker said it so harshly Ellery flinched.

"Money? I'm comfortable, but I don't have a lot of money like some of these old families. Oh. I get it. I have the Charleston pedigree, but not the fortune."

"Actually, it's Atherton who doesn't have money," Ryker said almost gleefully.

"His family is incredibly wealthy," Ellery corrected.

"And that's just it," Wade told her. "His *father* is incredibly wealthy. Atherton has been cut off. He only gets what he earns from working at the family business. And as Beatrice told me, that's minimum wage right now."

Ellery shook his head. "Bitsy has way more money that I do. Why does he want to get back with me?"

"Because Daddy said he'd give Atherton access to some of his trust fund if, and only if, he married a hard-working, nice, reasonable woman with a good name and reputation who will make him grow up," Ryker told her as his lips tilted into a smile.

"And I'm that?"

"You sure as hell ain't Bitsy Englewood," Ryker said, almost laughing now as Wade began to chuckle.

"You'd love to hear what Beatrice thinks of Bitsy. Her mom couldn't make it to the committee meeting last night. When Louisa suggested Bitsy for Atherton, Beatrice asked the group who else is amazed Bitsy doesn't sweat in church."

Ryker was full out laughing now. "And Louisa chided her mother-in-law for insinuating Bitsy is a whore."

Wade was clutching his stomach trying to stop laughing as Ellery's mouth dropped open. "And then Beatrice told her at least whores made money, but Bitsy gives the milk away for free."

Wade's phone pinged, and he looked down at it. His smile fell, his body went rigid, and in a split second he transformed. It wasn't only Ryker who had dark and brooding down pat. "There's an SOS call. I have to go."

And before she could ask, Wade was out the door.

"I better get to work too. But, Tibbie is worried about you. I couldn't pull her aside with everyone there. I thought you might want to reach out to her secretly. She's a sweet woman. Her husband was one of my first investors."

"Really?" Ellery asked as Ryker stood up.

"He took a chance on a kid with a fancy education and a knack for picking fights. I doubled his investment in six months and bought him out in a year. But it's because of his guidance I was able to do so. They're good people, unlike the Hawthornes. I don't know the Coldwells very much. They're old money and don't like to mingle with us new money types, but Beatrice seemed nice." Ryker squeezed her shoulder as if he were a big brother. "I'll see what Blair thinks and let you know." He winked as he headed for the front door.

"Thanks for the sacrifice," she called out sarcasm.

"It's a long, hard job, but someone has to do it," Ryker teased back.

The door closed as Ellery laughed. It felt as if she had a family again, and it felt good. Now, if everything stayed calm until Gavin got off work, they could think of a plan. Until then she would work on her own ideas of how to clear her name.

20

Ellery didn't get much time to herself. The doorbell rang fifteen minutes later. She thought twice about answering it then dropped to her hands and knees and crawled into the living room, using the furniture to hide her from anyone looking in the window. When she was close enough to peek out, she poked her head up and felt like an idiot.

She rushed to open the door for Reverend Winston, Ruby, and Winnie. Each smiled and handed her food as they came inside, talking excitedly of the gossip. Apparently Lydia's third child, Levi, had to be rescued from the top of a tree by Deputy King this morning. Then there was talk of another basketball coach coming to visit Quad Clemmons. And then Gator almost decked Professor Adkins for correcting him when he said, "ain't."

Winnie shook her white head as she sat down in the living room. "Bless his heart, he has a real stick up his ass."

Ruby nodded her agreement. "It's all that northern schooling. Educated the southern right out of him."

"What did Gator do?" Ellery asked, completely taken in with the gossip.

"Reminded Stephen of what happened the last time he was traipsing about in high cotton," Reverend Winston said with a shake of his head.

"What happened?"

"Bubba the alligator somehow got into Stephen's house," Ruby said, trying not to laugh.

"And Gator refused to get him out until the end of the day," Winnie said with nod of her head. "Serves him right for being too big for his britches."

"But we wanted to come check on you. Is there anything we can do to help?" Reverend Winston asked as everyone slowly stopped chuckling over Gator's beef with Stephen.

"I don't know," Ellery admitted after a pause. "I remembered more this morning, and I feel angry. I want revenge."

"An eye for an eye," Winston said knowingly. "It's been a common feeling for thousands of years."

"Exactly," Ellery said, relieved someone understood. "The trouble is, I'm not quite sure how to get it."

"Why don't you tell us what you know, hun, and we'll put our thinking caps on," Ruby told her as she picked up a brownie and handed it to her. "And you better eat something. You're skin and bones."

Not one to ever turn down a brownie, regardless of the fact that she was not skin and bones, Ellery took the brownie and told them about what she remembered and about her talk with Ryan Parker and the sheriff.

"There are some forces of evil at work, young lady," the reverend said solemnly. "But we weren't founded by pirates for nothing. If anyone can help you out of this, it's Shadows Landing."

"There's someone coming," Miss Winnie whispered.

"Winnie, you're deaf as a doorpost. There isn't anyone coming," Ruby said with a roll of her eyes.

"Ruby Jean, don't tell me what I can or cannot be hearing. I'm telling you, there's someone coming."

"Ladies," the reverend said as if he'd done this a thousand times. He got up and headed for the window. "Let's not argue. I don't hear anything, and I'm sure everything is . . . Well, I be doggone, there's some sort of law enforcement here. An unmarked car followed by the sheriff."

"Told ya," Miss Winnie said on a huff.

Ellery dove from the couch and plastered herself on the floor. "They can't find me here. I have to hide."

"You don't worry your pretty little head about a thing. Miss Ruby's got this."

Ellery crawled to the coat closet in the hallway and wedged herself inside, leaving the door cracked just far enough that if she closed one eye she could see out of it. The doorbell rang, and a minute later she saw Miss Ruby saunter over to the door and open it. "You want something?"

"I'm here to see Ellery St. John," a male voice said. She couldn't see who it was, but it wasn't anyone she'd heard before.

"There ain't no one here by that name. Now you better get to scootin'. I have things to do. Get on with you."

Ellery saw Miss Ruby try to sweep him away with her hands as the sound of another car door closing reached her.

"It's okay, Miss Ruby," Granger called out. "He's a friend of mine sent here via Keeneston."

"I don't know what any of that means," Miss Ruby said, putting her hands on her ample hips. Ellery shoved the closet door open because by Miss Ruby's rigid stance, she looked ready to charge out the door, sending law enforcement flying. The last thing Ellery wanted was Miss Ruby to end up in jail for assaulting, who Ellery thought may be, one of the good guys.

"Let him in," Ellery hissed from where she was hiding out of sight of the open door.

"I need to see some identification," Miss Ruby said with all sass and steel to her voice.

"FBI, ma'am. Peter Castle. I'm on Miss St. John's side."

"Miss Ruby, Agent Castle is here investigating the corruption of the higher-ups running the missing persons case as he believes she's being set up," Granger said patiently.

Miss Ruby looked over her shoulder, and Ellery motioned for her to open the door. Miss Ruby didn't like it, but she stepped back and let them in. A tall man strode in, wearing a wrinkled cheap black suit and somehow making it look good. His warm dark brown hair was the same color as his eyes. She expected him to look irritated, but instead she saw amusement. That was, until his eyes locked on her. The amusement fell away. While he kept his appearance easy-going, she saw that he swept her from head to toe and took in the entire room. He knew the location of every person and object. Then he relaxed again and strode the rest of the way into the room after deeming it safe.

"Miss St. John," he said to her, extending his hand, "Peter Castle."

After emerging from the closet, Ellery cautiously took his hand and shook it.

"Hi there, young man. You aren't from around here," Miss Winnie said more as a statement than a question with a flirty grin on her wrinkled face. Oh gosh, Ellery might die of embarrassment if she saw Miss Winnie climb onto Agent Castle like some of the women did to Wade. Well, maybe she'd cheer them on too. After all, when she was that age, she sure hoped she was still admiring hot men.

"I'm not, but I've quickly learned there is nothing sweeter than a southern belle." Miss Winnie preened under his words. "But right now, I need to have a word with Miss St. John."

"Of course, young man," Miss Winnie practically cooed.

Granger looked at his phone. "I have to call King. I'll be right back."

Ellery wrapped her arms around herself as she gave a weak smile to Agent Castle. "Why don't we talk in the kitchen?"

"Would you like me to get Gavin?" the reverend asked.

"Yes, thank you," Ellery said over her shoulder.

"I won't take too much of your time, Miss St. John, but I needed to see that you were safe and ask who you know with enough power to have you framed."

Ellery took a deep breath as Agent Castle indicated she should take a seat. "As you can see, I'm being well looked after." That got a smile out of Castle. "As for who is behind this, I'm not quite sure. Certainly Atherton Hawthorne, my ex-boyfriend, has enough power. Well, his family does. He doesn't. But from what I've learned, he's trying to get back together with me since his father approves of me. So, after that is Tibbie and Elijah Cummings, but they're like grandparents to me. They wouldn't have me framed for anything."

"Sheriff Fox filled me in on everything you remembered. Can you think of how your car ended up at Mark Vosslinger's house?" Castle asked as he casually crossed an ankle onto his knee. His shoes were scuffed but clean. However, there was no mistaking them as work shoes instead of the shiny leather loafers people wore into the gallery. Castle was a man of action, and that comforted Ellery.

"That's the thing. I don't think I was at Mark's house. One, I've never been there and he's never wanted me there. Two, I was heading to the gallery to roll down the shutters, not to Mark's house. And three, in the flashbacks I'm running on wet cobblestones. I want to go back to Charleston, and if I can find those cobblestones, which could be either at my condo or more likely at the gallery, hopefully I can remember what happened."

"What's going on?" Gavin asked as he rushed into kitchen.

Castle looked up at Gavin dressed in scrubs and wearing a stethoscope around his neck and stood up. "Agent Peter Castle. You must be Doctor Faulkner."

Gavin shook his hand and nodded. "Ryan said you were a friend."

Castle smiled as they dropped hands. "Yes, we are. I'm glad you called him. I think there's something going on for sure. I don't like being told not to investigate, and I was told under no circumstances was I to bother the hard-working police with this case. I went above my boss and got permission to shake the tree and see what falls out. Miss St. John was just telling me about the cobblestones. I think it's time for a little game of cat and mouse if Miss St. John is up for it."

"What do you mean?" Ellery asked. She wanted to do something, anything, to find out what happened to her. So if he had an idea, she was ready to run with it.

"I want you to go back to Charleston tonight. There's a chance of rain. When it's dark out I want you to drive from your condo to the gallery and see if you can find those cobblestones."

Ellery took a deep breath. It was action, and she wanted action. However, there was risk. "What if I get picked up?"

"I want you to be seen. I want to make sure you hit a city camera and look right into it. But then I want you to disappear. And that's where I come in." Castle smirked and Ellery couldn't help but smile. She wanted to rub her hands together because she was starting to see what Castle wanted.

"For what purpose?" Gavin asked.

"I want to see who comes running," Castle told them. "I'll be close by, but out of sight. If you get into trouble, I'll swoop in and take you into FBI custody. I can tell you where the cameras are and how to avoid the others."

"Where should we start?" Ellery asked.

"At home. I am going to set up hidden cameras in your condo so we can see who comes running if you are seen entering the building. And if they don't come running, I want you to visit Mrs. Cummings. After filling her in, have her call the police and say she thinks she saw you leaving the building. Then we'll watch and listen to whoever shows up. Is there a way for you to get to Charleston undetected?"

"We can take a drive," Gavin suggested. He looked to Ellery, and she nodded.

"Good. Then we'll meet and I'll pick you up and drive you. That will reduce your risk of being stopped accidently," Castle said with a nod. "Tonight then." He stood up. "Here's where we can meet."

He handed a card to Gavin as Granger walked in. Ellery didn't need to know what the conversation was about. It was written all over his face. Something bad had happened.

21

"What is it?" Gavin asked his friend. His lips pulled into a frown and his jaw was tight.

"King just called. Someone is asking around town about the new girl."

"Is it that officer again?" Ellery asked as Miss Winnie, Miss Ruby, and Reverend Winston came into the kitchen to listen.

"No. Dressed like a tourist. Private gun is King's best bet since he's well-built, but King can't find him now. The girls from Bless Your Scarf called King after the man left asking about you. King has scoured the town and can't find him. I think you two need to leave. Now." Granger tightened his jaw again, and Gavin was already in motion.

"I'll start the car and pull up the roof so we can hide you better. You get all your clothes," Gavin told Ellery. "And grab some of mine too. I don't care what, grab what you can."

"I can cool the car down and get the roof up," Reverend Winston said, holding out his hand. "You finish with your patients."

Gavin had completely forgotten about his patients. He

cursed repeatedly under his breath as Ellery tore up the stairs. He handed his keys to Reverend Winston. Miss Ruby and Miss Winnie opened cabinets and pulled out food in case they needed to go on the run.

"I'll move my car. I don't want them to see an FBI vehicle here." Castle stood and headed for the door.

"We'll be out of here in minutes, Agent Castle. Let's meet as planned tonight."

"Be safe. Call me if you need anything. I have my private cell on the back of this card. Use it." And then he was out the door and seconds later out of sight.

Gavin hurried into the patient room and finished with the little girl he was examining when he'd been called out. "Ear infection," he said, handing the prescription for antibiotics to her mother. He ushered them out of the office and called Sadie back.

"There's someone asking about Ellery. Someone dangerous. We have to go."

"You mean Emma, your friend from Kentucky, right?" Sadie winked and Gavin gave her a weak smile. Sadie would cover for them. "And her momma got sick so you're driving her back to Keeneston right now."

Gavin grabbed Sadie's arms and gave her a quick peck on her cheek. "You're the best," he said as he grabbed his newly packed medial bag.

"Remember that when it's bonus time," Sadie called out as Gavin ran from his office. He took the stairs two at a time while Granger and Reverend Winston talked in the living room and Miss Ruby and Miss Winnie bickered in the kitchen.

Ellery was in his room, pulling out his boxer briefs. "What do you need me to do?"

"I don't know where your bag is so I've been tossing things onto the bed."

"Got it," Gavin said, heading to his closet and reaching up onto the top shelf to grab a duffle bag. "Are you packed?"

"Yes, I never really unpacked," Ellery said with a sigh as she turned to help him stuff a wide assortment of clothes into the duffle bag.

"I'm so sorry about this. I was really hoping we could stay here. Ryker will let us stay at his home in Shadows Landing. It has a lot of security that may prevent people from entering the property. Even the dock has a gate on it," Gavin called out as he walked to his bathroom and scooped up all his toiletries.

"Right now I'm just mad. I want this over. I want to clear my name. I want to remember. I want the person who did this to pay," Ellery called out as he walked back into the bedroom.

Gavin stuffed the last of his things in the duffle bag and threw the strap over his shoulder. "We'll find them. Come on, let's go." He saw the garbage bags Ellery had sitting by the door and grabbed them. "We'll do this together." Ellery turned to say something and Gavin wouldn't be able to stand it if she were filled with doubt, so he kissed her before she could talk.

It wasn't a long kiss, but it was full of emotion. In it he told her he cared for her, he'd protect her, and he wanted to be with her. And then it was time to go. He'd kiss her again later tonight as he held her in his arms.

"Ready," he said, motioning with his head for her to lead the way.

"Let me help you," Granger said, meeting Gavin at the bottom of the stairs and taking the two garbage bags. "Hang on a moment. I have King doing a drive around, and the reverend went out for a stroll. Your car should be nice and cool for you, so let me make sure you're clear to leave without someone following you."

Granger took the bags and headed to the window as Miss Ruby and Miss Winnie bustled in from the kitchen carrying a cooler and a basket filled with food. "We can't have you going hungry on us," Miss Ruby said with a worried smile.

"Thank you," Ellery said to them and smiled a second before the whole house rocked on its foundation.

THE HOUSE SHOOK and Gavin dove to wrap his arms around the three women standing near him. Books and paintings fell from the shelves as things crashed all around them. Granger was already running out the front door with his gun drawn as the loud explosion caused everyone to cover their ears.

As soon as the shaking stopped, Gavin pushed the women under the kitchen table and ran to check on Sadie. He didn't know what had exploded, but he could smell smoke and the fire alarms were sounding.

He raced into his office, and then into the patient exam room before clearing it and heading to surgery. There he found the back wall that connected to his garage blown open. "Sadie!" Gavin looked around the rubble but didn't see his nurse. He shoved through the door leading to the waiting room and practically ran her over.

"Gavin! What happened?" she screamed, her hearing as impaired as his.

"There's been an explosion in my garage. Get everyone out. And make sure the oxygen is transported someplace safe as well."

Without question, Sadie took off to follow his orders as he grabbed a fire extinguisher and began fighting the flames licking the wall. As the ringing in his ears receded, he heard shouting and felt water spraying him through the hole in the wall. After emptying the fire extinguisher, Gavin looked through to see Miss Winnie, Miss Ruby and half his street pulling together garden hoses and spraying down his blackened garage. His sports car still had flames leaping from it as his friends and neighbors didn't wait for the fire department to try to save his house.

Gavin rushed into the house to find Ellery spitting mad. "They won't let me out to help!"

"It could be a trick to get you outside. Just stay put, okay?"

"What is it? What happened?" Ellery asked, grabbing his arm.

"They blew up my car. It was a good thing I wanted to cool it down before we got in it."

He could tell Ellery was fighting between anger and tears. "This is all my fault. I'm so sorry."

"It means we're on the right trail. Let's get to Charleston as soon as we can. We can take the boat."

Ellery nodded. "I'll take everything to the boat." She would be able to get on the water if she had Gavin by her side.

"No, wait for me. I need to check on everyone and let them know we're heading out."

"Hurry. I feel as if my time is counting down."

"I will." Gavin kissed her forehead quickly before running from the house. Reverend Winston was ordering people around as hoses were dragged from nearby houses. Smoke was pouring through the open hole in his roof, and a basketball on fire rolled from the garage.

His stomach plummeted. They'd almost been killed. Now he understood the anger Ellery was feeling. He wanted to tear apart the person responsible for this, limb by limb.

"Fire department will be here shortly." Granger tossed the empty fire extinguisher from his car onto the ground.

"Gavin!"

Gavin looked up to see Harper sprinting toward them. His little sister threw herself into his arms and cried, "I thought you were dead when I saw the smoke coming up from your house. What happened?"

"Shh, it's okay. They tried to kill Ellery again by blowing up the car. Luckily we were still inside and no one was hurt."

Harper stepped from his arms and punched Granger in the shoulder. "And what are you doing to protect them?"

"Easy, Harp," Granger warned her. "I know you're upset, but I'm doing everything I can."

"And so am I. I'm taking the boat to Charleston to meet with the FBI," Gavin said as Granger nodded his head in agreement with his plan.

"Charleston? Why would you do that? You need to go to Keeneston and beg our family for help." Harper was more worked up than he'd ever seen her. She handled bar fights with ease, but this had shaken her to her core.

"They're already helping. Ryan will be leaving soon, and we're working with Agent Castle in Charleston, who is Ryan's friend."

"You better not get killed or I'll haunt your grave for the rest of my life. And you know I can do that. Just ask Skeeter," Harper warned.

Gavin wanted to roll his eyes. Skeeter was of an undeterminable age and believed there were pirate ghosts around town. Ghosts had long been a fixture in southern lore, and everyone seemed to have a family member haunting them. You didn't hide your ghosts for fear of people thinking you were crazy. You set them out on the front porch and charged a fee to tell tourists about them. The Bells had Great-Great-Great-Grandma Ethel who they swore went around at night straightening up. Skeeter didn't claim to see a ghost though. He told anyone who would listen that he felt and heard all the pirates who looked out over the town.

"I promise, I won't get killed." Gavin looked down the road and saw a police car driving toward them. King and Fox were already here, which meant it was someone from out of town. Someone who had been close enough by to beat the fire department. "I have to go. You haven't seen me."

Gavin sprinted into the house, grabbed Ellery by the arm, and scooped their bags in the other. "What's going on?"

"Police are here," he said shortly, shoving his medical bag into Ellery's hand.

"I know that. I saw Granger come in—"

"Not them. Someone else. I didn't stick around to see who, but I'm guessing they're from Charleston," Gavin said as he grabbed the boat keys and quietly opened the back door. "Come on," he whispered.

He refused to let go of Ellery's hand as they ran down the hill in his backyard and out onto the deck. He glanced over his shoulder but didn't see anyone coming around back. The sound of oncoming fire engines helped conceal their escape as he tossed the bags into the boat.

Ellery didn't say a word as she went to work loading the boat as he untied it from the dock. "Life vests are under the bench," he whispered, knowing being on a boat might upset Ellery, but she seemed more intent on getting away than worrying about the water.

Gavin shoved the boat from the dock and leapt on. In seconds he had it started and Ellery in a life vest, hiding on the floor so she wouldn't be visible from the street as they started down the river. Gavin held his breath and steered toward the main branch of the Cooper River, which led straight to the Charleston Harbor and then out to the ocean.

Once Shadows Landing was far behind them, he breathed a sigh of relief. They were safe for now. "It's okay to get up," Gavin said, turning his head to look at Ellery huddled against the half wall of the center console of his fishing boat.

She was pale, but she stood on shaky legs and took a seat in the leather armchair next to his captain's chair. "Do you think it was Officer Hurst? Do you think he set the bomb?"

"I sure hope not. If it was, there's someone more powerful than we thought behind this. Someone powerful enough to drive an officer to kill."

Ellery was quiet for a moment as he steered them onto the Cooper River and headed for the ocean. "Is Castle going to put cameras in my condo now or tonight?"

Gavin handed her his phone and Castle's card. "Text him and let him know what happened."

Ellery was quiet as she texted. Gavin focused on the water around them. He tried to keep far away from other boats and kept his eyes open for any boats out on patrol. They could go to the meeting place Castle had told them about, but he thought it might be better to stay away from Charleston until nightfall. There was a popular place to fish where the harbor and the ocean met. He'd take them there, and they could spend the rest of the day fishing. They'd blend right in with the locals. Then when night fell, they could meet Castle and start to ferret out the people behind this.

"Castle said he'll go now and set it up. We'll meet him at eight tonight. He texted us the address," Ellery called out over the wind. "What will we do until then?"

"How do you feel about fishing?" Gavin asked with a grin.

22

Ellery handled the texts coming in from all Gavin's friends and family. She felt bad invading his privacy, but Gavin asked her to so he could focus on getting them to the ocean as quickly as possible. She relayed that Officer Hurst did in fact show up, and Ridge said he'd start rebuilding the garage as soon as he was allowed to. Ellery watched the shoreline fly by.

It seemed a whole lifetime ago she was completely unaware of the people from Shadows Landing. Now she felt as much a part of them as she did anywhere except when surrounded by art. But even then, it was as if Tinsley was her long-lost sister. Tinsley had immediately thought of Ellery out on the water again and told her she'd always be there for her. And there was one way she knew how to thank her for all she'd done. Once she was cleared, she was going to make Tinsley the hottest up-and-coming artist around. She was certainly talented enough to deserve it.

Ellery had also texted Wade who told them he'd keep his ear on the radio to make sure their boat wasn't called in. If so, he'd try to be the first to respond so he could get them out of the area. No one would stop and board a Coast Guard vessel. Ellery took a deep breath of the salty air. They were almost to Charleston, and she knew Wade would be looking out for them. He was a good guy. Funny, smart, sexy, loyal, protective, and kind. There wasn't a better combination out there. Well, except for Gavin. She saw glimpses of Wade's more serious side but wondered if anything ever truly bothered him.

Then Ridge said he would take care of the house without even being asked. And Harper texted every quarter hour to make sure they were both safe. And then Trent offered to let them stay at his place out in the country. And Ryker sent a simple text with the code to his Charleston house and the location of three guns in the house. He may be the opposite of Wade's laid back, happy-go-lucky attitude, but underneath his seriousness was fierce love and loyalty to his family and friends.

Ellery saw The Dirty Don Bridge, or the I-526 Don N. Holt Bridge to the tourists, spanning the Cooper River and instinctively dropped to the floor of the boat, tucking herself into the corner to hide as best she could.

"What is it?" Gavin asked with worry.

"We're getting close, and I don't want someone to look out their car window and see me. I know it's stupid, but I feel safer hidden."

"It's not stupid. There's a raincoat stuffed in there if you want to cover yourself more," Gavin said, pointing to a storage area.

Ellery opened it, pulled out the jacket, and put it on. She pulled the hood up and over her head and peeked out. She did feel safer this way. She took a deep breath to calm herself as they approached Charleston. From under the hood of the raincoat, she watched Gavin effortlessly guide the boat through the increased marine traffic and around Drum Island. She studied his muscled arms and the strong lines of his face as he drove. Somehow in the midst of the worst thing that had ever happened to her, she'd found the best thing that had ever happened to her.

Ellery's friends had long debated love, lust, and instant attraction. Ellery had never believed in love at first sight. And this wasn't a case of it either, but it was love very quickly. As she watched Gavin, she knew without a doubt she wanted him in her life forever.

Ellery rested her head against the wall as the busy loading docks came into view. Ryker was at one of them. She smiled thinking of him and the rest of the Faulkners who had become family to her in only a matter of days. The question was—was Gavin just being nice to her because of the situation, or did he feel something for her? Ellery watched his hands steer—hands that had been all over her body the night before.

They hadn't talked of their feelings, but Gavin didn't strike her as someone to sleep with a woman without feelings involved. She hoped they were enough to survive whatever was ahead of them. When all the danger was gone, would he still want her?

"We'll be through Charleston soon," Gavin said as he had to slow the boat in the bay. He glanced at her, and she tried to clear her face from the worry that Gavin might not be as interested in her as she was in him, but it wasn't fast enough. "What's the matter?" he asked, his voice and face filled with concern.

"Just thinking," Ellery said as she tried to smile.

"About what?" Gavin asked. "Please tell me it's about last night and your desire for another night together." Gavin winked at her, and some of the worry fell from her mind.

"I loved last night. I'm worried about what the future holds."

"Future as in making sure we catch who is behind framing you, or future as in you and me?"

Ellery gulped and was happy the long arms of the raincoat hid her hands' nervous fidgeting. She paused, trying to decide how to answer when Gavin looked over at her with such love and concern she gasped.

"You don't need to be worried, Ellery. We have a team and a plan to catch whoever is behind this. And as for us, you don't know me well enough yet, but I want to change that. Because I'm not the kind of guy who does one-night stands. I could have handed you over to Granger to take care of if I didn't care so much about you. But the thought of you depending on another man crushes me, even if it's on a professional level. I want to be that for you. I want to be the man you turn to. Now and in the future."

Ellery's breath was shallow as her heart raced to the same speed as the boat now flying out in the open water. She grabbed hold of the chair and pulled herself up. She held onto the chair as she stumbled over to Gavin. "If you're by my side, I have nothing to worry about," she called out over the wind. She leaned forward and kissed his cheek as one of his hands grabbed her waist and pulled her to his side. The hood of her raincoat fell back in the wind and Gavin turned his head to kiss her.

Ellery felt his fingers pressing into her hip as his short but passionate kiss left her heart pounding with excitement instead of fear. "For the day, it's only you and me out on a boat. Let's take advantage of this calm before the storm and pretend I'm just a guy taking his girlfriend on a date."

Ellery rested her head on his shoulder as he continued

to drive past Fort Sumter and out of the harbor. The title girlfriend had never sounded so good before.

GAVIN PULLED the boat into line with the other fishermen. Some had tourists with them as they fished, others were hanging out with buddies, and then some were serious about their fishing. He could tell which ones they were since they were glaring at anyone who got close to their spot.

Gavin pulled in near the tourists, but far enough away their faces wouldn't be clearly seen. "Why don't you set out the picnic while I get the rods out?"

Ellery moved to do as he asked while he got the tackle ready. He didn't bait them as he tossed them into the ocean and strapped them to the back of the boat. Fishing was not on his radar today. He had a whole day out on the open water with the woman he was falling in love with. He'd take every peaceful minute he got while trying to forget Ellery would be putting herself out there for someone to try to catch later that night.

"Here you go," Ellery said as he set the last rod in the holder and turned around. She'd laid out the spread on the floor where they could lean up against the benches. The cover from the console cast their blanket in shade so they could enjoy the nice day without melting in the hot southern sun.

They ate as they talked about themselves, their friends, growing up, and shared funny stories. As they finished, Gavin moved so Ellery was sitting between his legs and leaning against his chest. He wrapped his arms around her waist as they continued to talk. Eventually they fell into a comfortable silence and looked out over the water as the sun began to set. As the hours passed, they moved into the soft warm glow of the setting sun and were now overlooking the water with all the retreating tourists behind them.

Feeling Ellery's warm body under his hands was sweet torture. Gavin tightened his arms around her, and she snuggled into him. He was sure she could feel his hard outline pressing against her backside, but instead of pulling away, she wiggled against him.

Kissing her neck seemed the most natural thing to him. He pressed his lips against the base where her neck met her shoulder and worked his way to her ear. Ellery moaned softly and tilted her head, giving him better access as he kissed her gently. His whole body seemed to pound in time with her pulse beneath his lips. Gavin trailed his fingers up and down her arms, giving her shivers of what could lay ahead.

Ellery wiggled again as she tried to get closer to him. With no words spoken, she began to rub his thighs tantalizingly and he slipped his hands beneath her shirt. Her stomach was warm and smooth against his palms as he ran them along her stomach. He moved his hands slowly upward until he brushed against the bottom of her breasts. Ellery arched back, pushing her breasts against his hands in a silent order he happily followed.

He moved his thumbs in slow lazy circles over her bra. He heard and felt her breath hitch when they ran over her hardened nipples. Gavin was exhilarated but kept his pace slow as his thumbs brushed over her nipples again. Ellery let her head fall back against his shoulder, and Gavin felt her breath quicken with excitement.

He pressed kisses along her jaw as he cupped her breasts, pushing them up and then pulling down her bra cups to allow them to fill his hands. Ellery gasped his name and nothing had ever sounded so sensual to him before. Her hips rocked, her heart pounded, and Gavin did everything he could to keep himself in check. This was about her, not him, and he wanted to wring every little gasp and moan from her.

His body vibrated, and not in a good way. He wanted to ignore it, but it vibrated again. He stopped his hands from moving and smiled when Ellery groaned in displeasure as he reached for his phone.

"Yeah," Gavin said sharply as he let his hand run back up under her shirt.

"It's Castle. I have everything in place. Meet me at our location in thirty minutes then we'll head to her house. When we get there, you and I will go in a couple minutes after her. Make sure you're not identifiable. We are to stay out of the way as much as possible. We want them to think she's alone if they're watching the place."

A different type of excitement shot through Gavin. It was time to put their plan in action, and he hoped it worked. "See you then." Gavin hung up and pulled his hand from Ellery's shirt.

"Is it time?" she asked, suddenly serious.

"Yes. Let's get them."

23

Ellery stood outside of her condo building and stared at it as if she'd never seen it before. How had it been just days since she'd last been there, when it felt so foreign now? It hadn't taken long to know Shadows Landing was where she wanted to be. Right then she couldn't wait to get back. But first things first, she had to clear her name.

Ellery took a deep breath, crossed the street, and walked into the lobby. She used her keys that Agent Castle had grabbed from evidence to grab her mail and stuffed it into a fishing rod promotional bag Gavin had in storage on his boat. The lobby appeared how it always had as she slowly looked around. She didn't see any new cameras but knew the lobby had one that was monitored by a private security company. She gave it a wink knowing police would be looking at it before taking the stairs to her condo.

Her hands shook as she stood there listening at her door. Was someone moving inside? Was there a shadow under the door? She put in her key and paused. She heard the elevator ding and turned to look as Castle and Gavin stepped off. They both had hats pulled low with raincoats around them.

She looked out the window at the end of the hall and noticed rain had begun to fall.

Castle put his finger to his lips and motioned for Gavin to open the door. He pulled his gun, and the reality of her situation slammed into her like a freight train. This wasn't a nightmare. This was real life and someone, not only her, could be killed.

Gavin opened the door and jumped back as Castle stepped inside. Less than a minute later he was back. "I'd checked everything on the cameras I'd installed and it was clear, but I wanted to make sure. Come grab whatever you want and leave your calling card."

Castle had printed off small index card sized pictures of Mark Vosslinger paintings along with pictures from the party. Ellery stepped into her home and felt as if she didn't belong. She'd loved her condo. It had been her sanctuary, but not any longer. Now it felt like a prison.

Gavin and Castle stepped into the living room and looked out the window as she moved to her bedroom. She grabbed her suitcase and everything she could without looking at it or folding it. She stuffed it all in her suitcase before grabbing two tote bags. She filled one with toiletries and the second one with her jewelry and personal photos.

"Ready?" Gavin asked.

"We've got company," Castle said calmly. "We need to go."

Fear spiked as Gavin grabbed the totes, and she wheeled the suitcase to the front door. She pulled out an index card and dropped it on the floor in the living room.

"We can't go down. Is there a back way out?" Castle asked.

Ellery shook her head. "You can take the fire escape. But go up. Tibbie will hide us."

"Are you sure?" Gavin asked, sounding way calmer than she was feeling. They heard the elevator being called to the lobby and Ellery nodded. "She will protect me. Penthouse now."

Ellery didn't wait for them but quietly opened the door of the stairwell and proceeded up the stairs. She was relieved when Castle grabbed the heavy suitcase three steps up as they sprinted upward. Ellery stopped at the door to the penthouse and took a deep breath. She heard the door open below her and voices calling out to search the stairwell as she quietly turned the knob and opened the door.

They tiptoed through it, and Ellery silently closed it before they walked rapidly down the hall to the front door. Ellery rang the bell and shifted from foot to foot waiting for Tibbie or Elijah to answer. She heard Miss Muffy bark as the group kept turning to keep an eye on the stairwell door.

"Come on," she whispered under her breath.

Finally she heard the shuffle of someone coming to the door. "Quiet, Muffy," Tibbie ordered as she opened the door. The second the door was unlocked, Castle was pushing his way through as Tibbie gasped in shock.

"It's me," Ellery said, grabbing Tibbie's hands as Castle shut and bolted the door.

"Ellery?" Tibbie gasped. "Oh my stars. What is going on?"

"We don't have time to tell you. I need your help and then I'll tell you everything," Ellery said as quietly as she could as she practically dragged Tibbie from the front door.

"Gracious, Ellery?"

"Mr. Cummings, I'm sorry to burst in. I didn't kill Mark. Someone tried to kill me and tossed me in the ocean. Somehow I ended up in Shadows Landing, and Dr. Faulkner here saved me. But the people who hurt me are watching the building and saw me come in. We have to hide."

Elijah's wrinkled face filled with determination. "Back of Tibbie's closet. You all can fit, and no one will find you back there. I'll take care of this." The doorbell rang and Miss Muffy began to bark. "Go!"

Elijah pulled himself up from his leather armchair and grabbed his gold-topped cane. Ellery didn't wait to see what he would do. She led Castle and Gavin through the large penthouse and into the master bedroom. Off the bathroom was a giant walk-in closet. There was a closet within the closet, hidden behind floor to ceiling mirrors. That's where they were going. Tibbie used it to store out-of-season clothing.

Ellery slid open the mirrored door and then the three were engulfed by Tibbie's perfume covered clothes. "Just keep pushing back," Ellery whispered as she pushed through the wall of suits, sweaters, and dresses, not that she could see them. They didn't dare turn on the lights and were completely blind as she made her way to the back of the closet. She heard the men moving behind her and stopped when she hit the back wall. Gavin ran into her and pressed her body against the wall. He stepped in front of her to protect her in case anyone found them. Ellery heard the snap and then the sound of Castle's gun sliding against his leather holster as he pulled it free. The sound of him flipping off the safety echoed in her ears but was lost among the rows of clothes.

She lifted her hands and found Gavin's back. She wrapped one hand into his shirt and tried to control her breathing. It felt as if she couldn't stop breathing hard and the whole penthouse would hear her, but the more she tried to control it, the worse her panic grew. The fear of being caught because of her heavy breathing seemed to escalate her panic until she wasn't sure she could breathe.

Then lips were on hers. A tongue pushed its way through her lips and into her mouth. Gavin had spun and wrapped her in his arms and was kissing her senseless. It could have been five seconds or five minutes. But then the door opened, and Gavin flung her backward as he spun around to place his body between hers and whoever opened the closet.

"You can come out now. They're gone."

Ellery almost burst into tears at the sound of Tibbie's voice. Castle pushed his way forward as the light came on and Ellery noticed that while he'd flipped the safety back on, he wasn't putting it away as he dragged her suitcase with the other hand.

As soon as he was out of the closet, Castle dropped the bag and took off with his gun in hand to clear the penthouse. Ellery followed Gavin from the closet and was immediately wrapped in a hug by Tibbie. "You poor dear. Elijah wouldn't let them come in. He said I was sleeping, and he didn't want me disturbed. They tried to get in, but he squashed a toe with his cane and told them to find their manners before coming back."

"Oh, Tibbie. I'm so sorry. I've put you in danger by coming here."

"Pish," Tibbie said with a wave of her hand. "You're as close as family to us, and we take care of our own."

Gavin followed quietly behind as Tibbie led them to the informal sitting room. It was filled with overstuffed leather furniture, oil paintings of previous hunting dogs, and Castle grinning at Elijah Cummings, one of the most influential businessmen in the history of Charleston. His reputation didn't retire when he did. It was still alive and well.

"Mr. Cummings, thank you so much," Ellery said as emotion made her throat close. She rushed over to him sitting in his favorite chair and hugged him.

"Now, now, dear child. Of course I'll help you. What's all this about?"

"Are these the men who came to the door, Mr. Cummings?" Castle asked, handing him his cell phone.

"Yes. They said they were police officers, but I'm a regular donor to the police force and know many of the men on it. This one, he's a schmoozer. He's always at the fundraisers we have. Not an officer, but an administrator. He works with the police chief. But that one," he said, pointing to a cold looking man in a suit Ellery recognized as the man who tried to kidnap her. "He's not a police officer."

"I'm sending this to Ryan to run through facial recognition in the Lexington office. I don't want to do it here and have anyone find out," Castle said as he showed her the picture. "Do you recognize them?"

Ellery wished she didn't, but in the end she said, "Yes. The big one is the one who tried to kidnap me."

"It appears they have a key to your condo. They went in and immediately saw the calling card we left. Then they did a quick search and discovered your clothes missing. Two people went downstairs and two came up. Do you recognize these two men?" Castle said, pausing the video again and showing it to Ellery.

"That one looks familiar, but I can't place him," she said, tapping the picture of the professional haircut of a man who looked more like a banker than a police officer.

Castle showed the picture to Elijah and Tibbie. "I know I've seen him," Elijah said with a sigh. "Maybe with the mayor? I'm sorry, this old trap has sprung a leak." He tapped his head with his finger.

"Nonsense, you've already been a huge help. I'll find out who they are soon enough. Now, we better get out of here."

"Son, that dog ain't gonna hunt." Elijah tapped his cane on the hardwood floor for emphasis that Castle's plan to leave wasn't going to fly. "I think it's time you all sat down and told us what's going on. We've been worried sick, young lady."

Ellery automatically sat. "Yes, sir. I'm sorry, sir."

Tibbie sat next to her on the couch as Gavin and Castle moved to the chairs across from them. Ellery began with what she remembered, up to talking to Tibbie before heading back into the rain. Then it picked up with Gavin leaping into the river during the storm to rescue her. Miss Tibbie had tears in her eyes, and Elijah nodded his head solemnly as a sign of respect for what Gavin did to save her.

"And so that young Coast Guard officer was there to get information from us? Well, I be doggone. And both those young men are your cousins?" Tibbie asked Gavin.

"Yes, ma'am. They want to try to find out who would have enough power to pull the police strings to control an investigation like this."

"That must mean you're pretty serious about our Ellery. No man would do all this if he wasn't," Elijah said as he steepled his fingers in front of his chest.

"Elijah," Tibbie tried to warn as Ellery felt herself blush.

Elijah ignored his wife and kept his eyes drilled to Gavin's. "We're the closest thing to family our girl has. I want to know his intentions or I'll get my hunting rifle."

Ellery didn't want to look at Gavin, but when she glanced up he was smiling at her. He gave her a wink and turned back to Elijah. "I respect that, sir. I care for Ellery very much, and I'll do everything in my power to keep her safe."

Elijah was quiet for a moment and then dropped his hands to the chair arms. "That's good enough—for now. So what do you need us to do to help?"

"You already did," Ellery said as she patted Tibbie's hand.

"You said you needed to find out who's behind this. Darlin'," Elijah said to his wife, "put on something pretty. We're going to the club."

Tibbie smiled and stood up. "Wonderful idea, dear. We'll find out all the gossip there. Elijah, don't be stingy with buying the drinks for your friends."

"Yes, darlin'," Elijah said as he stood up. "Lay out my suit. I'll show them out and be right back."

Tibbie kissed everyone's cheeks. "Don't you worry about a thing. We'll get to the bottom of this."

"If you do get some information, please don't hesitate to call me," Castle said, handing his card to Elijah.

Elijah put his hand on Ellery's shoulder as they walked to the door. "You know, these old houses have been around since Blackbeard held Charles Town hostage for medicine, right?"

"Ghost stories?" Gavin asked with a smile.

"No, what they left behind are not just stories. Shadows Landing isn't the only town with a pirate history," Elijah said, opening the small drawer of an antique table that stood by the front door. He pulled out a thick iron key ring with two keys on it. "Piracy has a long history in Charles Town and even Charleston. In fact, some of these old historic houses have tunnels under them for smuggling. Now, a couple have been closed off when the sewage system was updated, but some weren't because no one ever knew about them."

Ellery felt herself smile. "And you happen to know of one?"

"There's a reason this house has been in the family all these generations. When my family settled here and built this house they made their fortune selling smuggled goods stolen from Spanish ships before going legit. Go into the basement. It's the last room on the right. Use this key to open that door and then this one to get into the tunnels. Just make sure you lock them back up tight," Elijah told them as he handed the heavy keys to her.

"Where does the tunnel come out?" Castle asked.

Elijah grimaced. "You'll need to use some muscle to get the door open. It's been fifty years since they were last used. And when it opens, you'll need to act like you belong. It comes out on the Coast Guard base in the old stone building they use for storage. It's only a short distance away. Once upon a time, that room was storage for smuggled items before the Coast Guard existed. The door is hidden, so as far as I know, it hasn't been discovered. Also, it's only one way access. Once the door's closed, you can't get back into the tunnel."

"Are you sure we should do this?" Ellery asked.

"You know they're out there waiting to see if you exit the building. I think it's our best chance," Castle told her. She was afraid that was going to be the answer.

"It's a good thing I have a Coast Guard connection," Gavin said with a wink as he pulled out his cell phone. "Wade, hey. We need a favor. Are you on base?"

24

The tunnel was creepy. Gavin wasn't one to believe in ghost stories, but if a pirate ghost came out right now, he wouldn't be surprised. In fact, he was seriously considering calling Skeeter and telling him he'd found the holy grail of pirate ghosts. The air was stale, and it felt as if it were reaching out and touching them. It gave him the heebie-jeebies.

No one talked as they had to duck their heads and move along the stone and earth tunnel. There were some wood planks here and there, and even some torches on the walls, but they weren't about to light them. Instead they used the flashlights on their phones as Castle led the way through the tunnel, which seemed to be a pretty straight shot.

"Where's the door?" Ellery whispered as if the entire Coast Guard was waiting for them on the other side.

"I think it's here," Castle said, handing his phone to Ellery. "Gavin, help me with this."

Gavin put his phone in his pocket and found the keyhole. Castle put in the old key and twisted hard. Finally there was the sound of creaking metal sliding free. "Push," Castle ordered as he and Gavin put their whole weight to the door. At first it did nothing, but then slowly it began to swing outward.

"No freaking way," Gavin heard Wade say, his amusement clear in his voice as his fingers appeared around the edge. Wade pulled, Castle and Gavin pushed, and finally it opened enough for Ellery to slide through. Gavin was next and then Castle.

Gavin was breathing hard as he looked at the hidden door. It was made of old wood on the tunnel side and the outer side was lined with heavy stone that matched the interior of the storage area. "We better close it," Gavin said with a sigh.

A few old bulbs with no covers lit up the windowless room. Stacks of supplies filled the space no bigger than fifteen feet by fifteen feet. Gavin put his shoulder to the stone and pushed. Wade and Castle joined and slowly they closed the hidden door and with a loud click of the lock sliding back into place they stood back. When Gavin stepped back it was impossible to tell where the door was.

"Amazing. We had no idea that was even here," Wade said with wonder.

"And no one will know," Ellery reminded him.

"I have to see inside it," Wade begged until Ellery smiled.

"I'll ask permission from the owners. But now, how do you intend to get us out of here?"

Gavin wondered the same thing.

"My truck is right outside. Hop in the truck bed and I'll toss a tarp over you and away we go. No one is on this side of the base. We're close to the old docking station, but that was closed eighty years ago or so . . . oh, it was the smuggler's dock. That makes sense. The Coast Guard secured this property because of its location to the harbor. The location made it perfect for ships to unload without having to come all the way into the harbor. They could make a quick escape if the British came."

Gavin placed his hand on the small of Ellery's back. "Are you ready?"

"More than anything. Can we start at Mark's place? It's not too far away, and on our way back to Shadows Landing, we can stop at the gallery and any other place Agent Castle wants."

"That sounds like a good plan," Agent Castle told her, and Gavin felt her relax a little under his touch.

"I'll drive," Wade said before opening the door and pulling down his tailgate. His truck was backed up to the door and all they had to do was crawl in. Gavin leapt up first and offered his hand to Ellery. In seconds, they were under the tarp, listening to the rain pelt the plastic as Wade drove them from the base, past Ellery's house, and into the suburb where Mark lived.

"This wasn't exactly how I envisioned tonight," Castle said with a little chuckle that had them all laughing. "Pirates, secret tunnels, smugglers . . . I knew I'd like Charleston when I was assigned here."

"Then I'll hook you up with Skeeter to take you on a Shadows Landing Pirate Ghost Tour. He also has a pirate living in his house. He calls him Eddie," Gavin said from under the tarp. Ellery was lying on his arm as he held her close to him. She was quiet, and he was worried she was thinking of running away instead of running toward the darkness. Not that he'd blame her. He'd help her run if that was what she wanted.

Before he could ask her about it the truck slowed down. They all stopped breathing as they heard the door open and suddenly the tarp was pulled back. The rain fell on them as they all sat up and blinked into the night. Street lamps provided a soft glow but left room for many swaths of darkness.

"It's right across the street. We're going to cut through this yard to get to it. I didn't want us to be seen if they're monitoring the house. Apparently there's a shrine of sorts started. At least that's what was reported in the news," Wade said, motioning them across the backyard of someone's house. The four of them kept to the shadows and stopped at the side of the house, looking across the street at Mark's place.

"There's no cobblestones," Ellery whispered to herself, but they all heard it.

"So, this isn't the place?" Agent Castle asked.

Ellery looked around slowly but shook her head. "No. I don't think I've ever been here before. Nothing looks familiar."

"Your car was parked in the driveway," Agent Castle told her as he pointed to the driveway.

"No. I'm sure. I've never been here before." Gavin heard the insistence in her voice and believed her. Someone had moved her car in hopes of framing her.

"Then let's head to the gallery," Wade suggested.

"Wait," Ellery said, stopping them. She dug around her purse and pulled out a pen. In the night she wrote, *RIP to a great man and talented artist. Ellery,* on the back of one of the index cards Castle had given her. She looked around and darted across the street. Gavin watched as she looked around and found a clear plastic bag a mourner had left with a note inside. She stuffed her own note in the clear plastic so the rain wouldn't ruin it and set it front and center of the house. "Let's go," she called out as she ran back across the street to join them in the shadows of the house.

CASTLE WAS GRINNING as they walked back to the truck and this time got inside the cab. Ellery assumed that meant he liked the calling card she left. They had agreed to cat and mouse games and Ellery was ready to play.

It took twenty minutes but soon enough, they were pulling to a stop where Castle instructed Wade to drop him so he could get his car. "Come on," Castle said as they got out of the truck. "I'll drive you to the gallery."

"I'm coming too," Wade told them as he leaned out the driver's window. The rain was falling in sheets, and Ellery and all the men were soaked, but no one seemed to care. They were on a mission, at least that was what it felt like to her. She liked having them with her, as if they were her team.

"Okay, follow me," Castle ordered.

Gavin held the door and she slid into the car. The windows were fogged and it took a moment of them sitting there before they pulled from the curb. "That was a nice move with the note," Castle told her.

"Thanks. I thought I could leave them all around, but it started raining."

"Leave one on the front door of the gallery. Turn to the upper left of the door and smile. There's a security camera there," Castle explained. "We can't park out front, but we can come in from behind. The back camera's visibility is only around the back door, and I'll try to cover it so they can't see you."

"How do you know that?" Gavin asked.

"I used my badge and talked to the security company who installed it."

"Then did they see what happened the night I went missing?"

"No. The cameras weren't on."

"But I saw Hollis arm the security system," Ellery said with frustration. She knew she saw him do it, or were her memories false?

"I'm sorry, but according to the security company the cameras were all off."

Ellery was quiet as they drove the short distance to the gallery. It seemed as if it had been a lifetime ago she'd last been there, but then she stared at the back of the historic building from the lot behind it. Castle left the car on and turned off the lights as Wade pulled in next to him.

Ellery almost jumped when Wade knocked on the window. "I have raincoats for y'all," he said, holding up three raincoats, but Ellery's mind was already running into the darkness as she opened the door and got out. Her eyes never left the back door of the building. Wade must have pushed a raincoat in her hand, but she dropped it on the ground as if someone was pushing her toward something— toward something no one had let her see.

"Ellery!"

She heard Gavin call out her name, but it seemed as if he were a mile away as she stepped into the back parking lot. She looked down at the cobblestones and felt the pressure squeeze her chest to the point she thought she'd black out.

Her heels teetered on the uneven cobblestone, but she ignored the twisted ankles as she raced for her car. She had her hand on the door when she looked into the window and saw it was too late.

Ellery stumbled forward, her feet carrying her quickly to the back door. She rested her hand on the door as the rain washed away the fog and the memories flooded her mind.

Ellery tossed her purse in the passenger seat of her car and pulled away from her condo. In less than five minutes, she was back at the gallery. And not a moment too soon. The rain and wind were really picking up. Ellery pulled into the narrow alleyway at the side of the building leading into the back parking lot. The tires bumped along over the old cobblestones as she pulled to a stop next to Hollis's luxury SUV and Mark's older sedan. She wasn't expecting anyone to be at the gallery, but with the three of them lowering the shutters, they'd be done in no time. It appeared everyone had been on the same wavelength tonight about protecting the valuable art inside.

Ellery grabbed her white raincoat from the backseat and slipped it on as she got out of her car. She was going to grab her purse to dig around for the gallery key when she noticed the back door was already open. Leaving her purse and keys in the car, she dashed across the small cobblestone parking lot and into the dryness of the gallery.

The lights in the back weren't on and Ellery was reaching for them when something made her stop. The sound of harsh voices arguing made her. Ellery didn't know if she should make her presence known, but when she heard the sound of glass breaking, she rushed forward along the back hallway until she reached the curtain that separated the back from the exhibit hall.

"I made you, and you better not forget that," Hollis hissed.

Ellery slowly pulled back the curtain to see Mark with his hands on his hips and a broken whiskey glass shattered against the wall. Hollis stared Mark down with his arms crossed over his chest. He'd changed into a pair of perfectly creased blue jeans and a designer black T-shirt, but Mark was in the same suit he'd worn to the gallery opening.

"I made myself and you took advantage! You bought all my old work slowly, week after week, before you offered me the Mimi Hollis grant. A grant that I didn't realize gave you fifty-one percent ownership of any work I created for five years! That's *insane and downright illegal. You have no ownership rights to my work!" Mark yelled.*

Ellery blinked with surprise as Mark pushed Hollis, causing him to stumble against a smooth marble statue of a palmetto tree. Hollis's hand clasped the teetering statue to prevent it from falling to the floor as his face flushed red with anger. "I told you to get a damn lawyer to review the contract, but you couldn't wait to get your grubby hands on the ten thousand dollars I was giving you. It's no one's fault but your own."

"You tricked me!" Mark yelled as he shoved his pointer finger into Hollis's chest, causing him to grunt. "You are now selling those old paintings of mine for fifty to ninety thousand dollars. Paintings you bought off me for a hundred dollars. That money should be mine, yet you aren't even giving me a cut of it, since you claim they are privately owned. Not even the paltry forty-nine percent. And I'll make damn sure everyone in Charleston knows you're no friend of the arts. You're an extortionist of the arts, stealing from artists to line your own pockets. And after tonight everyone will listen to the hottest new American artist since Norman Rockwell. You and your little gallery are done, Hollis."

Hollis slowly smiled as he shook his head. "Mark, you should have taken what you were given and be happy I gave you anything to begin with. Artists like you are a dime a dozen. This gallery is a drain to my finances, but according to the trust I have to keep it running to have access to the Hollis fortune. You want to take that from me, and I won't let you. I'll just replace you and continue making money while you struggle as another starving artist."

"Take your trust from you? Hollis, you have millions in a separate trust fund that you could live off. I don't have that and you're stealing my livelihood!"

"Do you know what makes art valuable?" Hollis asked

calmly. He didn't wait for Mark to answer, but Ellery already knew. He'd told her this before. "It's what people will pay for it. I could draw a line on a piece of paper and call it art and if I sold it for three million dollars, then that's what it's worth. You are worth nothing. Whatever your art is bringing in is because of me. Because I'm telling people what it's worth, and I'm selling it at that price. Without me, you and your art are worthless."

"It's still my art, Hollis," Mark said, crossing his arms over his chest. "And I deserve that money. You deserve your twenty percent, per normal terms, but not fifty-one. It's theft!"

"You know what else makes art valuable?" Hollis asked, ignoring Mark. "Knowing there will never be any more paintings made. Van Gogh only sold one painting while he was alive. The rest were all sold after his death when he finally became famous. Why? Because there would never be new artwork produced. The art world loves a good story. It drives the cost of the paintings sky high, especially when you're at the stage of your career that you're at. A rising star with demons he can't shake. That's the narrative that will be told. The promising artist who succumbed to his personal demons. It's just too bad everyone saw you tossing back drink after drink tonight. They were asking me if you were all right. I covered for you, of course, but I could see it in their eyes. The gossip. The questions . . . if you were losing your mind like so many artists have done before you."

The sound of the wind picking up should clue them into the storm approaching outside. Ellery narrowed her eyes as she watched Mark shake his head. What was Hollis up to? Should she tell them she was here? But something kept her back. Something kept her quiet as she waited for Mark to storm out. He did like his dramatic exits.

"Hollis, I'm not going to die. I'm just pissed off, and I want out of my contract. Even I remember that clause in the contract that states if I die, you own one hundred percent of my artwork. It's not going to happen, and neither is your ownership of me anymore. I'm taking you to court and shutting you down. You'll have to live with ten million dollars instead of the hundred million you have access to if the gallery is open. Face it, Hollis. I'm taking you down."

Ellery almost opened the curtain so Mark could make his dramatic exit. Mark turned around toward her and Ellery opened the curtain, but before she could say anything Hollis lifted his arm and swung the palmetto statute.

"Mark!" Ellery screamed as the statue crashed into Mark's head. He dropped to the ground as blood poured from the gash on the back of his head and pooled on the antique wood floor.

"You killed him," Ellery gasped and then realized her mistake. She was still standing there talking to a murderer. Her heart began to pound so loudly she didn't hear what Hollis said to her. She saw his lips move and then he shook his head. Before her body and mind could react he was striding toward her.

Ellery stumbled out of her shock and screamed. Hollis raised his hand and swung the statue. Ellery leapt back, feeling the breeze from the statue cutting through the air where she'd been standing. Her body slammed into the wall behind her as the statue ripped into the curtain, tearing it down from the rod above them. As Hollis struggled to free the statue from the curtain, Ellery ran. She bounced her body off the walls in the hallway as if she were a pinball. Her legs, mind, and body were all going in different directions. Her shoulders slammed against the brick as she zigzagged her way to the back door. The wind was howling, and the rain was falling as she slammed into the back door. The door flew open, and Ellery stumbled outside into the dark rain.

Her heels teetered on the uneven cobblestone, but she ignored the twisted ankles as she raced for her car. She had her hand on the door when she looked into the window and saw it was too *late. The palmetto statue arced through the air and then there was nothing but blackness.*

ELLERY WAS SUCKING in gasping breaths of air as she opened her eyes again. She had to see inside. The time had come for her to know if Hollis had killed Mark and tried to kill her. Ellery fought the door, but it wouldn't budge. The sounds of her friends shouting were in the air, but she ignored their questions as she ran back to them.

"Give me your gun," Ellery ordered. She knew she was losing control, but she couldn't stop until she knew it was true.

"No," Castle said calmly. "What's going on?"

"I know who killed Mark, but I have to be sure. I have to get inside."

"Who killed Mark?" Gavin asked before Agent Castle could.

"Hollis," Ellery said as the tears began to fall. "Hollis chased me out here. Hollis hit me with a Julia Duran statue of a palmetto tree."

"What are you looking for inside?" Castle asked as he tossed her a loose cobblestone. "Break the camera." She caught the cobblestone and with her middle finger raised to the camera, bashed it with the rock. And then Castle reached up to grip her arms. She realized they were all covered in hooded raincoats while she was soaked to the skin. She should have been cold, but instead she felt numb. Numb in her body and her heart.

"Blood. He hit Mark in the head, and I saw the blood pool. It should be on the statue and on the floor. Mark also threw a glass and shattered it. I have to know if what I saw in my flashback was true. You have to understand," Ellery practically shouted. Desperation filled her. They had to understand.

"Security could be here any minute if they bothered to look at the camera being out," Castle warned, but Ellery was growing near frantic. They weren't going to let her inside. She could break out the front window, but then the police would be there in less than a minute. The station wasn't that far away. "So, we better hurry."

"What?" Ellery asked, her breath stopping in her chest as she though she misheard.

"You two stay here. Let us know if anyone is coming." Castle ordered.

Ellery shifted from foot to foot as Castle made quick work of the lock. The door opened, and the beeping of the alarm sounded. Ellery rushed past Castle and entered the code and the beeping stopped.

"Unbelievable. He didn't change the code," Castle muttered.

"Why would he have to? He thought we were all dead." Ellery's stomach rolled as Castle followed her down the hall. The curtain was fixed. "It's a new curtain." She gasped as her shaking hand reached out to pull it back. Still a black curtain, this one had an inlaid pattern on it. The old one didn't. And she could prove that from the pictures at the party. She pulled back the curtain, and she could see them standing there. It was as if she were back there again.

"Ellery," Castle snapped, bringing her back. "I don't see a palmetto statue."

Ellery looked around, and there was now a statue of a sea turtle on the pedestal the palmetto had been on. "It had to have been sold or put away." But now she was frantic again. Was she making this all up?

Ellery rushed to the spot Mark had died and ran her

hands over the old wood floors. "This was where Mark was killed."

It was too dark, and she couldn't tell if there was any blood. Castle turned on his flashlight but said nothing. The floor spoke for itself. There was no blood.

On hands and knees, Ellery crawled to the other side of the room. "What are you doing?"

"They might have cleaned up the blood, but they would have just swept up the broken glass," Ellery said as she put her nose to the ground. Both relief and doubt filled her. "Does this smell like whiskey?"

Castle crouched down next to her and flashed his light. She didn't need for him to answer because there it was, a tiny shard of glass.

"Look. I'm not crazy. It was Hollis," Ellery said, grabbing hold of Castle's strong arm as if to force him into believing her.

"You're right. Ryan Parker will be here tomorrow morning and we'll serve a warrant on the place. Hopefully our lab team can find some blood to sample. These old floors will probably have some evidence in the cracks. You did it, Ellery."

Ellery felt like crying, but there was still one more thing she needed to do. "Come on. The records are in Hollis's office. Let's see if I can find that statue."

25

Ellery paced Ryker's massive living room that overlooked the water as she waited for news. Gavin's cousin, Ryan Parker, had arrived at six in the morning. He was as nice in person as he'd been on the phone, but he'd left almost immediately after checking on them. He was going with Peter Castle to get a warrant for Hollis's properties.

It was going to be an uphill battle though. Hollis's family was just as connected, if not more so, than Atherton's. Hollis's uncle was the mayor. His mother was a society icon. That wasn't counting the rest of his aunts, uncles, and cousins. There was a Hollis or Coldwell in power at practically every level of Charleston society from police officers to judges to newspapers. And there were the ones who ran every organization under the sun. They held influence, sway, and power.

Gavin sat quietly, watching her pace. They all hoped the two FBI agents could get a warrant from a judge that wouldn't try to protect the Hollis-Coldwell family name. Gavin's phone indicated there was a text message and both fear and excitement filled Ellery.

"Is it them?"

Gavin breathed out in relief. "Ryan brought along some of his team from Lexington, and the Columbia, South Carolina office is partnering on this task force. They got the warrants and are about to execute them."

Ellery's hands shook as she nervously twisted her fingers and waited. The minutes stretched to hours and finally Gavin's phone rang. She practically fell from the couch, trying to get to it to see who it was before Gavin answered.

"Hi, Miss Tibbie," Gavin said with a smile on his face. "Yes, ma'am." Gavin held out the phone for her and Ellery took it.

"Hello?" Ellery asked, both wanting to hear what was said and not wanting to hear at the same time. She was living in a constant state of fear that Hollis would get away with this, and she'd have to flee the state, possibly the country.

"Well, the Historical Women of Charleston are in a tizzy. And Elijah said it's all the Yacht Club is talking about."

"What is?" Ellery asked, trying not to sound too impatient.

"That the FBI is swarming the gallery, Hollis's homes, and his boat."

In that instant Ellery was transported into the past.

"No," she tried to yell as the hands gripped her. Hollis pulled her up and pushed her against the hard wall, and then she was falling. Her breath was taken when she hit the water. Pain exploded in her head as her legs dropped like anchors into the ocean water. Her eyes closed as the pain in her head called her into the darkness once again.

"Just let the water take you," Hollis called to her.

Now Ellery knew how she'd gotten into the ocean. Hollis

had taken her out on the boat and shoved her into the ocean.

"Ellery!"

"Sorry," Ellery muttered as she tried to calm herself. Her palms were sweating as she recalled the nightmare.

"Hollis's mother, Sylvia Coldwell, was at the committee meeting with me when her brother, the judge, called, giving her a heads up. She called her younger sister, the lawyer, who immediately went to Hollis's so he couldn't be questioned. Sylvia made it very clear—you are a spurned lover who murdered Mark, and you're trying to get your revenge on her son for turning you down."

"I can't believe this. Why would anyone think I had a thing for Hollis?"

"Because Sylvia and Louisa Hawthorne are painting you as a gold-digging hussy, that's why."

"And people are believing it?" Ellery sat down with shock. She'd never been anything but nice to people. She only wanted to share her love of art, and now her reputation was in tatters over lies.

"Not all of them. It helps that Beatrice Hawthorn, Louisa's mother-in-law, and I are countering the rumors, but we can't hold them back forever. Elijah said the same discussion is going on at the Yacht Club. You have a surprising number of friends yourself, including Atherton's father, which is a big deal for you. Now we just have to hope they find some evidence to support your claim of innocence."

"Thank you, Tibbie." Ellery collapsed on the couch. She had only thought about getting Hollis arrested, she hadn't thought she'd have to try her own case in the court of public opinion. She needed the smoking gun. She hadn't been able to find it last night, but maybe . . . "Miss Tibbie," Ellery said before her old friend could hang up.

"Yes, dear?"

"I need one more favor."

"Anything," Miss Tibbie said.

"I need to find a statue of a palmetto tree Hollis probably sold at some point after the gallery exhibit. I can't imagine he'd keep it since it's the murder weapon. If it didn't sell in three months, it would go back to the artist. And I found a carbon copy check to the artist dated on the Monday after the signing, which leaves me to believe it had to have been sold."

"On it! I feel the need to redecorate. I'll ask the ladies at the Women's Auxiliary Committee meeting in two hours. I'm guessing Sylvia will be too busy to attend, so hopefully I'll get more gossip."

"Thank you, Miss Tibbie," Ellery said before hanging up with a slight smile. She felt a little hopeful now. She had more faith in Miss Tibbie finding the statue than she did the FBI. Ellery had searched Hollis's office the night before, and while she found the copy of the check, she didn't find a sales receipt telling who bought it, and that was very unusual. However, as long as there was money going in, the commission being held out, and the artist being paid, accounting wise that was all that mattered. The name technically didn't. However, it was enough to be a glaring incident simply because they usually kept full records for provenance.

"Do you think she can find the statue?" Gavin asked as she handed his phone back.

"Do you think iced tea should be sweet?"

Gavin gave a little chuckle and patted the couch next to him. "The late morning news will be on in a couple of hours. Let's wait and see if they have anything about Hollis."

THE MINUTES TICKED by so slowly Ellery could barely stand it. Miss Winnie and Miss Ruby stopped by with food and words of encouragement. Harper and Tinsley also stopped by to check on them, but all Ellery could do was stare at the clock. Even when Wade tried to make her laugh, Ellery was too scared and nervous to smile. Wade gave her a hug before he left and whispered that everything was going to work out for her.

After what seemed like days of pacing, it was time for the local news. Ellery took a seat and pressed against Gavin for support as he turned on the television. His heat and strength gave her strength even though her stomach was doing summersaults.

The news started and Ellery grabbed Gavin's hand. The anchor came on with a serious face. "We have breaking news in downtown Charleston this morning. Ellery St. John has been found alive, but a rogue FBI agent is refusing to disclose the murder suspect's whereabouts."

"Oh no." Ellery gasped as her stomach violently rolled. "The Coldwells have gotten to the media first. I should have known. The family owns so much of the town, how could I have forgotten about the media?"

Gavin flipped channels and an image of Peter Castle flashed onto the screen. "Going against direct orders, FBI Agent Peter Castle has brought in FBI from Kentucky and Columbia to search Charleston icon Hollis Coldwell's gallery, house, and boat for signs of foul play. We've asked for a comment, but head of the local FBI, Randy McCarthy, has said Agent Peter Castle has been put on immediate suspension for ignoring a direct order to let local police handle the investigation into Mark Vosslinger's alleged murder at the hands of Ellery St. John, who has been missing since Friday night. Her vehicle was found at the victim's home, and local police have named her as a person of interest."

"Oh no," Ellery said, her world falling apart more than she thought possible. "I'm going to jail for a murder I didn't commit."

"However," the reporter continued to say, "we've learned from a source involved in the investigation that higher-ups have ordered no other suspects be investigated, which is why the FBI from Kentucky and Columbia have been called in by Agent Castle. If true, and the case is being manipulated at a high level, there could be a huge criminal corruption case not counting a civil case brought by Miss St. John, if she's still alive."

"It's okay, Ellery. Breathe," Gavin said to her as he rubbed her back. "There are four local channels, and only one is beholden to the Hollis-Coldwell family. Your story will be told, and you'll be vindicated. Just let Castle and Ryan do their jobs."

On the screen came live footage of Castle and Ryan standing side by side inside the art gallery's door looking to where people were on their hands and knees. They were partially blocked from view by Castle and the rest of the agents standing around. Crime scene tape was up and barriers set up around the front of the gallery were holding people back. However, that didn't stop all the reporters from screaming out to them for a comment.

"We're going to Shelly Jacobson for an on-scene report. Shelly?" the anchor requested, sending the interview to the onsite reporter.

"Thanks," Shelly said seriously. "I am at the Mimi Hollis Art Gallery in downtown Charleston where one hour ago FBI agents descended with a warrant and crime scene technicians. We do not know what they are looking for, but a source close to the case says there might be evidence of foul play inside. Now, we are unable to confirm if gallery owner, Charleston socialite and heir to the Hollis-Coldwell fortune, Hollis Coldwell, is the target or if person of interest Ellery St. John is. What we do know is fifteen minutes ago more lab technicians descended on the art gallery along with Mary Coldwell-Helmshire, Charleston's top defense attorney, and Mr. Coldwell's aunt. It's presumed she's here representing the Coldwell family."

"She's big trouble," Ellery whispered to no one in particular. Gavin nodded. Everyone in the state knew Mary. She was ruthless. "Who's that?" Ellery asked, pointing as an unmarked car pulled up. Apparently Shelly saw it at the same time because she turned to look and put a finger to her earpiece as an older man in a suit got out and looked around.

"I'm being told," Shelly said, "that Charleston FBI agent in charge, Randy McCarthy, has just arrived. Agent McCarthy! Do you have a comment?" The agent strode past the barricade and looked none to happy to be stopped by Peter and Ryan.

This time it was Ryan who didn't look pleased. In fact, he looked downright scary as his jaw clenched, and his hazel eyes narrowed. McCarthy went to grab Castle's arm, and Ryan moved so fast Ellery gasped.

Ryan shoved McCarthy up against the glass window of the gallery for all to see and had McCarthy in handcuffs in just a matter of seconds. Shelly stood frozen in shock, as did everyone outside the gallery. McCarthy rain downed a hail of threats as two FBI agents came forward to drag him outside and into a parked car.

"What just happened?" Ellery asked as if Gavin would know. Shelly was sputtering as she tried to explain with barely contained excitement at being live for this scoop.

"We don't have any details, but you're seeing it here—FBI agents from out of town have arrested the local FBI agent in charge. They put him in cuffs as he threatened their jobs, and he's being driven off."

Gavin's phone rang and at the same time they saw Ryan, with his phone to his ear, walking away from Mary Coldwell-Helmshire and getting into a car.

"Ryan, what's going on?" Gavin asked as soon as he accepted the call on speakerphone.

"We found blood in the cracks of the hardwood floor. It was well cleaned, but we pried up the floorboards and found it. It's on the way to the lab with one of my agents accompanying it. We also recovered glass shards from where Ellery said Mark had smashed the glass. Hollis's attorney is here, threatening lawsuits left and right and McCarthy tried to shut us down. However, the warrant for Hollis's properties weren't the only warrants we got this morning. We also got one for McCarthy's communications and one for the police chief's," Ryan told them.

"What did you find?" Ellery asked as her leg nervously bounced. She gripped her hands tightly together, thinking it had to be something if they arrested him.

"We found an email sent from the mayor to the chief demanding the investigation into you as the sole subject of the murder. The chief sent that to the FBI head, asking for a personal favor to let the local police handle the missing person case. In return, McCarthy would get a boat."

"Hollis's boat? The boat I was most likely tossed overboard from?" Ellery asked with anger and disbelief.

"Yes," Ryan answered as she watched his vehicle pull away from the scene. "We arrested the police chief already and now McCarthy for corruption charges. We're on our way to talk to Hollis and the mayor. I'm sure his attorney is on her way as well."

"Will it be enough to arrest him?" Ellery asked worriedly. "They'll say I killed Mark at the gallery. After all, I was there."

"I got a message from my lab techs that they've collected evidence from your car and from the boat. Your car apparently had blood in the trunk, which looks bad for you. However, I need to know if Hollis was ever inside your car."

"Inside my car? No, why?" Ellery asked.

"Ever? He never once rode in your car?" Ryan asked again.

"No. There was no reason for us to ever be in a car together. Why?" Ellery asked again.

"While we found blood and hair in your trunk, the front was entirely wiped down with bleach. But we found a fingerprint on the seatbelt buckle. He must have grabbed it to lock it in place. It belongs to Hollis."

"Oh my God. You got him!" Ellery's eyes shot to Gavin's with excitement.

"It's something, but I'd like more. We'll need to wait until the lab results come in to determine if we can arrest him."

The phone beeped and Ellery saw Tibbie's name. "Ryan, I'll call you back. We have someone looking into the case for us, and they're calling."

"Text me. I'll be questioning Hollis."

Gavin accepted Tibbie's call, his eyes never leaving

Ellery's. They were bright with hope, and Ellery crossed her fingers for luck as Gavin answered the call.

"I found it!" Miss Tibbie screamed in a whisper. "I'm at the meeting, and I was talking about wanting to redo a room with palmettos. Octavia Thorpe said she just bought a gorgeous one-of-a-kind marble palmetto statue for her living room. She rubbed it in good that she had it, knowing I wanted it. I offered to buy it from her, but she won't sell just to spite me."

"That has to be it." Ellery gasped as Gavin held up a hand to calm her.

"Miss Tibbie, we need to know when, where, and from whom she bought it."

"Sonny, do you think I was born yesterday?" Miss Tibbie chuckled. "Octavia said Hollis Coldwell opened the gallery especially for her on Sunday because he knew she had liked the statue when she saw it Friday night. He called her and offered her a special deal on it, since it was going to be sent back to the artist on Monday."

"Now we have him," Gavin said with a smile.

"Miss Tibbie, you did it. Oh my gosh, thank you so much," Ellery said as tears threatened to spill.

"Goodness, child. You're welcome," Miss Tibbie said, sounding a little choked up herself with emotion. "Now, I'll keep Octavia here while you get someone over to her house to get that statue."

"Yes, ma'am," Gavin said as he hung up and sent a text to Ryan.

Ryan: Going there now with a lab tech. Will let you know what we find.

And for the first time since Ellery woke up to Gavin giving her CPR, she had hope.

26

The next night Gavin and Ellery sat with Wade, Trent, Ridge, and Tinsley as they ate dinner and watched the continuing live news coverage of Hollis's arrest. Gavin didn't think Ellery or he had slept since Ryan and Peter had started arresting people the day before. Gavin was worn out, and he hadn't left the couch the whole day. His emotions were raw and he knew Ellery felt the same.

"We're live outside Hollis Coldwell's home in his elite neighborhood in downtown Charleston. FBI, assisted by the Shadows Landing Sheriff's Department, has escorted Mr. Coldwell from his home with handcuffs hidden under a sport coat and his aunt, famous attorney Mary Coldwell-Helmshire, following close behind. Agent Peter Castle, the new acting agent in charge of the Charleston office after the shocking arrest of his superior on corruption charges, has stated Mr. Coldwell is under arrest for the alleged murder of local artist, Mark Vosslinger, and the alleged attempted murder of art gallery director, Ellery St. John. Ms. St. John's whereabouts are unknown to the public at this time, but Agent Castle said in a brief statement she is safe and her report of the incident has been recorded," Shelly stated in front of the large Hollis-Coldwell mansion.

"Further, it is reported that there have been five arrests on corruption charges thus far. Various members of the police force, including the chief of police, the head of the local FBI office, the mayor, and his assistant have all been placed in custody. The FBI is asking for them to be transported to Columbia for trial since Hollis's uncle is a very influential judge in Charleston and could pose a bias for the case. "Shelly looked into the camera with a serious face. "We're trying to locate Ms. St. John for a statement and will be at the change-of-venue hearing to keep you updated on the latest."

Gavin turned off the television and sat back with a deep breath. "It's over. Hollis's fingerprints and both yours and Mark's blood were on the statue. It was Mark's blood in the gallery and Hollis's hair and fingerprint found in Ellery's car."

"And don't forget traces of Ellery's and Mark's blood on the boat," Wade said, setting down his empty plate of food. "How are you feeling?"

Gavin looked to Ellery who looked shell-shocked. "I need a drink," she said with a laugh.

"Well, it just so happens we know someone who owns a bar," Tinsley said with a little laugh. "Come on, you've been in hiding for days now. Let's go to Harper's and have a celebratory toast to the clearing of your name."

"Do you want to go?" Gavin asked Ellery, not wanting her to feel pressured into going out if she was too tired.

"I do. It sounds nice to get out of the house and have a nice tall drink with my friends. Hollis is in jail, my statement has been taken, and I'm ready to start moving on. I couldn't have done this without all y'all. The first round is on me,"

Ellery said as she stood up and reached for her newly recovered purse that she'd left in her car the night of the attack. Peter had gotten it out of evidence and handed it over this morning when he'd given them his update.

Gavin slipped his hand into hers as the happy group walked from the house together. It was only a short walk to Shadows Bar, and no one thought to drive on such a nice evening. It was seven o'clock and the sun was casting a warm glow about town. The smell of barbeque filled the air as they got close to Main Street. Pink Pig was wrapping up for the night. Wade had brought them dinner from there just an hour before.

Ellery was quiet as she held his hand, but his cousins were talking enough for them both. Instead he squeezed her hand and smiled at her when she looked at him. *I love you* he mouthed to her as if they were in their own world and not surrounded by people. It felt so natural to say, and he wished he'd told her sooner when she smiled so brightly she outshone the sun.

I love you too, she mouthed back and Gavin felt complete. His whole body relaxed as she leaned her shoulder against his. They walked past the park and marina before turning onto Main Street. They passed Pink Pig and the historical society on one side of the street and Gil's Grub 'n' Gas and the Daughters of Shadows Landing on their side before pushing open the door to Shadows Bar.

"Hey! Look who is out and about and looking like two lovesick teenagers," Harper yelled from behind the horseshoe shaped bar in the middle of the room. Booths lined the walls while tables filled in the middle of the bar. There were pool tables, darts, and massive televisions around the rest of the room. There was also a private event space on the second floor.

"Aww . . ." people called out in response. Gavin smiled and shook his head as Gator let out a catcall.

"Come on, our regular table's open," Wade responded as they made their way to the table near the dartboards. Harper strode around the bar and pulled up a chair.

"Hey, Edie," Ridge called out. "Why don't you join us?"

Gavin watched as Edie slid from the barstool she'd been sitting at talking to Harper and joined them. Before sitting down, she smiled at Ellery and asked how she was doing.

"What can I get you to celebrate?" Harper asked Ellery after giving her a hug. She sat in the one remaining chair and took drink orders.

"Sweet Tea Vodka with lemonade, please," Ellery said as Tinsley and Edie added that they wanted one too. Gavin and the guys ordered Palmetto Lowcountry Lager as conversation began to flow. Harper weaved around the two waitresses getting drinks for other tables and made her way back to the bar after promising to join them in a minute.

Gavin placed his hand on Ellery's thigh and smiled at her as his cousins continued to talk. He'd never felt anything so right as having Ellery beside him and in his heart.

ELLERY COULD BARELY CONTAIN HERSELF. She wanted to leap up and tell the whole bar she was in love. How, out of such a horrible event, had she found such happiness?

"I'm glad everything got straightened out, Miss St. John," Gator said with a tip of his Gamecocks hat.

"Thank you, Gator," Ellery said, looking up to see Gator and Turtle standing in front of the table.

"That was dadgum wrong what he did, ma'am. Too big for his britches, that Hollis was." This time is was Turtle who paid his respects.

"Yes, he was. Thank you, Turtle." Ellery smiled because she was so happy. She was in love, and she was already part of a town. She had always loved Charleston's small town feel, but Shadows Landing was completely different. It was a family. She looked at the missing part of Gator's finger and extra bandage bulging behind Turtle's zipper and revised her thought to a very unique family, but family nonetheless.

And they weren't the only ones who stopped by. Professor Adkins and all four of the Ball family hugged her and stopped to talk. Sadie threw her arms around her and said they were practically sisters since she was Gavin's nurse and Ellery was living at his house. That made Ellery pause. Was she still living there? She actually hadn't thought about what would happen to her now. The gallery was closed, so she didn't have a job. And would she want to go back to the gallery? Would that mean she had to leave Charleston in search of a job? And was she being presumptuous about staying with Gavin? She could go home now, but no matter how she tried to be excited about that, home was here—in Shadows Landing.

"Here you go," Harper said, handing out the drinks. Ellery sipped hers and felt herself relax. She would think about tomorrow, tomorrow. Tonight she was going to enjoy herself, the man she loved, and the new family she had gained.

"I'll tell you what," Harper said as she took a seat for a moment. "I think we need a drink named after you."

"Me?" Ellery asked. "No way. Why do you need a drink named after me?"

"Anne Bonny thinks it should be called St. John's Revenge. After you and the boat she was on," Skeeter called out as he sucked on a toothpick. He wiped his hand on his torn jeans and gave her a nod as if that was the final word on the matter.

"Anne Bonny, as in the female pirate?" Ellery asked on a whisper as if the notorious pirate would suddenly appear.

"Yup," Harper said with a nod. "Skeeter says a lot of the pirates who used to be in and around Charleston have ghosts here. Anne is one of them. She's usually very opinionated too."

"Anne heard that," Skeeter called out as Harper rolled her eyes.

"Well, tell Anne I actually like the name. I'm guessing she wants it made with rum?"

"And sweet tea. A little bit pirate and a little bit lady," Skeeter answered.

"Hmm, that does sound good," Ellery said with a laugh. "I like thinking of myself as tough enough to hang out with pirate ghosts."

"Well, then," Harper said, standing up and tossing back her drink, "St. John's Revenges for everyone!"

The small crowd that had gathered at the bar cheered and held their glasses up to toast Harper, Ellery, and pirate ghost Anne Bonny.

ELLERY HADN'T LAUGHED that hard in ages—even before her attempted murder. Their table had grown to include Skeeter, Junior, Gator, Turtle, and the Bell family as they played darts, drank, and laughed.

"I have to hit the little pirates' room. I'll be right back," Ellery said with a giggle as she slid from the barstool she'd been perched on watching Gavin and Wade taunting each other as they tried to win at darts.

Gavin leaned over and gave her a kiss on the lips and

only pulled away when Gage Bell let out a sharp whistle and chided them on being in a family establishment.

Harper pegged him with a lime slice to the head. "Family establishment? This is a bar," she joked.

"Well, this is where family comes to drink," Gage said with a wink before tossing the lime wedge back at the bar and hitting Harper right in the boob.

Ellery giggled again as she teetered to the bathroom in the back. The patrons talked to her as she walked by. Some she recognized and others she didn't, but they all said hi or that they were happy she was safe. And she did feel safe. Hollis was at the FBI office right now being questioned before his arraignment.

Ellery pushed open the thick wooden door with the picture of a female pirate on it. "Hello, Anne." She giggled as the door swung shut. Inside the bathroom were three stalls, a large rectangular sink with three faucets, and a window that overlooked the back. The window was cracked and let in the nighttime breeze that suddenly blew when she said hello to Anne.

"There are no such things as pirate ghosts," Ellery said, suddenly not laughing anymore as the breeze turned to wind and made the stall door rattle.

That was it, Ellery didn't want to stay in the haunted bathroom any longer than necessary so she hurried into the first stall and slammed the door. She went to move the lock when she heard a *click*. Ellery looked down at the lock on her door. It was still unlocked.

"Hello?"

Ellery paused and listened. There was no sound except for the wind whistling through the slightly open window.

"Anne?" Ellery said almost incredulously, but there was no response. She locked her door and shook her head. "I'm being silly," she said as she finished. She got up, flushed, and unlocked the door. She could hear a cheer from the bar and smiled. The darts game must have concluded.

Ellery stepped back, pulled back the door, and didn't even see the fist slamming into her face. Her whole body was flung backward as she landed hard on the toilet. A man filled the door.

"You," Ellery gasped. He'd been the one with the gun who Miss Ruby grabbed in Gavin's driveway. He was very large and very . . . rectangular. He looked like a refrigerator with muscles.

"And you are quite the problem. I should have been paid days ago. Now, let's go." He reached one meaty hand for her, and Ellery didn't know what to do. Until she would have sworn she saw Anne Bonny flash before her eyes. Anne wouldn't put up with this shit and neither would she.

"Not today, asshole!" Ellery yelled as she gripped her hands on the side of the toilet seat and kicked with all her might right into the refrigerator's ice cubes.

The man dropped to his knees as he cupped his balls and made this horrible dry heaving sound. Ellery couldn't get past him though. He blocked the door. What would Anne do? Ellery looked around until she had her answer. She carefully stood on the toilet, grabbed the top of the stall and jumped.

Her stomach landed hard on the partition, but it didn't matter. She was up, now she needed to get over. She kicked her feet as if she were swimming, and it tipped her forward. With a scream that was lost in the cheering of drinking games, Ellery crash-landed half on the toilet and half on the ground.

She pushed against the toilet to stand, pulled one leg from where it had landed in the toilet water, flung open the stall door, and ran. The man tried to grab her, but Ellery jumped him like a hurdle. She slammed into the bathroom door, wrapped her hand around the brass handle, and pulled. Nothing. She pulled again. The door didn't budge.

Ellery looked over her shoulders and saw the man gripping the stall door and pulling himself up. She spun back to the door and began to yell as she fumbled with the lock. Hearing it *click*, she pulled the door open only to have it slammed shut.

A large hand appeared above her head as the man effortlessly held the door closed. "Let's try this again. You're coming with me."

One hand kept the door shut and the other closed tightly around her upper arm. Ellery spun toward him and kneed him. But he'd learned and twisted his hips. Her knee slammed into his thigh as his hand gripped painfully into her arm.

Well, that didn't work. All Ellery could think about was the old children's song, *Head, Shoulders, Knees, and Toes* and she went with it. She closed her hand into a fist and punched him as hard as she could in the face before lowering her shoulder and ramming him. As he lost his balance and took a step back, Ellery kicked his knee and stomped on his toe.

"Fucking bitch," he cried out. He dropped his hand from the door as he clamped down on her arm and hobbled on one foot. Ellery charged forward then and locked her hand on the brass handle. When he pulled her back, she pulled the door open and screamed for all she was worth.

She felt her fingers loosen their grip and slowly slide from the handle. It felt as if she were being torn in two, but she held on and screamed with all she had. And then she heard it. Shouts, feet running, and she simply let go. The man stumbled back, falling to the ground, dragging her on top of him.

Ellery rolled off and crawled on hands and knees toward the door right as it was flung open. Harper stood with a baseball bat, Wade with a gun, and Gator with a knife that was big enough to scare the piss out of a fifteen-foot alligator.

The whole bar was crammed around the door as Gavin slipped in and wrapped his arm around her waist and pulled her up. "This is the guy that tried to kidnap her the other day."

"I know a place to put him," Gator said menacingly as he used the tip of the knife to pick at his teeth. "No one will ever find his body since there won't be none left."

"Get out of here, Ellery. Go get Granger or Kord," Gavin told her as he kissed her quickly.

"I'll go with her," Tinsley said and took Ellery's hand in hers. "Come on. Let's get you safe."

Ellery walked through a line of people holding darts, pool cues, large beer mugs, and anything they could use to hurt a person. They where all piling into the bathroom with a look of determination. As Tinsley took her from the bar, she heard the man scream but didn't feel a bit of remorse. They needed to find out who he was and why Hollis hired him. Did Hollis expect the guy to finish what he had started and kill her so she couldn't testify against him?

27

Gavin looked to where Gator and Turtle had the man hog-tied. Junior had his hammer out and was threatening to smash each finger as Harper smacked her baseball bat menacingly against her palm.

"What did you want with Ellery?" Gavin asked.

The man refused to answer. "Gator, can I borrow your knife?" Gator handed over the massive blade and grinned. Gavin crouched down so he could look the man in the eye. "I'm a doctor, and I know every spot to cut you to inflict the most pain without killing you. I'll make the CIA look like amateurs when it comes to interrogation. Do you understand me?"

"You're a doctor. You're sworn to help people," the man said with a smug tilt of his lips. That was until Gator drove his knee into the man's back.

"Not people trying to hurt the woman I love."

"Oh my gosh, you love her?" Harper asked, lowering her bat. "That's so great. I really like her."

"Yeah, I do too. She's a keeper," Wade said with a grin as Trent smacked Gavin's back and gave him a wink.

"I'll build a nursery above the garage so it will be right next to your bedroom," Ridge said.

The man let out a scream a second after everyone heard a *thud* and a *crunch*. Gavin looked to his right and saw Junior casually picking up his hammer. "Sorry. It slipped." The man's finger had been broken.

"So, what did Hollis want you to do with Ellery after you kidnapped her?" Gavin asked.

"Hollis?" the man asked genuinely not understanding. "No one named Hollis hired me."

ELLERY AND TINSLEY heard the man yelp in pain as they pushed through the front door of the now empty bar. Directly across the street was the art gallery and then the church. The sheriff's station was on the other side of the church, so as they walked out of the bar, Tinsley used her cell phone to call Granger.

Cars that hadn't been there before were lining the street on both sides now. "What's going on?"

"Ladies Prayer Group," Tinsley said as they looked both ways then stepped into the street. "Granger, this is Tinsley. A man attacked Ellery at the bar. They have him trapped in the bathroom."

Ellery tuned out Tinsley as they stepped around a car and into the street. Her mind was wondering what the man was saying. Why he wanted her? What Hollis had planned for her? A car engine revved and a massive pearl white SUV pulled away from the curb.

Ellery looked both ways and picked up her speed to get out of the street, but Tinsley had stopped walking and was looking in a different direction. Ellery followed her gaze to the right and saw the empty sheriff's station at the end of

Main Street."You're ten minutes away?" Tinsley looked nervously at Ellery before looking back at the station. "Yes, I can get her there."

Car tires squealed and Ellery's head snapped to the left in time to see the tires spinning on the shiny white SUV as the engine revved and the vehicle raced right at them.

"Tinsley!" Ellery cried as she shoved her friend backward. Tinsley fell back against the hood of a parked car and tumbled to the ground, but Ellery wasn't so lucky. She didn't have time to leap to safety. She stood frozen as the SUV was a hair's breadth away. It was the shock of seeing the person driving it that finally made her move. She pivoted so that she took a glancing blow instead of a full hit.

Pain shot from her side as she was flung sideways onto the ground. Ellery grunted as her knee and hand slammed into the street and the pavement tore into her skin, sending sharp prickling pain through her.

"Ellery!" Tinsley cried over the sound of the SUV slamming on the brakes. "Sanctuary!"

Ellery looked up from the ground at the church. Sanctuary. She tried to stand, but her breath hissed from her lips as she slowly stood, clutching her side. Blood trickled down her hands and knees as she took painful, stumbling steps forward. The door of the SUV opened right as Tinsley reached her side.

"Come on," Tinsley urged as she grabbed Ellery's arm and flung it over her shoulder. Tinsley might be small, but Ellery swore she practically lifted her off the ground as Ellery found herself somehow running to the church.

Ellery looked up as they climbed the steps toward the thick strong doors. The driver strode toward them with gun in hand.

"Stupid men. You can never depend on them to do the job right."

"Who is that?" Tinsley asked, looking at the woman in the five thousand dollar suit and carrying a pearl handled gun. Tinsley yanked the door open, and the first round of the gun lodged in the old wood.

Tinsley and Ellery screamed and then hands pulled them inside. "What in Sam Hill is going on out there?" Miss Ruby asked.

"A man tried to kidnap Ellery in the bathroom at the bar, and we were running to the sheriff but then this woman hit Ellery with her car and shot at us," Tinsley said in a rush as Miss Winnie dragged a chair over to the door and precariously stood up in it. "She's halfway across the street," she said as she looked out the small square of stained glass windows. "And she looks like she knows how to handle a gun. It's a cute little thing. I wonder if I can get one like that. That handle is lovely."

"Ladies!" Reverend Winston said, drawing their attention. "We have a member of our community in trouble. Grab your prayer books. You know what to do."

"Reverend," Ellery said as women went scrambling, "I don't think prayer is going to help. That's Sylvia Coldwell— Hollis's mother. She will not stop until I am dead. She refused to reschedule the debutante ball when Hurricane Joaquin hit in 2015. Sixteen inches of rain in one day, and she made it so the debutantes were escorted in on boats. She does not give up."

"Ladies, get in position," Reverend Winston said, ignoring her warning. A woman who looked like she needlepointed cat pillows stood at the door. Winnie had her position at the window. Miss Ruby and two others knelt down as the women lined up standing in three rows of three directly behind where Miss Ruby knelt. Each woman clutched their prayer book in their hands. "Miss Winnie?"

"Two o'clock." Miss Winnie answered so seriously Ellery hardly recognized her southern drawl.

"Now, Mildred," the reverend said calmly.

Mildred yanked open the door, and in a blink three prayer books were flung like Frisbees out the door.

The row behind Miss Ruby threw their payer books and then the door slammed shut. "Direct hit!" Miss Winnie yelled. "She's down, but she's not out ladies."

"Second group, take position. First group, get your things," Reverend Winston commanded. Two rows moved forward. "Miss Winnie."

"One o'clock."

"All at once. Go."

On Reverend Winston's command, cat lady opened the door and prayer books went flying along with bullets. Cat lady slammed the door shut as the bullets dug into the wood. "Oh, my," she said with a little grin. "I got a tingle from all this excitement. Is anyone suddenly craving those brownies Sissy King used to make?"

"Don't you worry, Kordell gave me the recipe," Miss Ruby yelled from the front of the church.

"Such a nice young man," Miss Winnie added. "Here she comes, ladies."

"We're ready," Miss Ruby called out. Ellery turned and looked to find the six women tipping over the tall floor candle stands that lined the altar.

Ellery felt her mouth drop open. "Is that a cutlass?"

"This church has never been invaded, and we won't allow it now," Reverend Winston said, tipping over another one of the floor stands and pulling out a wicked looking steel pointed pike. "Boarding pikes are up here, ladies. Cutlasses are by communion."

"Wait!" Miss Winnie yelled. Everyone stopped talking as the sound of an engine roared down the street. "We need a distraction."

Ellery grabbed the pike from the reverend and in three long strides was at the door. "Open it, just a bit. Miss Winnie, you keep a lookout."

"What are you doing?" Tinsley asked in a whisper, as if she was afraid Sylvia would hear her.

"Causing a distraction."

The door opened about a foot, and Sylvia froze on the sidewalk. She leveled her gun and smiled. She looked rather ridiculous standing in the middle of prayer books with what was looking like a cut cheek, two black eyes, and an egg shaped bump on her forehead. Her normally perfect hair was now falling from her jeweled barrettes.

"You realize we've all seen you. Right, Sylvia?" Ellery asked.

"Mrs. Coldwell," she snapped. "And that name means I can do whatever I want. Especially to a nobody like you. My brothers won't let anything happen to me."

"It wasn't Hollis who sent the men after me, was it?" Ellery asked as the sound of an engine grew closer.

"Of course not. He couldn't even kill you properly. Bless his heart, he's always needed his mother to clean up his messes. And that's what you are. A mess."

"He killed Mark. I saw him," Ellery called out the slightly open door.

"So what? Mark was a nobody just like you. But if you disappear, I can fix everything. If he'd just listened to me the other night, then none of this would be an issue. I told him when I arrived at the gallery to drive your car to Mark's, but he had to wipe it down. Did he listen? Stupid men. But I can still fix it."

"So you're going to kill me, but what about all these people inside the church?"

"I'll burn it to the ground. It's of little consequence to me. Although the stained glass is beautiful. I might buy it after the church is destroyed. It would look lovely at the plantation."

"You're unhinged," Ellery cried. The woman was probably planning the garden party she'd have to show off her new treasures, not caring a whit that she'd murdered fifteen people.

Sylvia shrugged one silk clad shoulder and raised her gun. "And you're all expendable."

The sound of a war cry sounded, and from the side of the church a red scooter driven by Mr. Gann slid onto the sidewalk. He revved the massive engine he'd built for his scooter and bolted toward Sylvia. She spun to see what was coming, took a step back in shock at the elderly man with three white hairs blowing in the wind and huge glasses on his face, and almost stepped on a prayer book. She braced herself and raised her gun as Mr. Gann reached down to pull his cane free from its holder. Ellery shoved open the door and threw her pike. It missed by several inches, but it caused Sylvia to briefly turn away from Mr. Gann.

"Motherf—" Tinsley began to whisper the curse.

"Favor us," Reverend Winston finished for her from where he and everyone else were crammed, staring out the door.

Using his cane as a jousting lance, Mr. Gann aimed it at Sylvia and then . . .

Ellery sucked in her breath as the cane struck Sylvia square in the stomach. The power of the hit not only doubled Sylvia over but pushed her backward. Her foot stepped on a prayer book and slipped. Her arms pinwheeled, and her gun sailed into the street as she let out a screech.

"Timber!" Miss Ruby called out.

The door to the bar opened and the patrons filed out. They took one look around and were running across the street. Except for Gator, who was carrying the hired goon over his shoulder. He dumped him in the wooden gator box and hammered it shut as the church doors were flung open and the reverend led the ladies' group outside armed with cutlasses and pikes.

"That was so sexy," Miss Winnie whispered as Mr. Gann sent her a wink. "He's been wanting my apple pie for months now. I think I'll finally give it to him."

"Miss Winnie!" Tinsley said as Ellery joined her giggling.

"It's really good apple pie," Miss Ruby added, and Ellery lost her battle of the giggles and broke out in belly laughs.

"What the hell happened?" Gavin asked as sirens wailed in the distance. He pushed through the crowd, circled around Sylvia Coldwell, and ran to Ellery's side.

"It's finally over." Ellery sighed with relief and rested her head against Gavin's shoulder. "Unless . . ."

"Unless what?" Gavin asked, but Ellery was already pulling away from him and walking to where Turtle was looking full of himself as he told Sylvia he was making a citizen's arrest.

"Did you send anyone else after me?" Ellery asked as she looked at Sylvia lying on the sidewalk surrounded by prayer books.

"I think my hip is broken, you bitch!" she cried out.

"I happen to have a doctor here who could give you

something for that pain, but he's not going to until you answer my question." Ellery motioned to Gavin and waited as Sylvia looked at him and then back to her. Her lip pulled up in disgust.

"You moved on from my son already? I knew you were cheap. And to a simple doctor? But even he's too good for the likes of you," Sylvia spat.

Harper used the toe of her boot to nudge Sylvia's side, and Sylvia screamed so loud Ellery was worried the beautiful stained glass might break.

"I bet morphine sounds nice right now, huh?" Ellery asked sweetly. "Now, did you hire anyone else?"

"No," Sylvia admitted through clenched teeth. "My brothers helped, but I only hired the one man."

Ellery looked around and saw most of the town had their cell phones out and were recording. "You hired one man after Hollis killed Mark, and you tried to frame me for his murder. How did you know Hollis hadn't succeeded in killing me too?"

"I answered your question. Give me the drugs now. This hurts," Sylvia snapped, and Ellery nodded to Gavin as Granger and Kord pulled up. Gavin jogged off to tell them what was happening.

"See, he's going to get it. How did you know Hollis didn't succeed in killing me?"

"I had sent my man there with one of my brother's assistants to see if the report from the local sheriff was really you. They said they were thwarted from getting a good look. I let it go for a while. After the Coast Guard started asking questions and nosing around, I got suspicious and later that night I went home and thought about it. I had been talking to Wade and Ryker Faulkner, and that was the name of the house a possible Ellery was spotted at. I had them go back and look for you, but you weren't there. I had them leave you a little surprise, but they messed that up too. No one saw you after the explosion. But then the police spotted you at your condo. I knew I had to do the job myself." Sylvia glared at Ellery then put her head down and closed her eyes. "Now, give me my morphine and take me to the hospital. Charleston Memorial. My niece is the chief of staff."

"Right after we do one more annoying thing, ma'am," Granger said with a grin on his face. "You have the right to remain silent..."

Sylvia waved her hand. "I know all that. Don't you know who my brother is? Call him for me, will you? He's Charleston's top judge. And while you're at it, call my sister, Charleston's top attorney. Oh, and our dear family friend, the Attorney General of South Carolina."

"Ma'am," Granger said, his smile widening, "after I book you into jail, I will happily let you decide which one person you'd like to call. But I can tell you, it won't matter much. You better like having a roommate. Maybe if you ask the Attorney General real nice like, he might allow a mother/son cell."

Ellery felt two arms wrap around her waist and someone at her back. She looked to her right, and Harper winked at her. She looked to her left, and Tinsley gave her a smile. She looked behind her and tears started to flow. Edie, Trent, Ridge, and Wade all had her back. Somehow she'd found a family in Shadows Landing.

28

Gavin administered medical attention to Sylvia Coldwell while she bitched at him continuously. An ambulance arrived to take her to the hospital in Charleston, and Gavin diagnosed her with a probable broken hip.

"Two out of three?" Kord asked as he and Granger stood over a glaring Sylvia.

"Let's go," Granger said as their fists hit their open hands. "One, two, three."

"Hell ya," Kord said as his paper covered Granger's rock.

"One, two, three," Granger said seriously now as their fists hit their hands. "Crap."

"Scissors for the win!" Kord celebrated.

"Fine. I'll escort her to Charleston and hand her off to the FBI. But you get to do the paperwork."

Kord groaned, and Gavin snickered as he stood up to deliver his report to the EMTs. The whole time he had been working, he'd kept an eye on Ellery. He hated that he couldn't be by her side right then, but as the town's only doctor, that was his job. Even if he didn't want to treat Sylvia and would rather see her endure twice as much pain, he knew it was his duty.

"Granger!" Gavin called out. "We forgot about the guy. He's in the back of Gator's truck."

Gavin and the rest of Shadows Landing looked around. No Gator. No truck. Granger grinned even larger now. "You're up, buddy. I have to get to Charleston."

Kord groaned dramatically. "I hate going to the swamp. You know that's where he's taken him. I won't come back with less that twenty mosquito bites and those bastards are bigger than most compact cars."

"Should have waited before issuing the rock paper scissors challenge," Granger taunted as he hopped in the back of the ambulance. "I'll be back with one of the agents. Just get that guy back before he's gator food and put him in our cell."

"Yes, sir," Kord grumbled as he opened up the car door and pulled out a massive bottle of bug spray.

Finally, Gavin had fulfilled his duty. Well, unless Gator had harmed the man they'd hog-tied. He made his way through the throng of people standing outside the church to find Ellery. He found her leaning down and giving Mr. Gann a kiss. The old man revved the oversized engine on his scooter in return. Ellery laughed and Miss Winnie sighed.

"How did you know I needed help, Mr. Gann?" Ellery asked as she stood up.

"I didn't. I was lucky enough to see the trouble. See, I'm always around here when the ladies' group lets out. It's the best place to pick women up. I can offer them a ride on my lap to their car."

Gavin saw Ellery struggling not to laugh. "So, you literally pick them up."

"If I'm lucky they give me a little pie."

"I'll give you all the pie you want tonight, my hero," Miss Winnie whispered as she leaned down to his ear.

"I can't tell if they mean actual pie or if it's an innuendo," Gavin said softly as he stepped up behind Ellery.

"I don't know, but when I tell you I'm going to give you my pie tonight since you're my hero, I mean sex. Lots of it. Even the kinky kind if you want."

Gavin stepped closer to hide his immediate reaction to her words. "Really?" he asked, letting his lips gently brush her ear. "What kind of kinky are we talking about?"

"The kind that involves pie."

"Have I told you I love you yet?" he asked with a laugh.

Ellery looked at him, and he knew this was his future. "Not out loud. I don't think I'll ever get tired of hearing you say it. I love you too, Gavin."

Gavin turned her in his arms and lowered his lips to hers. "Don't ever stop saying it and I won't either."

"That's a promise I can keep," Ellery said a moment before he covered her mouth with his.

The kiss went from loving to kinky pie level in seconds. He couldn't help himself. It was the rush of knowing he had found his forever.

"Oh my," Miss Winnie said with surprise. "That's giving me a whole other kind of tingle."

Gavin and Ellery pulled apart, embarrassed they'd gotten carried away. But when they looked at Miss Winnie, she wasn't paying them any attention. She was on Mr. Gann's lap, and he was revving his engine. Gavin pulled Ellery to his chest in a hug as they both laughed. This was perfection. His town. His family. His love. Gavin had never felt so complete.

ELLERY STOOD BACK and looked at the painting. She stepped forward and adjusted it slightly then stepped back again. Perfect. Tinsley's newest painting was the highlight of the newly opened St. John Art Gallery.

It had been eight months since Hollis and Sylvia took their plea deal. Sylvia had wanted a trial, but her sister convinced her she wouldn't make the most sympathetic witness or defendant. Plus, Gator had recorded the hired man spilling all he knew about Sylvia hiring him and her criminal intentions toward Ellery. When Gator showed them the clip, it appeared the man was sitting in a chair giving the confession. Turned out the chair was suspended over Bubba and Bubba was hungry.

After the plea deal, Hollis lost his Mimi Hollis inheritance, and, since Hollis had never had kids and the rest of the Hollis-Coldwell family wanted nothing to do with the now disgraced art gallery, a piece of Charleston history had died. That was until Gavin convinced her to go to the closing reception at the gallery. They'd quietly let the art world know they were getting rid of everything, including the building.

She'd been scared to death walking into the gallery with Tinsley, Gavin, Tibbie, and Elijah. Ellery thought she'd have flashbacks, but instead all she felt was sadness. That place had given beauty to the world, not death. Hollis's uncle, the banker, and one of the few besides his attorney aunt, who had not been arrested, had told her a company was interested in buying the building to turn it into small condos.

"How much are you selling it for?" Ellery had asked, torn at the idea of the beautiful building born from the love of art being broken up like that.

"The money from the trust gets divided now. We've

established a charity to help the arts with three quarters of it, and then the remainder is divided between those of us not in jail and a disgrace to the family name," he'd told her. "So, we're selling it for the taxable property value of two million dollars."

"That's a good deal," Elijah said as the brief spark of hope at buying the place died. It might be a good deal, but she could only come up with a half a million in cash and didn't know if she'd qualify for a loan. She had some in savings, some from her family inheritance, and then most from the sale of her condo. She'd been living with Gavin, and they'd finally made their living arrangement official when he told her she should sell her small condo and move in with him.

"Yes, it's very generous," she had said, sounding more defeated than she should over a spur of the moment idea.

"Why do you ask? Are you interested in purchasing the gallery?" Mr. Coldwell had asked.

Ellery had shaken her head. "It was just an idea. I thought I could keep it an art gallery, but I can't afford that price."

Mr. Coldwell made a "hmmm" noise and then waved his mother over.

"What's this?" Beatrice Coldwell asked after joining them.

"Ellery wants to buy the gallery," Mr. Coldwell told his mother.

"What a wonderful idea. But I can't allow her to buy it. However, she can be the first recipient of the Mimi Hollis Art Foundation grant. It's only fair after what she went through at the hands of our family."

"Oh, I couldn't—"

"Hush, Ellery," Elijah had told her. "I think that's a marvelous idea, Bea. What do you have in mind?"

"A grant of the property in full."

Ellery had gasped. Elijah had nodded, and Mr. Coldwell had called his sister over. "We have a majority of the foundation board, let's vote on it."

And just like that, Ellery had been granted the property. She knew it was their way of paying her off for attempted murder, but as Elijah told her, it gave them a way to say they were sorry and her a way to feel closure. So she'd taken it and used some of her savings to renovate.

Ellery looked around. The opening was the next day. She'd painted the exposed brick walls white and refinished the wood floors. She'd ripped down the curtain divider and put up French doors and installed all new doors and lighting. She'd also torn down some of the walls in the back and created an art studio for grant recipients of the Mimi Hollis Art Foundation. They also had a featured spot in the studio.

Beatrice Coldwell had been a fairy godmother to the gallery and to her. She'd never verbally apologized, but she'd done so by extending her friendship and her loyalty to Ellery and the gallery. Charleston society had noticed. Atherton had too. He'd begged her to come back to him, but Ellery had slipped her hand into Gavin's and told him she was in love, and he better grow up or he'd turn into a lonely old man who thought he was a playboy when, in fact, everyone laughed at him. It worked. Atherton was working his way up his father's company and living off the salary he'd been given.

"Everything looks perfect," Gavin said as he came up behind her. "But . . ."

Ellery spun around. "But what?" She looked at the

beautiful artwork hanging on the walls. The gallery was fresh, bright, and filled with color. It was perfect.

"You forgot a painting," Gavin said as he tapped his finger on the back of a canvas that rested on the ground.

"I don't think so." Ellery had been so busy. Had she forgotten something? "Is this one of Tinsley's?"

"It's a Faulkner, yes," Gavin said, holding up the painting for her to take.

Ellery took it, turned it around and then cocked her head. It was ugly. Actually, it was hideous. The strokes were a disaster and the colors were horrendous. Her eye went to the bottom and sure enough it was a Faulkner, but it wasn't Tinsley's name there. It was Gavin's.

"You painted something for me to sell?" Ellery asked with fake cheer. It was dreadful. In fact, she wasn't really sure what it was.

"Here," he said, taking it and hanging it on the last open spot—the spot where she was about to hang a simply stunning work by a local artist. Gavin hung it up and then stepped back to where she cocked her head and examined it.

There were blues, greens, browns, grays, golds, and silvers. She stepped forward and squinted. "Is that the ocean?"

"Yes," Gavin said excitedly from behind her. "Do you like it?"

"Umm," she said, squinting more. "Is that brownish thing the ground in the middle of the ocean?"

"It's a dock."

"Oh!" Ellery exclaimed as she stepped closer and stared. What in tarnation was this? Okay, so there was a dock going out into the water. That meant the gray things were probably clouds. Did that make the gold hoop and silver ball at the end of the dock a basketball goal and ball? But silver rays were shooting upward from the ball and why was it on top of the hoop? No, maybe a ball and chain that lightning was trying to break?

"Gavin, what is—?" Ellery turned around and found Gavin on one knee with a diamond ring.

"Ellery, you've had my heart since that stormy night, and I would be the proudest, happiest man alive if you will do me the honor of marrying me."

"It's the ring!" She gasped.

Gavin smiled a little uncertainly. "Yes, it's an engagement ring."

Ellery looked back at the painting and laughed. It was the most beautiful painting she'd ever seen. It was of a large engagement ring on the dock they'd first met at during the storm. "The painting! It's the most beautiful thing I've ever seen."

She leaned down and kissed him as he kept the ring held out. "Is that a yes?" he asked against her lips.

"Yes!" she cried as Gavin placed the ring on her finger. "I love you so much!"

"I love you too, future bride."

The French doors opened, and his family and their friends spilled in with bottles of champagne, whiskey, and Gator with a six-pack of the cheapest beer he could find. Tibbie looked horrified as he held it up. "Sonny, I think I'll pour the first toast." Tibbie handed him the bottle of champagne. "Can you open this for me, dear?"

"Yes ma'am," Gator said as he pulled out his knife, and with a slice faster than Tibbie's gasp, popped the cork.

"Now that was neat. The girls at the Magnolia Brunch would love that."

Ellery had never seen Gator blush before, but he did as

he adjusted his twenty-year-old Cocks hat. "Anytime, ma'am."

Ellery caught Ryker standing behind the crowd, smiling as his shoulders shook. Wade and Harper began pouring drinks and passing them around. "To my brother and his beautiful fiancée!" Harper said with her glass lifted in the air.

The rest of the evening was a blur of laughter, joy, and love. It was the perfect way to start her happily ever after.

Gavin looked into the eyes of his bride. She was radiant in her white dress. Her hair was swept up with tendrils of blonde framing her face in a beachy look that went with the small blue forget-me-not flowers woven into her hair.

"I now pronounce you husband and wife!" Reverend Winston cheered as the congregation stood, clapping and whistling.

Gavin took his wife's hand in his as Walker Greene, his best friend since childhood, gave him a slap on the back. His cousins, who were also groomsmen, cheered as Harper handed Ellery her bouquet. Tinsley and some of Ellery's friends he'd gotten to know over the last year followed behind Harper as they walked hand in hand down the aisle.

Gavin smiled at his family, both from Shadows Landing and from Keeneston, who sat together clapping and talking. Walker's sister, Edie, was with them. Not only as part of his Shadows Landing's friends, but Keeneston had adopted her as well since Walker married Gavin's Kentucky cousin, Layne Davies.

Gavin turned to look at the other side and saw Tibbie's

and Elijah's eyes glistening as they sat with Beatrice Coldwell, the matriarch of the Coldwell family. He'd heard Miss Bea tell Ellery over and over again that Ellery's compassion, forgiveness, and inclusion in the gallery had given her a second lease on life. And they weren't the only ones on her side. She'd ended up having more friends than she knew about. Artists, art collectors, and members of the art community had been behind her since she came forward with her story.

The wedding was filled with love, and they pushed open the doors, ran down the stairs, and into the horse drawn carriage Skeeter used for ghost tours. The crowd gathered outside the church and bubbles were blown as the happy couple waved to their friends and family. The Bells had insisted the reception take place at their plantation. As the carriage pulled away from the church, the people they loved had smiles as large as Gavin's and Ellery's.

"So, Mrs. Faulkner, are you ready to start your next adventure?"

"As long as it starts with a kiss and not CPR, I'll go anywhere with you."

Much to the delight of their friends and family, as the carriage drew away, Gavin kissed his wife with all the love and happiness of their future.

WADE FAULKNER HAD BEEN to his fair share of Davies weddings in Kentucky. Now it was his turn to introduce his cousins to Shadows Landing. The married ones were already talking to many of the town's couples along with Edie, Miss Winnie, and Miss Ruby, who they'd met at pre-wedding events. But now was the fun part.

"Hey, Greer," he called out to his cousin who was Ryan's

little sister. Well, she was in her twenties, so she wasn't that little.

"These fancy folk aren't going to have anything to talk to me about," Gator whispered nervously. What he didn't realize was while his cousins were fancy when they wanted to be, they weren't what they appeared.

"Hi, Wade," Greer called out as she joined them. She gave a pointed look to Gator who had dressed in an actual suit with alligator boots. Gator shifted nervously. Greer was as pretty as a picture with her honey brown hair and greenish-gray eyes. She was tall and fit and dressed in a beautiful light green strapless dress that stopped about two inches above her knees. "Cocks, really?"

Wade pursed his lips, trying not to laugh as it hit Gator she wasn't glaring at him but at his South Carolina Gamecocks hat he never took off.

"Kentucky is so going to beat y'all this year," she teased.

That was all it took for Gator and Greer to fall into conversation. And when Gator escorted her to the dance floor, Wade heard them setting a time for him to teach her how to wrestle an alligator. Oh, crap. Great-Aunt Marcy and Aunt Paige would kill him.

"Did you say, hunt an alligator?" Paige Davies Parker, Greer's mother asked, stopping the couple. While he and Paige were technically cousins, they'd been so much more than that over time, and it seemed natural to refer to Paige and her brothers as aunts and uncles, and their children, all around Wade's age, plus or minus ten years, were the long-lost cousins they'd grown as close to as they possibly could over the past two years. "Can I go too?"

Wade shook his head as his uncles, aunts, and a fair number of cousins joined the conversation, and soon it was decided they'd all go out tomorrow to learn how to catch and release alligators. Gator blushed red when he became the center of attention, and knowing his friend was now occupied, Wade looked around the dance floor. Granger was talking to Matt, who was the sheriff of Keeneston, and Kord was dancing with a younger Davies cousin named Cassidy. Finally, Wade turned his attention to Gavin dancing with Ellery. They only had eyes for each other.

"I know that look," Walker said, joining Wade and handing him a drink.

"What look?" Wade asked as Walker's father-in-law, the very intimidating Miles Davies, joined them.

"Oh, I know that look," Uncle Miles said, stopping next to Wade.

"What look?" Wade asked again, not knowing what they were talking about.

"The *I want that* look," Walker said. "I've seen many a man fall to that look recently."

"What?" Wade was affronted, even though he'd been thinking the same thing. "I don't think that will happen."

"Think what will happen?" his great-aunt Marcy asked as she, Miss Winnie, and Miss Ruby joined them.

"Hey, Ma," Miles said, pulling out a chair for his mother. "He has *the look*."

"Oh!" Wade's great-aunt said, perking up with a dangerous glint in her eyes.

"What look?" Miss Ruby asked.

"The *ready to settle down* look," Great-Aunt Marcy explained.

"How do you know it's that look and not the *I want to tingle* look?" Miss Winnie asked as Wade, Walker, and Miles suddenly found the dance floor very interesting.

"It's in the eyes," Marcy explained. "They soften instead of harden."

"Oh, like they do when they look at my apple pie," Miss Winnie said, nodding her head.

"You make apple pie?" Marcy asked. "I do too!"

"Do you use cinnamon?" Miss Winnie asked and with a shake of their heads Walker and Miles pulled Wade away from the women.

"They'll be talking about pie for hours," Miles said on a sigh. "And now I'm hungry."

"Sometimes I don't think they're talking about pie," Wade said with a grin.

"You're right, they're probably talking about every eligible woman here to set you up with," Walker said on a laugh, but then stopped laughing. "And that better not include my sister."

"What won't include your sister?" Ryker asked as he joined them.

"Getting her pie," Wade answered.

"She doesn't make pie," Ryker said with knit brows. "Doesn't she make cake?"

Wade laughed as Walker teasingly shoved Ryker's shoulder. "No one touches my sister's pie or cake. Got it?"

"But it's a good cake," Ryker complained.

Wade laughed harder. "Her figurative pie."

"Ah," Ryker said, taking a sip of the whiskey he'd gone home to get. He wasn't a champagne kind of guy. "Why are we talking about Edie's *pie*?"

"Wade has *the look,* and Walker doesn't want him to look at his sister with that look," Miles filled in.

"What look?" Ryker asked as Trent and Ridge joined them.

Wade groaned. "I don't have a look, okay? Just drop it. And I won't eat Edie's pie—or anyone else's at the moment."

"Edie doesn't make pie," Ridge said, confused, and Wade groaned again.

Miles was fighting valiantly to not laugh.

"Wade wants a serious girlfriend," Walker clarified. "And that won't be my sister—got it?" Walker looked pointedly at each of his childhood friends who were now his cousins-in-law.

Trent held his hands up. "Got it. I'm not really that big into pie."

"I like cake better," Ridge said as Walker growled.

"When it comes to my sister, no pie or cake!"

"What about her?" Miles asked, using his eyes to direct Wade's glance.

"That's Maggie Bell. Her parents own this plantation," Wade answered. "I've known her my whole life."

"So," Miles said with a shrug. "I've known my wife my whole life too."

"Yeah, but Maggie is more . . ."

"She's perfect for someone a little more . . . well, like us," Walker explained. "She's an Olympic medalist for shooting and tough as nails."

"Really?" Miles sounded interested. "Excuse me. If you're not interested, I know many a nephew who would be."

"So, you're ready to settle down?" Ridge asked after Uncle Miles left.

"I didn't say that!" Wade said, exasperated.

"Twenty bucks he'll be married by next year," Walker said.

"You'd bet on something like this?" Wade asked incredulously.

Walker just grinned in response.

"I got twenty on six months," Ryker said.

With a roll of his eyes Wade left his cousins as they placed bets on his love life. His phone vibrated in his pocket and when he pulled it out, he saw it was a Coast Guard update. There'd been a report of a boat on fire a couple miles down river from him. He was being called in to see if he could get eyes on it before the on-duty team could arrive. He set down his drink of tonic water and lime and slipped quietly out of the party. He loosened his tie as he ran down to Ryker's dock and felt himself relax. He knew his job and he loved his job. There was one thing he didn't know—love. He saw it in Gavin and Ellery, as well as some of their other cousins. But Wade didn't really know what it was that made a relationship so special.

Wade entered the gate code to Ryker's private dock and ran along the wooden planks. Ryker's flashy speedboat wasn't great for fishing, but it would be perfect for a rescue. Putting aside all thoughts of love, marriage, and pie, Wade went to work navigating the waters by heart. Now if only he could be as sure in his navigation of women.

"THERE GOES WADE," Gavin said to his bride.

"I can't believe the Coast Guard would call him in tonight," Ellery said as they watched him slip from the reception.

"He's the best they have. And it must be something very important for them to call him in when he had the night off."

"I hope he's safe," Ellery said as she looked away from the night's shadows and back to her husband.

"He needs a good woman like I have to come home to," Gavin said before placing a sweet kiss on her lips.

"I couldn't agree more. But right now I was thinking of being a very bad woman," Ellery said, lowering her voice.

"Oh, yeah?" Gavin grinned. He loved his wife with his whole heart. "What did you have in mind?"

"How about a taste of my pie?"

Gavin scooped up his wife and carried her from the reception. After all, what man could turn down pie?

THE END

Bluegrass Series

Bluegrass State of Mind

Risky Shot

Dead Heat

Bluegrass Brothers

Bluegrass Undercover

Rising Storm

Secret Santa: A Bluegrass Series Novella

Acquiring Trouble

Relentless Pursuit

Secrets Collide

Final Vow

Bluegrass Singles

All Hung Up

Bluegrass Dawn

The Perfect Gift

The Keeneston Roses

Forever Bluegrass Series

Forever Entangled

Forever Hidden

Forever Betrayed

Forever Driven

Forever Secret

Forever Surprised

Forever Concealed

Forever Devoted

Forever Hunted

Forever Guarded

Forever Notorious (coming in 2019)

<u>*Shadows Landing Series*</u>

Saving Shadows

Sunken Shadows (coming later in 2019)

<u>Women of Power Series</u>

Chosen for Power

Built for Power

Fashioned for Power

Destined for Power

<u>*Web of Lies Series*</u>

Whispered Lies

Rogue Lies

Shattered Lies

ABOUT THE AUTHOR

Kathleen Brooks is a New York Times, Wall Street Journal, and USA Today bestselling author. Kathleen's stories are romantic suspense featuring strong female heroines, humor, and happily-ever-afters. Her Bluegrass Series and follow-up Bluegrass Brothers Series feature small town charm with quirky characters that have captured the hearts of readers around the world.

Kathleen is an animal lover who supports rescue organizations and other non-profit organizations such as Friends and Vets Helping Pets whose goals are to protect and save our four-legged family members.

Email Notice of New Releases

https://kathleen-brooks.com/contact

Kathleen's Website
www.kathleen-brooks.com
Facebook Page
www.facebook.com/KathleenBrooksAuthor
Twitter
www.twitter.com/BluegrassBrooks
Goodreads
www.goodreads.com